PRAISE FOR THE

De

"Every woman who's ev
balancing independenc
Emily." —*Kirkus*

"Emily and Dolly's developing friendship, the particulars of small-town Michigan life, and the eccentric characters enliven the story." —*Booklist*

"Debut author Buzzelli is notable as one of the growing number of women writers who use female protagonists trying to make a life for themselves, such as Sue Henry." —*Library Journal*

"Well-plotted . . . Emily grows more likeable as the mystery progresses and the town and its residents more endearing throughout the investigation." —TheMysteryReader.com

"More Carolyn Keene than Agatha Christie, Buzzelli captures the quaint quirkiness of country folk with a not-so-far-fetched twist on the things they'll do for money." —The Detroit *Metro Times*

Dead Floating Lovers
"[An] enjoyable sequel . . . " —*Publishers Weekly*

"A mystery that keeps you guessing, together with the story of a woman slowly finding her voice." —*Kirkus*

"Quirky characters, the life of a journalist and a developing writer of fiction, and the focus on a woman ready to choose her life's direction all add to the story." —*Booklist*

DEAD
DOGS AND
ENGLISHMEN

An
Emily Kincaid
Mystery

DEAD
DOGS AND
ENGLISHMEN

Elizabeth Kane Buzzelli

MIDNIGHT INK
WOODBURY, MINNESOTA

FIRST EDITION
First Printing, 2011

Book design by Donna Burch
Cover design by Ellen Lawson
Editing by Connie Hill

Midnight Ink, an imprint of Llewellyn Worldwide Ltd.

Library of Congress Cataloging-in-Publication Data

Buzzelli, Elizabeth Kane, 1946–
    Dead dogs and Englishmen / Elizabeth Kane Buzzelli. — 1st ed.
        p. cm. — (An Emily Kincaid mystery ; #4)
    ISBN 978-0-7387-1878-1
    1. Women journalists—Michigan—Fiction. I. Title.
    PS3602.U985D432 2011
    813'.6—dc22   2011005658

This is a work of fiction. Names, characters, places, and incidents are either the product of the author's imagination or are used fictitiously, and any resemblance to actual persons, living or dead, business establishments, websites, events, or locales is entirely coincidental.

Midnight Ink
Llewellyn Worldwide Ltd.
2143 Wooddale Drive
Woodbury, MN 55125-2989
www.midnightinkbooks.com

Printed in the United States of America

DEDICATION

To friends and family who make my books possible: my sister Mary Lou Kane Colucci, Rainelle Burton, Carolyn Hall, and Annick Hivert Carthew.

To Higher Self Book Store, where they gave me my teaching start in Traverse City.

To Bernard Hanchett for his help on crows.

For my good friends Mardi Link and Aaron Stander—my intrepid "Murder Takes a Road Trip" buddies.

To Ken Bryson for his amazing knowledge of area history, and Cathy and Fred Rowe for letting me move their property to a different location, and then hide dead bodies on it.

To Arlene Heffelfinger for the canned fish; Eva Sears for great stories—if she doesn't find them in this book they'll show up in Emily's future; and Linda Radtke of the Kalkaska Museum and Margaret Beebe of the Kalkaska Library for their wealth of great local lore.

And Greg Hughes, a good friend in law enforcement.

And, as always, for Tony.

ONE

THE DEADLY SUMMER OF the worm began in spring when the tent worms crawled into my northwest Michigan woods after May blossoms faded on the wild cherry trees and tiny leaves first appeared on the Juneberry; when the trees bloomed again with thick, gauzy webs at every fork of their branches. Each of the sticky, white webs woven into the blackened and sickly trees writhed with thousands of worms. I tried not to notice the moving webs when I walked with Sorrow, my happy lump of a mixed-breed dog. I hoped the worms would go away, that maybe the birds would feast on them. Maybe, I thought, they'd turn into moths and be nothing more than a nuisance after summer dark, pulsing around my porch lights and bombarding the window screens with buzzing thumps.

That wasn't what happened. None of that.

In June, the worms tore open their throbbing webs and marched up the newly leafed oaks and maples, chewing as they climbed, stripping every tree—these evil, voracious, Bernie Madoffs of the natural world.

By July, the forest was turned upside down and backward, as was my life. The oaks and maples were bare. Bright sun poured into places that should never see the summer sun: damp places in deep woods; small caverns under the exposed roots of old basswood trees; thick beds of leaf mold where the morels grew in May. Other mushrooms tried to poke through last year's leaves but dried and disappeared quickly. Wild flowers were sparse. The loamy earth slowly turned brown. In places it cracked open.

We tried, Sorrow and I, to stay happy as he snuffled chipmunk houses and howled at fox holes now caught in pools of sunshine. My shady paths were where ideas for novels simmered, my mysteries that didn't sell although I thought them great—or maybe not great, but pretty good. Now, sadly, the only thing I found as I walked were steady, tinkling streams of black tent worm shit falling on the old leaves and on my head. I wanted to stay with the usual paths but had to give them up as, spitting and angry, I took my sad dog back to our little golden cabin near the shore of Willow Lake to give us both a shower, getting the slime out of our respective hair and fur, and off my skin.

In early July I gave up the woods completely and we kept to roads, to gravel and cement, and looked longingly into the suffering forest. Sorrow didn't seem to mind worms pooping on him; and didn't mind if shady walks were sunny, if no mushrooms grew, if wild leek and purslane patches were few and far between. He was a creature who decided early on to be happy and never let go of happy thoughts as he bounced merrily through life—unless he got caught chewing one of my sandals, or sneaking away from a steaming pile he'd left, inadvertently, I'm sure, in the middle of my living room Oriental rug.

The quiet woods were one of the many reasons I'd left Ann Arbor and the newspaper I worked on to come to northwest Michigan after a bad divorce left my ego bent back on itself like a piece of cheap wire. Jackson Rinaldi, my ex-husband, a good-looking, forty-one-year-old, cheating jerk of an English professor from the University of Michigan, was one of the biggest reasons I'd run to the north woods to find peace and write the mysteries I'd been dying to write, and to live a life I'd only dreamed of living back when every day was filled with appointments and meetings and interviews and deadlines and I had no idea who I, the real Emily Kincaid, was beyond a journalist and an aggrieved wife. Mid-thirties, starting over, and still not sure I could make it in the woods by myself. Sometimes everything was too much—like winter and being jobless. Sometimes I regretted that I'd tossed my old life away. But there were those other times, times when I wanted to pat myself on the back and wanted to click my heels in the air. Times when I wanted to shout out how happy I was.

Now my ex had come to stay near Traverse City, on sabbatical, writing his giant tome—to end all tomes—on Chaucer and his pilgrims on their way to Canterbury. He was far enough away from Willow Lake to keep from being a pest. Close enough by phone, e-mail, and need to be a nuisance.

That particular hot morning, 83 degrees at nine a.m., Sorrow and I climbed to the top of our gravel drive. Up on Willow Lake Road I waved halfheartedly to three noisy crows sitting in a white pine. The crows had become a source of solace and inspiration for me since I'd convinced myself they were my muse and my guardians. Woods people came to me with stories of crow intelligence, crow ingenuity, and crow prescience. I believed it all. Crows gave me the mystery novel I was trying desperately to sell, and seemed always to be around when I needed a bird to lean on. Today they shook their black heads and cawed, probably commenting on my white legs in old denim shorts and my washed-out tee shirt and my blond and brown hair caught up on top of my head with a tortoiseshell clamp.

I checked my mailbox. The mailman hadn't been yet. The thought of an empty mailbox made me smile. No bills. No threats to shut off one thing or another. But also nothing yet from the agent I'd sent my mystery to. Not a word since she'd requested changes months before. I'd done everything she'd asked me to do and got the manuscript back to her in record time.

Still waiting.

I shut the mailbox door as Sorrow romped ahead down the road. Old Harry Mockerman—my handyman, neighbor, and teacher of woods smarts—was out on his usual morning quest, bent over at the far side of the street with a shovel and a coal scoop in his hands, a silhouette in the streaming sunshine. He was salvaging a dead raccoon—road kill from the night before. Harry found road kill an easy supply of meat for his soups and stews. Kind of like the crows who hung around for the same reason. Harry ate everything except skunk—or so I liked to think. Rabbits were at the top of Harry's list, he'd once told me. Then came birds. In a jumble behind those two were raccoon, squirrel, chipmunk, and once, a fox. I'd tried most of them. Not bad. Not good. Harry knew how to live off the land around him, and was teaching me—though there were still some things I wouldn't stoop to, like stuffing a flattened chipmunk.

"Hey, Harry," I called down at him.

He straightened, a hand at the small of his back, his very shiny funeral suit jacket (which he wore in case of his death in the woods) falling open as he leaned back, stretching his old bones and muscles.

"Emily." He waved, picking up his shovel and tucking it under one arm. Carrying the scoop straight out in front of him, he ambled over to have our morning talk, as all people in the north country do. He put a bony knee up to stop Sorrow's overly effusive greeting, nodded to me a few times, and then looked off into the woods, shaking his head.

"Awful, ain't it? Them worms and what they're doin'? Get 'em two years in a row and the whole woods could die. You hear that?"

I shook my head.

"Truth. Read it in that newspaper you write for. Eugenia, at EATS, showed me. Everybody's talking. Damn things crawled right into Dumphy's attic. Took 'em out with a snow shovel. That's what I heard." He nodded his skinny head on his long, skinny neck a few times to impress me with the importance of his news. What he meant was the *Northern Statesman*, a Traverse City paper whose editor, Bill Corcoran, threw work my way—keeping the wolf and the gas shut-off guy from my door yet another month. That Harry got his news through Eugenia Fuller, who owned the only restaurant in Leetsville, didn't surprise me. Everybody went to EATS for the latest news, for the latest trouble bedeviling anyone within fifty miles of Leetsville, the latest grumbling about the mayor, about deer foraging town gardens—whatever was going on, was going on strong at EATS.

"Mushrooms aren't growing with all that sun in the woods," I said.

He clucked a couple of times. "Tell me about it. 'Course they can't grow. You findin' any leeks?"

I shook my head. "They're too strong. Taste like rotten onion. My pantry's going to be pretty empty by winter. No mushrooms. Garden's not doing too good."

"Thought about fish?" He lowered his thick gray and white eyebrows at me.

"What about fish?"

"Cannin' 'em."

"Never heard of such a thing."

He shook his head a few times though he was used to me. "Don't know how you lived up to now," he said as he bent to pat Sorrow's head. "I'm going fishin' in a couple a days. You want to come? I'd be happy to have the company."

"Okay, but..."

"Get us a couple a suckers. Bring 'em back here and we'll can 'em. I know how to do that and make 'em taste like salmon by the time you open 'em next winter. Got me a secret." He looked up slyly and I knew I was going to be the lucky recipient of a long-held family recipe.

"I got jars," he said. "You get us some new lids. Old ones don't seal right."

I agreed. Might as well move on to canning fish since my morel supply was low, no leeks, cattail root for flour not quite ready, and my vegetable garden, behind a wire fence Harry put up to keep the animals out, wasn't flourishing.

"Say, Emily." Harry, with a bent finger in the air, had a sudden thought. "Meanin' to ask you. What's up with your friend, Deputy Dolly?"

I made a face. I hadn't seen Dolly in weeks. Happy weeks without the little flea of an officer on the two-person Leetsville Police Department calling me out to play—or investigate yet another dead body. A few weeks without her blazing siren screeching down my drive, without her frantic and angry phone calls. I shook my head at Harry.

"Eugenia was asking what's going on with her."

"Like—what did she mean?"

"Says Dolly's meaner than ever. Growls at everybody. She's not giving out no more warnings to speeders, only tickets. And those for the full speed they was goin'."

"Sounds normal enough to me—for Dolly."

"Yeah, well ... people in town are kind of worried. She almost never comes into EATS no more. And, you know, Eugenia offered her free donuts in the morning."

"Bet she didn't take them." I laughed at the thought of straight-edged, law's-the-law, Dolly Wakowski taking free donuts. Be like a New York cop taking kickbacks from a drug dealer. I could see her slapping the cuffs on poor Eugenia, Leetsville's only restaurateur, just for offering. The one thing Dolly never tolerated was law breaking. "Not on my watch," she'd say and shake her head until her police hat wobbled.

Harry shifted the heavy scoop to his other hand, then flexed his fingers a few times. "Arthur-itis," he explained. "Storm comin', I'll bet. But, as I was sayin', lots a folks noticin'. Something wrong with the deputy."

"Her grandmother's living with her now. Maybe it's hard for Dolly to get used to having somebody in the house. She's been alone a long time."

"Yeah, and the old lady's nuttier than a fruitcake, you ask me. But, the way Dolly always carried on about havin' no family of her own, you'd think she'd be happier."

"Then it's probably something else. If I see her, I'll ask."

Harry waved his shovel at a crow creeping from the high grass toward the dead thing in his coal scoop.

"Got to get this down 'fore it gets too ripe to use," he said. "Ya just got so much time, ya know. One minute—fresh as a daisy. Next—shot to hell."

While Harry shuffled off through the picker bushes and straggly raspberries lining his overgrown, two-track driveway, I whistled to Sorrow, figuring I could get back down to my house and begin work on a new book I had in mind. Or I could make phone calls—I had a couple of human interest stories Bill Corcoran assigned me. Or I could do laundry. Or I could do nothing. Maybe go swimming.

Or, I could just stand there as Deputy Dolly Wakowski, in her battered blue squad car, drove in behind me.

TWO

"*THE ICEMAN COMETH* ..." I muttered under my breath, meaning the messenger of death, as Deputy Dolly Wakowski, in her rickety squad car, turned in the sloping driveway behind me.

I grabbed for Sorrow's collar and missed. If I'd been a little faster, I told myself, I could have gotten back to my house. I could have escaped down into the crawl space, dragged Sorrow in behind me, slammed the trap door behind us, and hid long enough to avoid her.

Sadly, even hiding wouldn't shake her when she was on my trail. Being rude wouldn't get her off my back. Saying I was busy and had work to do, or "just don't have the time"—all polite excuses from my Ann Arbor days—didn't penetrate Dolly's head. Like a bloodhound, Dolly stomped straight on whether it was with phone calls, pounding at my door, or pulling in behind me and tooting her horn when I tried to ignore her. I was Dolly's special project, like it or not. She was single-handedly going to see to it that I didn't starve to death in her territory. And she was determined to have a friendly journalist covering her police stories so when it came to filling Chief Lucky Barnard's post as head of Leetsville's police force, she'd be the first in line.

Sorrow, indiscriminate greeter that he was, went bounding back up the drive as her car door opened with the squeal of metal on metal. Dolly stuck her heavy black shoes out toward the gravel then pushed her square body, in summer blues, off the seat to stand, frowning, next to the car, under what should have been a shady maple but was instead a mass of bare sticks. I thought of the falling tent worm poop she was going to get on her hat and smiled, then waved.

I was stuck. Dolly didn't drive all the way out from Leetsville, wasting taxpayer's gas, unless she had an urgent and significant reason for doing so. Lately, the urgent and significant reasons always had to do with murder.

She put one pudgy hand squarely on top of Sorrow's head, keeping him away from her. "Told you, gotta get him trained" were her first, squeaky-voiced words. When he sat quietly, tail beating small puffs from the gravel, she folded her arms across her bountiful chest, and muttered, "No such thing as bad dogs, only bad owners."

"Thanks," I said ungraciously, giving her my best tight-lipped smile. "And 'hello' to you too."

"I got something for you. Tried to call," she groused, then bent to pull her cop pant legs down over her big shoes. Dark sweat circles stained her blue short-sleeved shirt. "Guess you bought one of those machines that warn you who's calling. Dumb. Especially if it's me, with news you need to hear."

"Check your paranoia, Dolly. Sorrow and I were out walking."
I sighed, then watched as tent worm pellets fell on her blue hat, bounced a couple of times, and stayed there.

"Thought maybe you was ignoring the phone again. You know, like you do sometimes."

"When I'm writing," I said. "Can't write and talk on the phone."

"Yeah, well, hope it all comes to something—your books. Not that I want you mentioning me in any of them."

"I'll change your name."

"To what? Do I get to choose?"

"How about 'Millicent.' I think it means 'mouthy' in Latin."

"What the hell kind of name is that?" Her pale blue, red-rimmed eyes went wide. The left eye wandered off a little, as if it had a mind of its own.

Another poop skittered across her hat. I knew I should tell her to move, or I could just count the drops gently raining down on her.

I shrugged. Maybe I even rolled my eyes. "What have you got for me? I'll call Bill, see if it's anything he …"

"Yeah, sure. Like he don't want a murder."

I shook my head and worked my feet from under Sorrow's large, warm butt, where he'd decided to plant his body. "If your person is really dead and … well … was murdered, sure I'll go with you."

"What do you mean 'if'? Unless she shot herself in the back of the head, dragged her body through high weeds with her hands and feet tied, broke down the locked door to that abandoned house over on Old Farm Road, and laid herself out inside—I'd say it's a safe bet she's dead, and was murdered."

I'd already had enough of Deputy Dolly Wakowski, who, when she finally glanced up at me, looked worse than I'd ever seen her: eyes sunken with dark half moons beneath them. She blinked hard against the bright light.

"Guys from Grayling still there, doing their thing. I'm the officer in charge but the chief's covering for me. I said I'd be right back. I'll get you in—but no pictures of the body, ya hear?"

I nodded. No pictures of the body.

"Drive your own car," she ordered. "I don't wanna be stuck having to bring you back."

I looked longingly toward my tiny studio halfway down the hill. Any ideas of writing shifted to a far back burner.

"And Emily…" Dolly sniffed, glanced up at me, and quickly away. "Maybe later… well… I got something I need to talk about to somebody."

"Somebody like me?"

"Guess you're my friend." She thought awhile. "Yeah, like you. But later. Or maybe I'll change my mind…"

"Whatever, Dolly. Give me a minute." I reached out toward her hat, making her duck. Dolly didn't take her hat off much since she'd shaved her head to join a cult and catch a killer. The hair was still short, like a little boy's, with thin, pink scalp showing through.

"Tent worm shit," I explained, brushing off the top of her hat.

"You could've said." She frowned hard, then shuddered, pulling her hat off and striking it against her knee. "Just let me stand here like that…"

"Be right back," I called over my shoulder as I turned and hurried off toward my house.

I set Sorrow up on the screened-in porch with dog bones and water, which wouldn't keep him busy long—he'd be out the newly repaired screen and running around the lake before I got to the top of the drive. But hope does, after all, spring eternal. Some day he'd be nicely trained. He'd be dependable. He'd be a really good dog. Just not yet.

I stopped to call Bill Corcoran at the paper. I told him I was heading over to where a dead body had been found—so he didn't send another reporter.

"Try to get something to me as soon as you can. Tomorrow's paper, okay?" he said, probably leaning back in his crooked desk chair and running his hand through his thick, uncombed hair the way he did, and then pushing his dark, heavy glasses up with that middle finger he sometimes left leaning against his large nose—as if to emphasize the comment.

I grabbed my camera, notebook, keys, and purse. I was out of there, backing up the drive to where Dolly waited. We took off in a shower of gravel. Me, in my aging yellow Jeep, following behind Dolly's patrol car with a big dent in the trunk and a wobbling back tire.

THREE

THE HOUSE ON OLD Farm Road, half-hidden by a tall clump of a long-dead woman's overgrown lilac bushes, was one of those abandoned farmhouses waiting for one last wind storm, one last snow, to finish it, weight it down to broken boards and twisted windows. Michigan State Police cars had nosed in along the road between unmarked cars and a white van—probably the techs from Grayling. Men and women—some in protective suits— stood around in the yard, behind police tape, talking, working, photographing.

I pulled in next to Dolly, got out, and waited beside my Jeep.

The blackened house stood to the front of a once-plowed field. The land was a mass of tall wild grasses stretching over a low rise to where the farmland ended and the forest began. I covered my eyes against the bright sun. In a far corner of the land three birds circled, soared, and circled again, wings barely beating as their heavy black bodies rose and fell. Even I could recognize these kings of the sky. Turkey buzzards. Ugly and clumsy on land but in the air they floated endlessly, circled gracefully, dipping, rising, turning sidewise and turning again. As I watched the birds I thought about Dolly—so graceless in most of her life but utterly at home as a cop, in charge, magnificent in her own Deputy Dolly way. But then I told myself Dolly probably wouldn't appreciate being compared to a turkey buzzard, so kept my observations to myself.

I didn't like abandoned houses. Driving by one, I could smell the mold, and the disrepair. Places where families used to live brought up questions—the whys of everything. But then I sometimes don't have a lot to do while I'm out driving and my imagination runs to the philosophical dark side.

"You comin' or what?" Dolly yelled as she started across the road.

"See the turkey buzzards back there?" I pointed.

She tipped her head. "Yeah? Turkey buzzards. So what?"

"Because of the body inside?"

She kept her head turned away from me, then shrugged. "Who knows? Something out there, I'd say. Dead animal probably. They got theirs. We got ours."

We ducked under yellow police tape strung along the road frontage, down both sides of the house, and probably across the back too. Crime scene. The officers would be very careful, collecting evidence, recording finds, impressions, names of people at the scene—what each had done, when they arrived and left. Dolly had studied police procedure recently, through an online program, and was into dotting every I and crossing every T. "So those bastards' lawyers can't trip me up in court," she'd groused and slapped her log book against her thigh.

She motioned me to hurry as she made her way toward the house. The first thing to hit me inside was just what I'd always imagined about abandoned houses: the overwhelming stink of mold and dust caught in dead, wet heat. And then the unmistakable smell of a rotting body. Enough to make me retch; only I tried never to do things like that in front of cops. Later, when I got back home and washed the stink from my clothes and skin, maybe I'd give my stomach the go-ahead, but for right now I put one hand over my nose and mouth and tried not to breathe too often.

The room we walked into wasn't large, maybe nine feet by twelve feet. Smashed beer cans, old rags, and yellowed fast food bags testified to who had been using the place lately. Peeling, blue flowered wallpaper hung in streamers from the walls. The ceiling, having fallen some time ago, exposed narrow wooden slats overhead. Piles of old plaster lay strewn across the bare, wide-plank floor. In the middle of one of the piles of fallen plaster lay the curled body of a woman. She was dark-skinned—maybe Hispanic or Indian, and lay on left her side, facing away from us, knees drawn up. She wore white shorts, streaked in places with dirt and grass stains. If her hands had been tucked beneath her chin she could have been sleeping except for her yellow cotton shirt, stained dark red with dried blood.

Half of her face had been blown away. Gunshot. I walked around the body, as close as the cops would let me get. Her hands had been pulled behind her and tied with something that looked like jute roping. Her legs were tied at the ankles with that same coarse rope. I took her to be in her forties. Dark hair—what was left of it—that looked to be neatly cut. Her nails were trimmed and painted a soft pink. The sandals on her feet were fairly new, though the heels were scuffed and worn equally, as if she'd been dragged in them. An execution-style murder.

I'd seen plenty of dead bodies while on the Ann Arbor newspaper, but it never got any easier. Just the faces—always ugly in death, eyes staring off beyond everyone, involved elsewhere. I tucked my emotions down inside me and looked at what I could see of her face. A skewed blood trail, like a trail of tears, made its way down her cheek. Another trail led from the door to the body. Even I could tell she hadn't been killed where she lay. No blood spatter on the walls, nor on the floor around her. No tissue. No pool of blood beneath the body. The crooked blood trail down her face meant she'd been leaning or sitting up when she was shot. A killing you might expect in Chicago or Detroit but not your average murder in the quiet countryside of Northern Michigan. Up here people got shot in the heat of an angry fight over a snow blower, or a man strangled his wife when she bad-mouthed his sainted mother, or meth buddies hallucinated and had an old-fashioned shoot-out. From time to time we had hunters shooting each other. Nobody got shot in the back of the head like this woman, their bodies weren't tied up, and most were left where they died.

This old house was obviously only the killer's crypt of choice, not the scene of the murder.

I stood behind Dolly and made my notes. Woman in her forties. Slight build. Not enough blood under that half of head to have been killed here. No tissue in the blood that was there. No spatter up the wall beside her. No spatter across the floor.

She was dressed neatly, despite the bloody stains. A gold cross hung around her neck.

"Emily Kincaid." Detective Brent, from the Michigan State Police post in Gaylord, pulled his single, dark eyebrow tighter over his nose as he turned, saw me, and called my name. He left his place beside the body. "I understand why Officer Wakowski wants to include you. You've been a help to us in the past. But stay out of the way as much as you can ..." He waved a large hand at me, motioning me back from the body.

"Anything on who it is? Why the body was brought here?" I got my questions out as fast as I could.

"You noticed she didn't die here."

I nodded.

Brent gave a deep sigh. "Anyway, nothing on her. No ID. Sure not from around here. Looks Hispanic, or maybe Indian, or even Arab. Can't tell. Only thing is that gold cross around her neck. You see that? Wasn't robbery. Clothes in good order, far as I can see. Unless the M.E. finds something we aren't seeing, I'd say it wasn't rape. But we'll wait on that one.

"That gold cross might help," Brent went on. "I'll send your paper a picture—if we don't ID her right away. You could run it. Otherwise, until we get something more, just go with the usual."

We'd worked together a few times now. There was a grudging respect for me on his side, and a careful wariness on mine. He would shut me out of a story if he had to, when he didn't want something in the *Northern Statesman*. And I wasn't above running with something he wanted to sit on. He had his job and I had mine. We both knew that and liked each other in spite of it.

18

Officer Omar Winston, also from Gaylord—a little guy I had trouble liking—stood beside Brent with his hands crossed over his pants zipper, feet wide apart, his shaven head settled down into thick shoulders, like a turtle. Omar Winston rarely smiled. And rarely was he more than minimally polite. He kept his almost lidless round eyes firmly on the world around him, ready to take on any and all miscreants and reporters—whichever gave him the most trouble. Dolly said she thought he was a good guy, but then Dolly stood up for all cops, at all times, and in all places. I'd had a couple of run-ins with Winston and they hadn't been pleasant. He was an unattractive man with a snarly face and a sycophantic way with officers ranked above him. If he'd shuffled along instead of marching, if he'd been just a little more self effacing, he'd have made a perfect Barkis, a character from *David Copperfield*. Ahhh but, *Barkis is willing*. Yes, *Barkis is willing*. Though I liked Dickens's Barkis, this one annoyed me.

"Anybody check out those turkey buzzards in the back?" I asked, to a round of startled and incredulous cop faces.

"What the hell, Miss Kincaid, we've got our hands full right here." This from little Omar Winston. I noticed his left cheek was ticking away. That was what I liked best about the guy, that I made him nervous.

"I just thought … they're back there. Could be something…"

Brent turned from talking in low tones with the coroner. He sighed. "Dolly, maybe you and Emily should go take a look. They were out there when we got here. Nothing like checking—be on the safe side. Let Emily get a couple of pictures of the house. But keep her out of the way of the investigating officers, all right?" He turned to me. "No disrespect, Emily. Just, you know, don't want some lawyer saying we let you foul up the crime scene when this comes to court."

I nodded. I knew the drill.

Dolly looked at me, her face bunched with distaste. She wasn't happy being sent off to check on birds, but she was a good soldier, did as she was told, dragging me out of the house and around to the back where those birds still circled.

In the yard, as I leaned against a broken clothes pole half-fallen in the weeds, I asked Dolly if Lieutenant Brent was leaving her in charge and if I should call her for updates.

Her eyes brightened for the first time though there seemed to be something missing there. She toed an ancient pile of rags on the ground. "Yup. We got our reciprocal agreement on cases like this. Though sometimes you wouldn't know it, the way those state boys throw their weight around. Chief Barnard says to make sure we hold on to this one. We'll get forensics through them, but that's about all." Her little face drew in with distaste. "They know who's got near a 100 percent solve rate on murders over here. I'm not pushing it in their faces, mind you. But it's out there. I'm doin' a damned good job." She hesitated, then added a grudging, "With a little of your help."

I smiled.

"I think you've got everything we got, so far." She pushed off. "Give me a call later. I'll let you know if we get anything on the victim. Could be some migrant grudge playing out here. She looks Mexican. Maybe somebody's girlfriend. You know, a jealous fight. Something like that. But then … we don't know. Wouldn't be a bad idea to visit a few of the orchards and farms that employ Mexican workers. But don't put anything about that in your story." She snapped her head up, realizing she was thinking out loud. "I'll let you know what you can print."

She took one big sniff and went back to business, striding off over the overgrown farm field toward the woods.

The birds were still there, graceful shadows against a silvery sky. I put my head down and made my way behind Dolly through tall weeds that caught at my ankles. She was kind of pissed at me for making her leave the real scene of the crime, but even though I was new to this wild northern world, I knew that circling buzzards spelled something dead. If she wasn't interested, I was. And I was willing to be laughed at later if we came on a dead possum.

Dolly stopped just ahead of me. "Hey," she yelled, then bent over, pointing toward a path in the grass. She traced a straight line through the weeds, out to where we were walking.

"Drag trail," she said. "Watch where you walk. Either somebody dragged the body to the house this way, or there's another body out there. Stay behind me, you hear?"

I moved over, avoiding the straight path of broken weeds leading toward where we were heading. Something had been pulled along, all right, and not too long ago. The weeds were still flattened, but rebounding slowly. Eventually they'd be standing straight with only a hint of what had happened here.

When we got close, the buzzards paid us little attention. They were into what they fought over, there on the ground. The ugly, red wattled things with skinny necks and dull eyes flew at each other, sprang into the air, then settled ahead of us in the tall grass.

21

One of the birds glared forward, as if fixated by something. Another leaped back atop a thing lying too still to be living. The bird took a long moment to pull himself away from what he'd found, giving way grudgingly, only as we got almost to where he stood.

A dog lay among flattened grasses, a pale furred dog—probably a pit bull, I thought, from the configuration of the snout and thick body, and from the pink-rimmed eye I could see, one pink-rimmed, oozing eye the buzzard had been pecking.

"Wha ... the hell?" Dolly said. Her expression caught the revulsion I was feeling. My stomach gave a single heave and then another.

The dog's body was pretty much intact expect for what looked like scrapes and a few open wounds, the worst being a black bullet hole into the brain at the back of his head. A small cloud of flies, disturbed by the buzzards, hung in the air just above the dead animal.

"Jesus ..." Dolly's voice was strange. When I looked at her I saw the palest face I'd ever seen. Well—pale edging toward green. She bent forward, one arm across her stomach.

I hurried to where she stood, the turkey buzzards scrambling awkwardly away.

I put my arm across her back though she waved a hand at me. She turned and vomited into a clump of weeds behind her.

"Geez, Dolly, it's bad. I know that. But you've seen a lot worse ..."

She raised her hand to quiet me. Her eyes, when she looked up, were wet with tears. Her face turned a bright shade of red. It didn't seem she could stand straight so I tried again to help her.

Again she shook me off, keeping her shoulder between us. If I'd ever seen misery written across someone's whole body, this was it.

"Maybe you need a doctor or ..."

She shook her head violently and pulled a tissue from her pants pocket, wiping it across her mouth.

"I'm gonna go get Chief Barnard ..." I started to say.

She shook her head again. "I don't need nobody."

"It's a dog, Dolly. Sad, yes. But ... there's a woman back in that house in a lot worse shape than this animal."

"Dog's just as dead," she said, avoiding my eyes as she blew her nose.

"I don't get it ..."

"You don't have to. Just mind your own damn business and don't say a word to nobody."

"Are you sick? Is that what you wanted to talk to me about? I'd like to help."

Her head snapped up, eyes wet and angry. The weak eye wandered off as if looking for a way out. "Where you headed from here?" she demanded.

"Traverse City, I guess. I want to get the story in."

"Okay. Never mind. It wasn't nothing anyway."

"Why don't you come on out to my house later? We could talk ..."

"Yeah, sure." She nodded but it didn't sound likely. "Maybe later. Or maybe not. Just something I got in my head ..."

I knew better than to push her. If she was in some kind of trouble, if she hated living with her grandmother and wanted help getting her out of the house, if she had a disease—I'd have to wait until she was ready. Dolly was as stubborn as a bulldog and moved at about the same pace.

I put my hands in the air and stomped off, yelling over my shoulder,

"Fine. Just … well … I thought we were kind of … you know … like friends."

"Yeah, sure." She pulled in a couple of deep breaths and steamed past me. "Like you'd ever be my real friend. Think you're so smart, all that college …"

Dolly, grousing along ahead of me, still avoided the drag path. I watched her back going up and down, big boots tripping in the grasses. Something different about her sloping shoulders, about that oddly shaped rear, and that head under her official hat. Something gone from Dolly. A certain sharp edge that had always been her protection. She was snappish—as usual—but the snap was blunted, turned half on herself. I'd never seen anyone who needed help more than Dolly at that moment. I knew that if Leetsville people, like Eugenia at EATS and all her customers, caught on to this Dolly problem they'd be forming support groups and rescue groups and driving Dolly crazy. At that moment, watching the tight little blue-shirted back ahead of me, I wished them well.

FOUR

FIRST CAME A LATE lunch and a kind of reconnoitering on the Dolly problem. That meant EATS, Leetsville's finest restaurant. I had a few questions for Eugenia Fuller, the large, blond, contentious owner, or Gloria, her sweet little waitress. If anyone knew anything going on in Leetsville, it was that pair. They were the unofficial presidents of every civic association and every social service—psychologists to the masses. Before anyone officially knew that Doctor Henley, at the small clinic between Leetsville and Mancelona, had delivered bad news to a patient, word went around EATS. Planning how best to help began; figuring what could be done for a woman fighting breast cancer, how her kids could be taken care, meals planned, deliveries set up, and a caravan of rides to Munson Medical Center in Traverse City put down on paper. Every municipal government in the United States could learn logistics from the women at EATS. It was simple, cost little, and came from giving hearts.

If Eugenia didn't know what was going on, I would get over to Dolly's house and call on her grandmother, Cate, who'd been living with her for a couple of months. The old woman had to have noticed something if everyone in town was already talking.

EATS was clearing out when I got there. I nodded to the people I saw going in. I seemed to know them all. A few years ago, when I first walked into the foggy restaurant filled with smokers, complete silence had fallen. Curious eyes turned my way. Puzzled glances were exchanged. Lips hovered over the stained edges of coffee mugs a little too long. I'd looked around then, nodded if I caught someone staring, and settled into one of Eugenia's red plastic booths with a sigh—me and the red plastic.

Little by little I'd been accepted. Dolly paved the way, bringing me into her investigations because she'd figured she had a better chance of holding on to a case, not having it go over to Gaylord, if she had help. The chief of police, Lucky Barnard, had his hands full of the day-to-day police work in a small town: those pesky marijuana growers, a kid with a new BB gun shooting out car windows, mailbox destruction, wife beatings, runaway kids. Plenty to keep him busy. Dolly sold me on helping her by telling me I had a better chance of a fulltime job on the newspaper if Bill saw what a good crime reporter I was. Maybe things didn't actually work that way in the journalism business anymore, but I'd figured it wouldn't hurt.

Eugenia, as always, stood behind her glass counter near the door. She glanced up, frowned, and stuck a pencil into her huge mop of blond hair that covered her ears, most of her forehead, and cascaded down her neck.

"Haven't been around much, Emily. Seems like ages." Her frown didn't go away. I got the feeling not being around was a kind of sin in Leetsville—or cause for major alarm.

"Ya know," she went on. "People who live alone back in the woods should see to it they call somebody or come in to have a talk from time to time. Otherwise, we get to thinking maybe you're dead out there."

I shook my head. "Eugenia. Don't you think Harry would, just maybe, call somebody if he found me dead?"

She bit at her bottom lip, punched a button on her cash register, then surveyed the contents before closing the drawer and giving me a dead-on look. "Emily. I know you're new up here ..."

There went the last five years down the drain.

"... and maybe you're not onto the ways of the woods, yet." She hesitated, nodding to Jake Anderson of the Skunk Saloon as the tall man came in and took a booth by the front windows. "But if you want to keep us from worrying you gotta check in from time to time. That way we don't waste time thinkin' about you. You see?" She raised her plucked and drawn-in eyebrows at me, and gave one of those tight smiles people give when they're mad as hell but not willing to own up to it. "I got a little story for you."

She rested her forearms against the counter, above a handwritten sign that clearly said: *Please do not lean on glass.*

"Old Selma Tompkins from down south of Kalkaska. Take her for instance. Lived alone well into her eighties. Tough old bird. Never wanted any help, not even somebody looking in on her once a day or so. Always had this woodstove to keep her warm in winter. Lugged the wood in herself, she did. One winter—and it was a bad one—she went out to get her load of logs, and the shed door closed and locked behind her. There she was—sitting alone until they brought her out feet first, stiffer than a board. Came from that shed bent like a chair. Now, if she'd just not been so stubborn and let folks help her a little bit, maybe drop by once a day, she coulda been found and got out of there before she turned into a popsicle."

Instructive story. Chastened, I nodded. "Sorry. Been busy."

"Still trying to write them books?"

I nodded.

"No luck?"

"Some. I'm waiting to hear."

She stood back, her face lighting up. "Be great if you sold something. I'll tell you what. You ever want to have a party to announce your book selling, or when it comes out, or whatever you writers celebrate—why, you can have it right here, at EATS."

I thanked her for the offer. She was too many steps ahead of me. First came acceptance by the agent, then word of an offer from a publisher, then making changes and getting the book turned in on time—so many steps to having a published book in my hands and actually celebrating. But EATS was a fine place to start dreaming.

Most of the booths were empty so I took one off in a corner by myself. Gloria came over, her tennis shoes sticking to the brown linoleum with a sucking sound, and took my order for a BLT and diet Coke. I tried to catch Eugenia's eye, to beckon her to join me, but she was busy talking to a group of women from the Leetsville Library.

My sandwich came in record time so I settled into eating. I really had to get to Traverse, to the *Northern Statesman*. I'd write my story there at the paper, turn in the film I'd taken of the house and the body being brought out. Most of all, I needed to talk to Bill. I had two small stories to do, but I could use more. I'd figured my August bills ahead of time and had a slight shortfall that could be taken care of by a couple more human interest pieces. Maybe I'd call Jan Romanoff at *Northern Pines Magazine*. She paid better, but most of the work there was done by staff.

This waiting to hear if I had a chance with my manuscript was driving me crazy. What I should have been doing was beginning a new book. That's what writers were always told. I was thinking maybe not another mystery. Maybe the great American novel instead. Something that would knock Jackson Rinaldi's Chaucer book right out of the literary waters.

Not that I was competitive or anything.

But I had an idea to write a book about a bunch of homeless women living in a small wood down in Detroit. There was a time, back when I was in Ann Arbor, that I volunteered at a homeless shelter and sat with women who always had a new dream to tell me about, the biggest dream being a home of their own. Maybe I could get a good novel out of that. I had notes. I had characters. I had my place. All I needed was the time, and the actual belief that I could ever compete with my ex in the literary world.

What I seriously had to do, beyond a competition that lay only inside my head, was get busy finding a job that paid enough money to keep me there in Northern Michigan, although soon I'd have a few jars of fish—since Harry was willing to teach me how to can the stuff. With such bounty I'd surely live to gripe another year. And dream another dream of publishing a novel that would turn Jackson Rinaldi green with envy.

"You know, Emily…" Eugenia shook me right out of my writing reverie as she sat across from me with a heavy plunk against the plastic seat.

"Heard you and Dolly found a dead woman over on Old Farm Road," she said.

I didn't even bother to wonder how the news had gotten back to town so fast. Something in the water, I was beginning to think. Or a kind of specialized Leetsville radar—picking news from the air.

"Know who she was yet?"

I shook my head.

"If you describe her maybe I can help."

I read her my notes. She shook her head. "I'll start asking," she said. "But you know how these workers come and go. If she was a wife or a girlfriend… well…" She shrugged. "And, hey, I heard there was a dead dog out there, too. Now that's a really sad thing."

I nodded, used to Leetsvillians's take on news, and launched into what was foremost on my mind. "Harry said something that's got me worried. You know, just what you were talking about— how we have to watch out for each other."

She nodded. "You mean the deputy, don'tcha."

I nodded. "He said people are saying she's different."

"Meaner, I'd say. Well… not exactly." She thought awhile. "Short with everybody, is what I hear. Don't come in here hardly at all. She's got that grandmother with her. Maybe Cate's doing some cooking. Don't even see Cate much any more."

"You said 'not exactly meaner.' So what is it exactly?"

She thumped her hands on the table top. "Something different. We all seen this kind of thing before and that's why we're worried. Not in Dolly, mind you. But the gettin' mad stuff. Something's going on that's got her in a twist. We're just hoping it's not bad. You know, like cancer." She leaned closer. "Seen enough of it and we don't want Dolly goin' through anything. And not all by herself. She's so damned hardheaded. Never opens up to anybody about anything."

"Comes from her background," I said, not having to remind Eugenia that Dolly's childhood had been a series of bad foster homes until she turned eighteen and was sent out on her own. Then a marriage to Chet Wakowski that lasted six months and the guy was gone. No family. Until the grandmother showed up— thanks to Eugenia's constant delving into genealogy and producing relatives—wanted and unwanted—for Leetsvillians.

"Yeah, well. It's time to get over all of that. You know something, Emily? If you let people come into your life, and you let 'em care about you, a responsibility is owed. That kind of caring doesn't get turned on and turned off. Dolly's been one of us since I can't remember when. She's been there for a lot of people. Mostly she's not easy, but she takes care of the innocent ones and hunts down the others. Think she owes us just a little bit more of herself—like sittin' down and tellin' us things are okay, or letting us help her if they're not."

"She wanted to talk to me but then told me to forget it. I don't know how to help her. She's impossible ..."

"Yeah, well … maybe you should just sit her down somewheres and make her tell you what's going on."

I had to laugh at that one.

"You got any other ideas?" She frowned.

"You really think it's medical?" I asked.

She nodded. "That's what we're thinkin'. She's got her job—so it ain't financial. Got her grandmother with her—so she's finally got some family. What the hell else could it be?"

My turn to shrug. "Anybody talk to Cate?"

"Seemed too much like intruding."

"I'll stop by there. I haven't seen her in a while."

"Be okay, I suppose." She set her hand on mine as I pushed my cleaned plate away. "Would you just let us know? One way or the other—whatever it is. We'd like to stop worrying. If she don't want help, that's fine. But just don't leave us hanging like this."

I agreed, left money on the table to cover my bill, and my usual tip, and made my way out of the restaurant.

I drove over to Dolly's place, a straight up-and-down, no-nonsense white house with cement steps that sat right on the sidewalk. No front yard to speak of. A two-track dirt drive with no car. She had an ochre plastic pot with one tired-looking geranium sitting on a top step and her last year's Christmas wreath—plastic greenery with a couple of shiny pine cones—still hanging in a front window. I was going to stop but got cold feet at the last minute. If Dolly suspected I was asking questions about her, I would never hear the end of it. I drove on past the house. Another time, I told myself.

FIVE

LET US VOTE MY ex-husband the man I least wanted to see in Bill Corcoran's office when I sauntered in, notebook in one hand, roll of film in the other, proud to have scooped even Bill on this new murder.

"Got something for you..." I began, then stopped to take a deep breath when I saw Jackson, lounging in a chair across from Bill's desk.

How I rued the day I'd introduced him to Bill—the day I thought it might be nice to help Jack make friends in the north while he was up here slaving away on Chaucer's penitents, lost in Middle English. How could I have known he would become a more or less permanent fixture in my territory, with my friends— except Dolly, who despised him—and in my life?

"Emily! My sweet Emily. I was on my way out to your place." Jack rose languorously to his feet, stretched his long body, pushed his shoulders back, and opened his arms wide to greet me.

Let's just say my knee came up slightly, aimed at his groin—just in case. An old reflex, a defense mechanism women are born with, like growing spikes on our elbows to keep guys from pulling us in too close to feel our breasts; or wearing pointed shoes for a well-placed kick when a hand went where it shouldn't go; or knowing how to roll into a ball: knees to forehead, like a hedgehog, if we have to; or that magical wishing reflex: praying hard for someone to simply go away.

Anyway, I'd convinced myself I was finally over this jerk who couldn't keep his hands off other women despite once having a charming, talented, intelligent wife who loved him dearly back at his own home.

"What are you doing here?" I let him hug me as I looked over his shoulder at Bill, his dark-framed glasses slipping down his nose, hair as wild as a raccoon's, and a wide face trying to say 'I'm sorry.'

Jackson held me against his perfect white shirt opened a button or two, just enough to show a little of the dark chest hair. He nuzzled my cheek. I knew the smell of him: shampoo, rosemary bath gel, detergent, touch of a fresh iron, shaving lotion—all of it. Even while holding my breath, when that close to him, his scent worked into my head. The feel of that hard chest against mine brought on atavistic flutters; tiny curls of old temptation, down in an ill-used place I tried not to think about any more.

I gave in, for just a second, to the pressure of his hands on my back, then I took a deep breath and stepped away from him, leaving him to pout a little—just the smallest of pouts that I wouldn't stay there, in his arms, forever.

"What a pleasure," Jackson gushed and backed off, his arms still wide as I stood smiling at him for reasons of my own. "I have news for you. I dropped by to see Bill a minute but ..."

You couldn't help but marvel at the guy. Still the academic he'd always been: that slightly superior smile, that shrugging lift of one shoulder, that shake of his head. A good-looking man with a romantic swagger to him, even if the edges were a little worn from too many romps with willing coeds. He had that thing about him that blinds women. Some men are blessed, or cursed, with it. Nothing about looks and nothing about being young. It's just there—in the smile, or the eyes. A touch on your back. It's a kind of knowing that women fall for every time, me included. What I'd come up with, as a weapon against my inane genital flutters when I got near him, was a coded list of remembrances of things past: *A is for asshole, B is for bastard, C is for cunning, D is for devil ...*

Devil was fitting, since I'd once been drawn into typing all that damned Middle English blather into a file for him, then sending the file to his publisher. I'd spent months with Chaucer's pious characters, most of whom I'd have loved to throw into the Thames, or any nearby river in England. And then there had been his pontificating voice if I complained:

"*'Sondry folk,' Emily. Much like your people. The real thing, don't you think?" "Perfect frame narrative, Emily." "Something you might emulate, in one of your books, Emily." "Father of English literature, Emily." "Really, you know so little of literature and yet you aspire to write it"* (with a shake of his perfectly coiffed, dark head).

"Whatcha got, Emily?" Bill cleared his throat and asked.

"Murder." I turned to him fast, hoping my face wasn't red. A couple of deep breaths and I spit out the rest, "Body in an abandoned house on Old Farm Road. Could be a feud—think the woman is Mexican. But she seemed better dressed. I mean, this was no apple picker's wife."

I took a step back toward the door.

"And a dog," I said.

"Dog? What's the dog got to do with the murder?"

I shrugged. "We don't know…"

"By 'we' I'm assuming it's not a royal address…" Bill frowned.

I gave him a withering look. "Me and Deputy Dolly Wakowski. We're working together."

"Woman found outside?"

"In the house."

"And the dog?"

"In the field behind the house. Both shot. Dolly should know soon if they were shot by the same caliber gun. Could still be a bullet in the woman's head. Or maybe in the dog. He was shot where he fell. The woman was killed elsewhere, her body dumped inside the house."

"I'll get it in the morning paper."

"Can I borrow one of your computers? Just came from the scene. I'll write it up."

He nodded. "Give me a daily update, okay?"

"Lieutenant Brent said they might need help with the ID—in case they don't get anywhere."

He nodded, and told me to use the desk across the hall from him.

Jackson, who'd settled back into Bill's plastic chair, sniffed. "Another murder, Emily? My God, you do get yourself into things."

I didn't dare open my mouth. Bill didn't need to know that I could be churlish and vindictive. With him I cultivated an image of a woman in control; a solid reporter able to handle any story, from covering an old woman's tea cup collection to tracking the most vicious of killers. I smiled at Jackson, top lip pasted against my dry teeth.

"Actually," he went on, "I was just telling Bill, here, I needed to talk to you." He tented his fingers then settled them against his chest. "I may have found a job for you."

I waited.

"A new friend of mine. Quite wealthy. And learned. British, you know. He's taken a magnificent home over beyond Torch Lake—grand vistas, a thousand acres. He's running an authentic Australian sheep station, even a kennel. I think that's what he said. But better than any of that, he is writing a book. Name's Cecil Hawke. Have you heard of him?"

I looked at Bill. He shook his head.

"Me either," I said. "What's the job?"

He got up from his chair, unfolding slowly. "Well, for that part you'll have to go to dinner with me. I won't say a word unless it is over a glass of merlot ... "

Bill stood, obviously wanting both of us out of his office. "Great idea. Why don't you two go off somewhere and talk this over." He pushed up at his heavy glasses, giving me a get-this-guy-out-of-here look. "Just do the story first, okay?"

I nodded, pulled my notebook from my purse, then stopped a minute as Jackson waited patiently, eyebrows raised in expectation.

"Amical?" I suggested, meaning the restaurant down on Front Street, past the State Theatre. "I won't be long. A few phone calls, get the story done. I'll see you in ... oh, maybe thirty minutes. Is that all right? You're buying, right?"

Jackson nodded. "Of course. Not that the divorce left me with much ..." He gave Bill a conspiratorial smile. A two-guys-together kind of thing. "I'll see you there."

I called Dolly.

"Looks like the dog and woman were shot with the same kind of gun, but not where we found them," she said. "Dog was. Not the woman. Dug a bullet out of the ground under the dog and the pathologist got one out of the woman. Both were brought to that abandoned house. Woman dead when she got there. Dog killed out in the field. Can't figure why. Same kind of up-close shot. Back of the head. Dog's got other wounds on him. Woman's Mexican, all right. I'm on my way out now to talk to some of the farmers around here who hire Mexican workers. No photo though—you saw her face. Gold cross around her neck. Nothing else."

"Any fingerprints in the house?"

"All kinds. Most won't do us any good. Too many transients. Too many local kids. But go ahead and call Brent. Could be something new from the lab—least a time of death." She stopped to take a deep breath. "And Emily, just want you to know, that dog's being sent down to the Michigan State University Vet School in Lansing. One of the state boys is taking it down soon as they're through with it up here. Wants what they call a necropsy done. That's an autopsy on an animal. The vet school does 'em long as one of us brings the body in. Brent wants to get an idea of the condition of the dog—stuff like that. But you go ahead and call 'im. He'll fill you in on anything I missed."

Brent had more on time of death. Post mortem lividity, temperature, lack of rigor—all led to at least three days dead, maybe four. The body was found by a couple of teenage boys looking in the windows of the old house, probably with the intention of breaking in. "Said they were only curious and weren't going to do any more than take a look. Either way, it doesn't matter," Brent said. "Nothing to do with the murder."

I had all I was going to get, typed up the story, and e-mailed it over to Bill. On the way out I waved, though he did little more than glance up from copy he was editing and give me a distracted smile. I forgot to ask about other assignments.

———

Front Street teemed with tourists: straw hats, dark glasses, plaid shorts, and the smell of coconut suntan lotion. The tee-shirt shops were booming, as was the fudge shop. The Cherry Stop, where they sold products produced by our local cherry growers, had a full house.

At Amical, near the State Theatre with its brightly lighted marquee, and just down from Horizon Books, people sat at outdoor tables having drinks. Jan Romanoff from *Northern Pines Magazine* was at one of the small, wrought-iron tables on the front patio. She called out, "Emily! How are you doing?"

I stopped to talk to her for a minute, asking if she had any stories I might take on. She told me to keep in touch. "There's a possibility of a story on turkeys, for the Thanksgiving issue—if you're interested." She leaned her blond head on one fist and looked up at me. "Or—since I need that, like, tomorrow—how about something on a new ski lodge?"

I told her I'd be in touch—probably work on the ski lodge story since I didn't feel like sitting in the woods, in a blind, waiting for turkeys to wander by. Been there. Done that.

I went into the coolly dark restaurant and stood just inside the door as my eyes adjusted.

The restaurant wasn't full yet. Early for dinner. At the wooden tables lined down one side of the long room, a few intrepid shoppers rested, bags at their feet, iced teas and salads on the white tablecloths in front of them. A young couple held hands across their table. An older couple sat at the tall back windows, the man, obviously Italian, engaged in lively conversation with his plump wife.

Jackson called out from a table back by the dead fireplace. He paused his deep discussion with a willowy waitress and stood to greet me. This time I got a slight peck on the cheek but no hug. When the waitress, with a Trudy nametag on her chest, came back I ordered a glass of pinot grigio and sighed at the thought of resting after a very full day.

"And how is Regina?" I asked brightly, happily returning to the thought that he was soon to marry the typist/researcher who had recently taken my place working on his book with him. His falling face made me want to groan. *Oh, no, not again…*

"It just isn't going to happen," he said and knocked back half of his merlot, while giving me one of his more sorrowful looks.

"So sorry." I liked Regina. She was young and tough. She would have kept Jackson in his place; no nonsense. "What happened?"

He shrugged. "Probably the age difference."

"Yeah," I said, enjoying myself a little too much. "Like—what is it? Twenty years?"

"And her father raised some objections." Insults had a way of sliding right off Jackson's back.

"Too bad. I liked her. At least this one was intelligent. And funny." The sad thought struck me that maybe she'd already quit her job, that this whole business was to get me as his unpaid typist—yet again. "She's still with you, isn't she?"

"Who knows for how long?" He lifted both shoulders and dropped them slowly. "As you might imagine, things are a bit … well … strained, you might say."

I wanted to groan but Trudy was back and Jackson, into impressing the babes mode, asked about the preparation of just about everything on the menu. I ordered chicken and settled for another glass of wine.

"Now," Jackson said and thumped his hands on the table. "Let's get off the past and on to the future. I must tell you about Cecil Hawke. He's writing a book on Noel Coward. You know who he is? Noel Coward, I mean."

I nodded. Noel Coward was an English entertainer my father had idolized, a quirk that came straight down from his own father, along with an old collection of vinyl records that had now come down to me. From the 1920s right through the 1940s, Coward had been that suave, musical gentleman in spats and white suits with short, blunt-cut blond hair, and a wispy look to him. He wrote wonderful, funny songs and acted in British musical comedies of the time and even some American films. The songs he'd written rang through our house, with my dad singing along, until I could have sung them all and not missed a word. Noel Coward: with a cut-to-the-bone sophisticated humor, probably a gay man, brittle, and witty.

"I've heard of him," was all I was ready to give up to Jackson, who, if he'd bothered to remember anything, could have remembered me singing Coward's "Mad Dogs and Englishmen" on happier days.

"He has a doctorate from Oxford, if I'm not mistaken. Man's a genius."

"Is he here permanently?" I asked.

"I don't know that for certain but he has established this amazing residence, with his sheep barns and all. I think he's creating a hunting preserve too. He mentioned friends from all around the world who were here for a spring turkey shoot. And, of course, this fall they're coming for deer. Mentioned riding to hounds…"

"Not fox hunting?" I was aghast.

"No, no, no." He shook his head and clucked at me. "More a kind of geocaching on horseback. He told me about a Saudi Arabian sheik who came for one of the treasure hunts. The man's got friends everywhere." He cupped his hand to outline the whole world. "And you'll just adore his wife, Lila Montrose-Hawke. Oh, and best of all, wait until you see his home. Gorgeous! You would never even know it was there—back in the hills north of Torch Lake. Gated. Guard on duty—all of that."

"How'd you meet him?"

He laughed slightly, "Funny story. I was browsing in Horizon Books one afternoon. Cecil and I were looking for the same book and got to talking. After that we had a latte and he invited me to visit and view some of his Noel Coward collection. I, in turn, invited him and his sweet Lila to my cottage on Spider Lake to look over my Chaucer materials. He's interested in everything. A true scholar and yet a true raconteur. Much like a Noel Coward figure himself. You know, funny and bright, with an edge to him. A man of the world. He'll simply charm the pants off of you, Emily…"

Since that wasn't a compliment, in my book, I frowned and waited for a point to be reached.

The food came. We ate while making a few comments on the food, the wine, the weather, and then back to business.

Jackson drew a deep breath, took a quick glance at the dessert menu, stopped himself from ordering—and me from getting a crème brûlée—and went on.

"This is the part for you." He gave me a broad, even genuine, smile. "He's looking for an editor. Someone to edit as he writes—give opinions on character, structure. Well, you know what's expected. You've done enough of it. Sort of—always the bridesmaid kind of thing." That made him settle his chin into his neck and snicker.

"What you'll do is see if he's missing the obvious—the usual things editors do. And he pays well." He reached across the small table and put his hand gently on mine. "I know it's been tough up here for you. I would like to help … if you'll let me."

Being nothing if not direct, my first question, after easing my hand from his, was, "How much?"

"Fifteen hundred—and that's just for the first ten chapters."

I leaned back and gave him an incredulous look. "Is he nuts?"

Jackson laughed. "Not crazy, Emily. Rich. He needs someone to bounce ideas off—give him some feedback. That sort of thing. He was looking for a connection with a New York editor—but I might be able to talk him into hiring you. Proximity and all of that." He finished his wine with a single toss of his head. "Of course, I'll have my work cut out for me, convincing him, I mean. He isn't particularly impressed with the quality of those he's met up here. That's why he was so surprised to meet me. I mean—so many embrace the simple life, as you do. I'll skip over that aspect of your biography when I speak to him. We've become friends— of a sort. I'm pretty certain I can convince him. If you play things right, could mean at least a few hundred a week for you. And more, as he progresses with the book."

A few hundred a week had the ring of pure gold to me. A few hundred a week—in the upcoming winter—would take care of my snowplowing bill, my gas bill. I did cartwheels in my head as I signaled the waitress to bring me another glass of wine.

"You should really acquaint yourself with Noel Coward's work. He has a tendency to quote the man constantly. Not to the point of annoyance, mind you, but he will expect a certain level of knowledge and intelligence…"

Yeah. Sure—keeping my temper under control. "I know Coward's work. Read *Blithe Spirit*, among others, in college. I've even seen some of his old movies—in college. Modern English Literature, I think. I did graduate from college, Jackson. You do remember? I, too, have a degree in English Literature and Language from U of M?"

He ignored me. "I'll tell him, being a writer yourself, you'll bring a fresh eye to his book. Just think, Emily, you'll be working on a book that will probably be the ultimate work on Coward."

What could I do but sigh? There are people so oblivious, so lost within their own head—Jackson could wear me down to the point I just gave up. "Have you mentioned me to him at all? I mean, tell the truth, Jack."

He gave one of those smiles that would have made me melt in the old days. "He wondered what brought me up here. I told him my ex-wife, Emily, thought this was the perfect place to write. The quiet and all."

"So he knows nothing else about me?"

"I may have mentioned journalist. And that you were attempting to write fiction. His first question to me was whether you thought you were an intelligent woman. Wasn't that odd?"

I thought about that one.

"Cecil Hawke is a bit of an—I guess you might call him an eccentric."

"Did he really say 'does she think she's an intelligent woman'? I don't get it. And if I do think so, is that supposed to be the mark of a big ego?"

"I wouldn't worry. He's British, you know. They sometimes have a funny way of putting things."

"But what did you say to him?"

"I said of course you thought you were intelligent, and so did I." Jack waved a hand as if chasing the subject from his head. "But, let me call him. Maybe we can get out there in a day or two."

"Jackson." I needed to know everything I was getting into. "What did you tell him about our divorce? Not the usual BS, right?"

He frowned hard at me. "If you mean how you took almost all my money, sold our home, left me practically destitute ... I may have ..."

"We shared equally, Jack."

"If you say so."

"So he thinks I'm a woman with a big ego, a money grabber ... but he wants me to edit his book. Am I getting it right?"

"Lots of money," he reminded me.

I took a deep breath. As long as it didn't mean working with Jackson. Maybe I would make enough money to keep me out of the hole for a while. I had a checking account and a savings account. The checking account took care of my present. The savings account was for the future. Both were getting leaner as the months passed.

"The money will be appreciated," I acknowledged, smiling a tight smile.

He shrugged. "Who else would I think of? There is one more thing." He gave me another smile meant to melt the hardest of hearts. "I hate to mention this, but ... well ... I wasn't quite honest with you. Regina is leaving this week. I think it was her father's idea. I might … well … perhaps I'll need your help with my manuscript again. Just until I find someone, you understand."

He slipped his eyes away from mine to watch as a very young blond in tight shorts came in, waved to a man by the back windows, and wiggled her way through the tables.

He cleared his throat, thought a minute, and came back to me. "I wouldn't expect you to do research, just some typing. Maybe get some of my new work to the publisher for approval …"

I hesitated a long moment. "But Jack, think of what I could have charged you for all the work I've done so far."

He made a face. It was close to the aggravated face I'd seen from time to time when we were married. "Don't you think you owe me at least this much?"

"Owe?"

If I hadn't seen Jackson as my pipeline to a fifteen-hundred-dollar job I would have let his last remark send me straight out to the street. But there was no turning my nose up at real money. Not me, who dug wild leeks and hunted mushrooms for frozen soups. Not a woman with a dryer down to its last tumble and sheets on my bed so threadbare as to be almost transparent.

I nodded, then nodded again. The nod changed to a head shake, and a sad look on my face. "But Jackson, let's be realistic. You see the kind of money I can command …"

"Don't be funny," he growled and stood.

"I'm not being funny. If you'll agree to pay me hourly. At least minimum wage. Don't you think that would be fair? How about ten dollars an hour?"

"Is that really the minimum wage?" He stuck his nose in the air and sniffed, turning to see if anyone was watching.

"Yup," I lied, crossing my fingers beneath the table. Sometimes lies can be such fun. "Ten dollars an hour."

"Well, I suppose ... that's never been our ... way ..."

I gave my best sad smile. "Business. It's only business. And I seem to be in the editing business."

"Thanks to me," he groused.

"I'm so appreciative. Will you let me know when I can meet this Cecil Hawke?" I stood, starting toward the door as he signed for the tab and tucked his credit card back into his wallet.

"This isn't quite what I had in mind ..."

I hurried back and planted a big, wet kiss on his right cheek. "Oh, Jackson, I just know you wouldn't want to take advantage of me."

"Emily ..."

I was gone out the door, dancing through the crowd on Front Street, and over the Boardman River bridge with a huge "YES" bouncing in my head.

SIX

A MORNING SWIM IN Willow Lake made me feel clean again. The dead woman, the dead dog, and then my ex at the pinnacle of yesterday left me in a funk. Dolly, on top of that, deepened my funk. The best thing for times like that was being alone in my lake, floating on my back, watching the high white clouds move slowly against a raw blue sky.

Sorrow, paddling beside me, long stick in his mouth, made me laugh. He gave me light moments. He gave me a kind of spiritual freedom I got from no one else. Not from dead women and not from dead dogs. Not from a closed-mouth friend in trouble. And not from an arrogant ex-husband; no matter that he might be my road to financial stability—at least for a couple of months.

I flipped over and swam awhile, for the exercise, then turned on my back again, sunshine beating against my face and outlining red veins on the inside of my eyelids. I moved my arms enough to keep me afloat, kicking my feet when necessary. Another part of living up north, I told myself as I wallowed in cold and warmth;

exquisite freedom of mind and body. As good as sloughing off an old skin—these minutes of peace with my new world and with my dog. The aloneness that had plagued me for years—even when I was married, and certainly when I first moved up to this place—was a gift now that I knew the difference between being lonely and being by myself. One cried out for other people to make me feel alive. The other meant just being me—wearing what I pleased, eating what I pleased (maybe cereal for dinner) whenever I pleased, going to bed when I wanted to go to bed, planning my own day, thinking and thinking and thinking, and when I got tired of thinking going out to find company so I wouldn't be alone.

A cranky beaver, as irate as ever, slapped his tail on the far side of the lake, over by his growing, conical house. He didn't need to worry—I wasn't out to hurt even the least of the creatures. I'd stood up to Jackson. I was in imminent danger of being fairly solvent soon. I was going to be all right. I patted the water, then dripped shining drops from my long fingers on to my face—cool paths to my ears. I touched my tongue to my upper lip—water and my own salt.

"Emily! Hey, Emily!"

Dolly. There isn't a groan deep enough for what I felt right then.

She stood on the end of my dock waving me in. Sorrow, always the first to respond to company, headed back to shake a greeting as Dolly yelled and brushed water from her uniform.

I swam in slowly, struggling out of my half-asleep place. I hoisted myself up to the dock, grabbed a towel, and buried my not-too-happy face in it. I took plenty of time to dry off, then turned to Dolly, who waited impatiently.

"Called you again. I don't know why in hell you even have a telephone if you won't answer it..."

"Yeah, yeah, yeah." I wrapped the towel around me, and whistled to Sorrow, who was headed back around the lake to give that beaver a last 'woof' or two.

She followed me up the sandy path, through the bowing ferns, to the house. Then into the house and on to a seat at my kitchen island, hardware clanking, boots planted on the narrow rungs of the stool. She grabbed her hat off and ran a hand over all that new growth of hair.

"Got a farmer who might know the dead woman. Thought you'd like to go out with me."

"Now?"

"You doin' a story or not?"

"Well, I guess..."

"Then let's get going. The guy's waiting for us. He said he'd talk to some of his migrant workers. See if they can help. He's got one guy been with him a long time. Said if anybody knows anything, this guy will."

She clapped her hat back on her head and slid off her stool.

"Can I get dressed first?" I let the sarcasm drip.

"You better. Hard-working people up here will think you're a nut case—going around like that."

"You know something?" I didn't wait for her answer. "You are the biggest mood killer I've ever known."

"Yeah, well, sure, I guess..."

I was dressed. Sorrow, tired from his long swim, seemed happy enough to rest on the screened porch. We were out of there, headed back over to Leetsville, then on toward Elk Rapids, to see this farmer who wanted to help in the investigation of a woman and dog I had almost put out of my mind.

SEVEN

THE FARM WAS ONE of those going concerns that dot the rolling Michigan landscape: silos and many barns, and a yard filled with big green and yellow equipment. The man's potato fields stretched over one hill and up another as far as I could see. Rolling slowly through his endless fields were huge watering machines, tracking back and forth among the rows.

"He won't be in the house," Dolly said when we pulled up a circular drive beneath dying Lombardy poplars and parked in front of a red barn with wide double doors. "Unless he's having lunch…"

One of the barn doors slid open and a tall, thin man in blue overalls, plaid short-sleeved shirt, and straw hat came out, waving us over to him. He had that farmer look: lined face; narrow eyes lost in folds of wrinkles; shoulders, in stained overalls, drawn halfway up to his ears. He could have been in his late thirties or his early sixties. Or no age. Farmers—after a few years—took on the eternal sense of the soil. They plant food crops and harvest food crops. They talk food crops and weather. Endless dialogue of an ancient brotherhood.

"Deputy." He nodded to Dolly then turned to me, dark eyebrows shooting up.

I introduced myself and told him I was with the newspaper, covering the story.

"Joshua Sutter," he said, dipping his head and fixing me with a pair of very sharp blue eyes. We shook hands.

"Terrible thing you got goin' on there." He turned back to Dolly. "Like to help, if I can. Might as well go over to where my workers live. One of 'em been with me years now. He knows all the yearly pickers up here. If anybody can help you, I'd say Miguel's the one. He's probably back at the house where he lives, having his dinner. Get in the truck." He motioned toward a red extended-cab pickup. "No sense taking two vehicles."

In the truck, I rolled down my window; the air inside thick with the smell of oil. The man revved the motor, ground the truck into gear, and we were off—out behind the barn, around a couple more huge gray outbuildings, and on to a barely visible track leading through the fields back to a far tree line. We bumped along through the fields, a rough ride made endurable by the fresh air blowing through the cab.

Mr. Sutter made no small talk, only kept his eyes focused on the road, swearing under his breath when he swerved to avoid a covey of partridge he stirred up.

A row of identical, small white houses, more rustic cabins than houses, stood in a line beneath a stand of tall oaks. Wet clothes hung on sagging lines from the houses to poles in the grassless yards.

"Talked to him earlier," Joshua said as he pulled in, parked, and turned off the motor. "Miguel Hernandez, one of my best workers—comes every year. Said he doesn't think he knows this dead woman of yours. Said he hasn't heard about any trouble among the migrant workers, like maybe a husband and wife fighting. Not that many of 'em come yet—not 'til harvest time. But, like Miguel, who helps me with the equipment and just about everything else, there are some who get here early, ahead of their families. If Miguel can't help he can sure give you names of other men to talk to."

He got out of the pickup, as Dolly and I slid out on our side. Dolly hit the ground kind of hard and stumbled, catching herself. She didn't straighten right away, only put an arm across her middle, and took a couple of deep breaths.

"Dolly," I put my arm across her bent back and leaned down. Her face was red. She bit at her bottom lip. "What's going on?"

"Nothin'," she growled and straightened, settling her shoulders. "Tripped. Thought I was going to fall."

"Look…" I started to say but was interrupted by a short, dark man who came from one of the houses, letting the screened door snap shut behind him. Two tiny children stood on the inside of the screen, watching the man make his way over to shake Joshua's hand and be introduced to me and Dolly.

We took seats on logs ringing a dead fire pit.

"Rain tomorrow," Joshua said after a while.

Miguel nodded. "I got plenty to do on that engine in the barn."

Joshua agreed, then, after a minute, asked, "You know why these women are here?"

Miguel turned to first Dolly and then toward me. "Somebody found dead. That's what Mr. Sutter told me."

Dolly cleared her throat and moved to get comfortable on her log. "Found a woman with a gunshot to the back of her head. Over near Leetsville."

Miguel nodded, glanced over his shoulder at the house, called out to someone in Spanish, and the children were pulled away from the screen. The door closed.

"What did this woman look like?" he asked.

Dolly gave him a brief description, ending with the gold cross. Each part of the description brought a deeper frown, until Miguel was rubbing his hands between his knees, biting at his lip, then glancing back at the house, to us, then to Mr. Sutter.

"I don't think I know her." Miguel made a face as he shook his head.

"There's something else, Miguel," Joshua said. "They found a dog killed with her—well, nearby. Shot, the way the woman was shot."

A look passed between the two men. Miguel drew in a deep breath. He blinked again and again, looking from me to Dolly. If I've ever seen a man with pain trapped behind his eyes, this was that man.

Joshua saw it too. His voice went lower, softer.

"We had that incident ... remember ..." he said. "I don't mean to put you on the spot but ..."

Miguel looked away and shook his head. "I don't know ... anything ..."

56

He got up. "Mr. Sutter, I got work to do..."

"Not right now, Miguel." Joshua cleared his throat then stood, stretching his shoulders back. "It's about that dog someone dumped here. That dog was shot in the head. Are we looking at some kind of war going on? I really need to know if there's something..."

Miguel's eyes burned. "There's nothing for you to worry about. If I knew even one thing, I would tell these two women. You've been good to me and my family for almost ten years now. You know I wouldn't let anything come close to hurting you."

Joshua Sutter shrugged and wiped his hands down the sides of his coveralls. "It's not me I'm worried about."

Miguel shook his head. "I don't know anything. I would give my life before..."

Dolly stood, hands resting at her gun belt. "Miguel, I'm sorry but I'm going to be puttin' pressure on you. You're not tellin' everything you know, are you? Somethin's going on. That's plain. You should be tellin' us right now, before this gets worse. If there's some kind of vendetta, or somebody's threatenin' people..."

Miguel shook his head and backed away, tripping over a tree root. He turned and hurried into the house. He closed the door carefully, and quietly, behind him. A white sheet was immediately draped across the front window.

"Hope I didn't just lose my best worker," Joshua Sutter said, digging the toe of one heavy shoe into the dirt beside the fire pit. "Never seen Miguel like that before. He's a good man. I'd say a brave man, but he's scared. I can't figure out what's doin' it to him."

EIGHT

"SCARED SHITLESS." DOLLY TURNED her squad car back toward Leetsville, pulling out onto US-131 and heading south. The car was hot and smelly. This hot spell had been going on for a couple of weeks now. It was the time of year when I began praying for rain, even a couple of cool nights. "That's what the guy is."

I rolled my window all the way down and leaned back against the hairy seat, grateful for the fresh air, no matter how overheated. Anything was better than the smell of Dolly's car which must have been inhabited recently by a sour old drunk, a sick old drunk, and maybe a couple of teens chewing cinnamon gum.

I sighed. "Sometimes migrant workers are not comfortable around authority figures like you. Could be an illegal. That would make him a little difficult to communicate with."

"Don't think Josh Sutter would have an illegal on his place. Said the guy had been coming back for ten years or more."

"Still, you don't know for sure."

Her radio crackled and Chief Lucky Barnard launched into a message.

"I gotta leave, Dolly. Charley's got a doctor's appointment…"

Lucky's son had been sick for a couple of years. He came first in Lucky's life. Everyone in Leetsville knew and tried to keep their real emergencies to days when Charley was feeling good.

"On my way in," she answered.

"How'd it go with Sutter?" he asked, voice cracking.

"Okay, I guess. The guy Josh Sutter wanted us to see was awfully nervous. Emily Kincaid thinks it's because I'm a cop."

"Could be. She still with you?"

"Yeah," I called out. "I'm here."

"How ya doin', Emily?" We exchanged a few more pleasantries and he was back to business with Dolly.

"Get your report on my desk by morning, okay? I got to call Brent or that Winston guy and see if there's anything new on their end. I'm getting a strange feeling about this case. It could go a lot deeper than we're thinking."

He signed off and Dolly hit the steering wheel with the pad of her hand.

"Damn it to hell. More paperwork. Wish he'd just let me write it up my own way and give it to 'im. A form for this. Form for that. Be a lot more productive if I didn't have to fill out forms all the time."

I broke into the tirade. "Mind stopping at the IGA before you take me home? I need canning lids. I promised Harry. We're going fishing tomorrow."

"You're actually going to can fish?"

"He said it's good."

"Yeah, that's from a man who eats roadkill."

I sighed. "Just stop, will you? I need some groceries, unless you want to go have lunch at EATS."

"I don't go there much any more. Too nosey for my tastes. Always gettin' into my business. Decided I'd just stay away for a while. Cate likes cooking anyway."

"They're worried about you."

"Why?" She made a face at me.

"Eugenia thinks there's something going on." My back was itching from the seat cover, hairy bits sticking through my light cotton shirt. I moved around, scratching my skin as best I could. "You and Cate getting along all right? You've been alone a long time. Must be kind of hard. I mean, it's nice to have your grandmother in your life after all these years, but it can't be easy …"

"Cate says she's leaving."

"Huh? I thought she was happy to find you."

She shrugged and whipped the car into the IGA lot, pulling between a couple of pickups.

"Wants to go back to France. See if she can get my mother out of that cult thing—the reason she gave me up when I was a baby. Don't see the point of it myself. What's the use tryin' to change her now? Don't mean a thing to me."

I ran into the store, got a frozen turkey dinner and a box of canning lids, stopped only a minute to talk to one of our fine librarians, and then back to the car. Dolly headed up Maple toward Willow Lake.

Halfway home she looked over at my grocery bag and said, "Too hot for canning. I'd wait 'til fall."

"We're going tomorrow. Don't think dead fish will wait until fall."

"You actually going to eat that stuff? Rather starve myself."

"Well, that's you."

"Yeah, somebody with common sense."

I kept quiet and let the warm air rush in and hit my face. Heat in Northern Michigan was the damp kind. Being surrounded by lakes made for hotter hots in the summer, more lake-effect snow in the winter, and great, wide skies filled with either fluffy clouds or thick, enclosing gloom all year round. I didn't have air conditioning at my house and Sorrow, with his warm hairy body, liked to sneak into my bed at night. I'd taken to sleeping out in the living room, on my narrow couch where, as hard as he tried, Sorrow couldn't quite fit himself next to me.

"You know, there's this thing about the women in my family," Dolly said as we passed Arnold's Swamp.

I knew by her tone of voice that this was one of her bits of hard-won philosophy and she was going to spit it out no matter what.

"We don't hang around when there's trouble. I know that much. Like Cate taking off on me."

"What do you mean 'taking off on you'? She's got something she wants to do. Not everything's about you, Dolly."

"Not me exactly, I guess you could say." She thought awhile. "Nope, I got that wrong. It's me she's deserting all right. Like none

61

of us hang around when somebody needs us. Like my mother dumping me the way she did when I was born."

"Since when do you need anybody that badly?"

"Since now, I guess you could say."

I took a deep breath and waited.

She was quiet a minute, then pulled to the side of the road, took the car out of gear, and turned to face me.

"You'll find out soon enough, I guess." She thought awhile. "I'm in … well … some people might call it trouble."

"Ooh," was all I could bring myself to say, half dreading what was coming.

"Yeah, that was what I said. Then I said a few more things."

"What is it? If I can help …"

"Nobody can."

"You're not sick, are you? Nothing like that?"

She shook her head, sniffed, and looked back out the front window.

"Nothing wrong with your job. You couldn't ever do anything that would jeopardize that. I'd never believe …"

"Hell, no. You think I'm crazy?"

"So?"

"Pregnant. That's why Cate's leavin'. She says she's disgusted with me."

'Pregnant' wasn't a word I expected to fall from Deputy Dolly Wakowski's mouth. It wasn't just an anomaly, it was an impossibility. Square little women in blue cop suits didn't get pregnant. And if she had—how? No guy in her life. No visits to a fertility clinic that I'd heard of. No immaculate conception—this wasn't a saint I was looking at.

I opened my mouth and closed it a few times. I knew my eyes were wide. "Not you," was all I could think to say.

She shook her head up and down. "Me."

"Who's the father?"

"Not sayin'."

"Ever?"

"That's right. Nobody's business but mine."

"Maybe the ... eh ... baby's business."

"Just mine."

I watched her face: smug, determined, almost angry at me, as I let her news sink in. "Are you having it?"

"Sure am. Wouldn't do that to a baby, not after all the stuff done to me."

"Did you set out to do this, Dolly?" I asked, not knowing what else to say. "I know you've got this thing about family ... I mean, wanting a family of your own. I thought—with your grandmother showing up the way she did—maybe you were all right."

"I didn't ask for it. Nothin' I went lookin' for. It happened, that's all."

I sat quietly awhile, trying to take in news I never expected to hear. When I glanced over at her, seeing only the side of her face, her mouth was set in a grim, hard line. Her small eyes stared over the wheel at the vanishing point where the road disappeared and the woods all came together. "I've never even seen you with a guy who wasn't a drunk or a pervert or a suspect in something or other. This is way beyond anything I can grab hold of."

63

"That's too bad, I guess." She took a deep breath and turned the car back on, then pulled out onto Willow Lake Road.

I couldn't let it go. I didn't even know what she needed from me. I wanted to be a friend but how do you do that with a person who shuts down after dropping a bomb like '*I'm pregnant*'?"

"You tell Lucky yet?"

She shook her head, glanced in her rearview mirror, and signaled her turn down my driveway.

"Doesn't he have to know? There are questions of insurance. I mean, you're on his payroll. Are you covered with medical insurance? What if you get hurt on the job now…?"

"That's all stuff I can't think about. I've got to keep my mind on the baby growing in me. All the rest of it—even Lucky, well, that's not something I'm gonna worry about right away."

"Some of it's got to be…"

She pulled down my drive and stopped next to the rose arbor, beside a car I didn't want to see in my driveway. She didn't turn off the motor, just looked over as if she couldn't wait to get me out of there. Dolly was done with me. If I had questions, that was my problem. If I had concerns about her, that was my problem, too. Dolly had accomplished what she'd had in mind for that day. Anything more would have to wait.

I got out and stuck my head in the open window to give her a weak, half smile. "Any way I can help…"

"Don't worry," she said, returning the weak smile, as if she didn't believe it any more than I did. "It'll all work out."

I wanted to add something supportive, at least something kind, but I heard voices behind me, coming from out in the garden. I turned to see Harry Mockerman and Jackson Rinaldi standing together—an unlikely duo. Harry was watering my flowerbeds. My ex watched a while, then finally waved.

Dolly peeled back up my drive, shooting stones and dirt behind her. I was afraid it was her way of saying how sorry she was she'd told me about the baby. Maybe her way of telling me to keep my mouth shut. Or maybe it was just Dolly's way of celebrating what was sure to be a major change in her life.

NINE

"Storm tonight," were the first words out of Harry's mouth as he turned off my hose, rolled it into a coil, and stored it under the faucet. "Still, we're going fishing in the morning, Emily. 'Less it's raining hard."

I stood in among my canna lilies, surrounded by phlox and hostas. Jackson stood beside me, hands crossed at his crotch, one finger impatiently tapping the other hand as he waited for Harry to leave.

"Probably not tomorrow," he said to Harry. "I've got a job lined up for Emily. The appointment with the gentleman is for tomorrow afternoon."

Harry shook his head and leaned back stretching his neck to look up at the darkening sky, as if for patience. "Tomorrow's when I'm going, if she wants to come along. Guess you'll just have to choose, Emily." Harry smiled one of his rare, tight smiles.

Jackson leaned back on the heels of his very expensive deck shoes and laughed. "I'm afraid she really has no choice. The man who wants to employ her isn't the patient sort. I don't think..."

I looked from one to the other of my bristling bantam roosters and put up a hand.

"I'm going fishing with you, Harry. That's just what I need. This other thing might not come through, but a jar of fish is a jar of fish."

"You're kidding." Jackson gave me a disbelieving look.

I shook my head. "Please set it up for the day after tomorrow. Just explain that I had a previous engagement."

"Maybe I should tell him you're too busy and don't need the money..."

"Don't be a jerk. I promised Harry I'd go fishing with him. He's going to teach me to can fish for next winter. I'm not turning my back on him just 'cause something else came along."

"Well... well..."

"If your man needs my help, I'm sure he can wait."

Jack shrugged and gave up. "I left a few of my chapters inside." He motioned toward the house. "On the counter. Whenever you can get to them... maybe this weekend?"

I made a face at him. "I'll call. And I'll get you a bill."

He closed his eyes and threw his head back as if pleading for patience from some place outside of him. He turned and walked to his car.

"You seem out of sorts," Harry commented after Jack was gone. "Heard about that dead woman over to Old Farm Road.

And a dog too, eh? I got an idea about that. Don't like to say too much."

He gave me a smile—this one with a bit of a gleam to his eye—and walked off the other way, around my fading vegetable garden and toward the drive and his home. He stopped once to call back at me, "See you at six-thirty a.m. You be ready. Take your car, if that's all right. Otherwise that friend of yours'll be chasing me 'cause I got no license on mine. And we got no fishing licenses either, so I'll pick the spot where we go in. That all right with you?" He frowned and added, "Unless it rains. I ain't standing in water with water coming down on my head."

I nodded—if it rained I was not going to get my fish and I wouldn't get the job either. I hadn't thought about licenses—cars or fishing. If we got caught I could be fined. My name would be in the newspaper.

I sighed. That's the chance you take when you've got a friend like Harry Mockerman. The rest—well—like Scarlett, I'd think about that tomorrow.

For the next few hours I picked tent worm cocoons off my house, my tool bench, my work gloves, and the statue of a little girl holding a rose behind her back that I'd brought with me from Ann Arbor. The cocoons were everywhere—this next stage of the awful creatures' life cycle. I poked them, peeled them from where they had been stuck on, and dropped them into the can of gasoline I carried around the garden with me. I thought about Dolly and this situation she'd gotten herself into and had now dropped in my lap. Then I thought about Jackson. When the can was filled with cocoons, I threw a match in, lighting the gas. I watched them burn with deep and evil pleasure.

———

When it was almost dark I called Sorrow from a foxhole he had his nose stuck into and went inside to find my message light blinking. Couldn't be Dolly—I didn't expect to hear from her for a while. Maybe Bill, with an assignment. Maybe one of the magazine editors. I could use the money in case this book editing thing didn't come through. I needed some new jeans without holes at the knees and back pockets. If I didn't cut back on the mashed potatoes at EATS I was going to move up to a bigger size. That's what I was thinking about as I pushed the play button: a bigger behind.

A woman's voice said, "Emily, this is Madeleine Clark. I finished going over your material and love your changes. The novel works beautifully now—those poor elderly women. Awful thing that they couldn't be left alone to enjoy their small pleasures out in the woods. Could you please call me? We've got to talk before I begin sending the book out..."

There was a slight hesitation as if she waited for me to pick up, then a sigh and the phone went dead.

I took a deep breath, holding on to the edge of the desk, gulping a couple of times. Madeleine Clark wanted to represent me. I had an agent. What did she want to talk about? Probably if I had any thoughts about publishers. Maybe if I had any thoughts of a second book. I'd heard that always got a publisher's attention.

I dialed the number she'd left. A woman, who must have been Madeleine Clark's assistant, said Ms. Clark was gone for the day. I left my name and promised to call in the morning. I hung up and took a deep breath.

Tomorrow then. Early. What time did agents get into their offices? No earlier than ten, I was certain.

Okay. So ten o'clock.

Oh, no! I'm fishing in the morning.

Okay, okay, okay—when we get back.

Well, after we can the fish. Then. Shouldn't be too late.

She'll think I'm not excited, that I'm not a professional writer.

Oh no, she'll probably want to scrap the whole thing.

Okay. Right after fishing, before we start canning.

I'll call her then.

Maybe we won't catch any fish and I won't have to worry about canning.

I'll starve next winter.

Yuck. I probably wouldn't eat canned fish anyway.

I heard the roll of thunder off to the west. From the sound of it, the storm was close. I smiled. It was like someone clapping for me, or a cheer from heaven, or fireworks to celebrate.

All I had was my no-longer-frozen turkey dinner to microwave. A glass of wine. A couple of extra Milk Bones for Sorrow.

A grand celebration for my dog and me.

Until the electricity went off, thunder shook the house, lightning scored the sky like crazy strobe lights, and Sorrow and I went off to sit in the bathtub until it was over.

TEN

ALL THE STORM DID was clear the sticky air. The morning was hot. I picked Harry up at six-thirty sharp. He stood outside his crooked house waiting with two fly-fishing rods, a cooler, a slouch hat with flies hooked to the brim, and a pair of waders for me, folded and sitting on the cooler. I took one look at him, in his fishing hat and dark green waders, and knew I'd made the right choice. If it cost me that editing job—so be it. The day ahead, fishing with Harry, would be priceless.

———

Quiet fishing rivers running through close trees and steep banks have a smell all their own, and a presence. It was very much as though Harry and I intruded, being where the water rushed on, leaving behind the feel and odor of coolness. There was a sense of something—a watching thing, or a sentient breath-holding—as we stepped into the current, waders up to our armpits, lines flicking out and back through the thick air, the tiny splash of contact, and then out again and behind us. Over and over.

I sensed mustiness beneath the clean scent of early morning dew and the feel of heavy damp on my skin. I'd had a few fly-fishing lessons so could pull in my line and send it arcing out beside me, but not the way Harry did. He was good—the rod and line a part of his arms and hands, his body knowing how to swivel gracefully as he cast.

I wasn't into the spirit of the rod and line and fly. For some guys it was a kind of religion. For me it was a matter of not twisting my line so it fell with a thud a few feet from where I stood. Or not catching it in the trees behind me. Or not catching a fly in my own backside. I worried that the slippery rocks beneath my feet would upend me, or that I'd step into a deep hole. Then, as I teetered on the rocks, I worried about catching a fish that required quick movement landing me face down in the fast water.

I moved carefully out into the river and found a flat rock to stand on. I planted my feet and felt secure. Harry kept walking from shore to shore, doing a zigzag through the water, casting and recasting. There was a lot to be said for a fly-fisherman who knew what he was doing and a lot to be said for a woman who knew her limitations. Harry was precise, even stylish, in the slow arc of his arm, the dark suit coat he wore under his waders taking nothing from belonging to the river. With ballet-like movement his line snapped beside him to curve overhead and land exactly where he wanted it to land. I couldn't help but admire a guy who knew what he was doing. But then Harry, as rough as he was, had this side of him in the wilds that was pure artistry. That was one thing

I'd learned since coming up to the woods: art comes in all forms, sometimes without an easy manner or nice clothes but still with a deep knowing.

Harry moved further downstream. I stayed where I was, figuring the fish would come to me as fast as Harry would stumble on one.

I flicked my line sideways, getting the hang of it in my wrists and shoulders and feeling pretty good about how professional I looked out there, up to my hips in cheap green waders. I was beginning to smile a smug smile as something took my hook and ran with it. The pole slid out of my hands and sailed off down river, smacking the water and bobbing under and up until it got to where Harry stood. He reached down in one easy movement and grabbed the pole, holding it in one hand as he held his in the other. He pushed a gloved finger hard on the line and hung on.

I left my flat rock without a thought to my own safety—now that I was embarrassed—and made my way through treacherous water until I stood beside him. I grabbed his fishing pole so he could concentrate on mine, pulling back hard again and again until a shimmering sucker broke the surface and leaped about in the air. It was gray and big, with the look of a carp to it. Harry grinned at me, then waded in to shore to release the hook and string the fish. I wobbled along behind him, watching how he pulled the fish carefully from the hook and strung it through the gills.

When he'd finished and I was pretty sure I could do that much—if not really catch them—he turned his faded eyes, lost in a network of wrinkles, to me. "Why don't you sit on the bank awhile and rest yourself. I'll catch a few more of these boys and we'll get on home."

I happily sat on the high bank, hugging my arms across my chest. I was dressed for heat in only a worn muscle shirt and shorts under my damp and mushy waders. I hadn't remembered about river water. Always a sliver of ice buried in a river. That sliver of ice made me think of the dead dog Dolly and I had found. So still and empty. Not dog-like any more. What kind of person shot a dog in the head? What kind of icy human being felt nothing for an animal in his or her care? Or was so removed from feeling as to look down into a pair of hopeful brown eyes, then put the gun to the back of the creature's head and pull the trigger. All I could see was Sorrow looking up at me, tongue out, eyebrows going up and down as he waited to see what I wanted to do next, how he could please me, how we could discover an old bear's den together. Sorrow was all about the present. All about laughing without laughter. Even more than one man killing another, the thought of a man deliberately hurting a child or an animal drove me insane.

By the time Harry had what he called "a decent catch," I was shivering and beyond caring if I had jars of fish standing on my pantry shelves on not. Thank God, I told myself as I helped pack the fish into a cooler, for the IGA. I'd get through the winter and up the hill of April; maybe with a book contract under my belt. Maybe there was a nice, fat advance in my future. Why worry about a few dead fish when, happily, I had a future of possibility?

I dropped Harry and the fish off at his driveway and drove down to my house to let Sorrow out and call Madeleine Clark. Thoughts bounced through my head—what I needed to say, how I needed to sound, how cool and blasé I needed to be.

There were two calls waiting on my answering machine. I hoped one of them was from Dolly. She'd been on my mind. I was worried about her. There were questions I wanted to ask: had she been to a doctor? Did she have a due date? Was she feeling okay? I remembered that green face when we found the dead dog. Her telling me her secret was like being sand-bagged. I was left with a load of my own feelings, that I wasn't allowed to talk to her about and I couldn't tell anybody else. No advice—if I had any. No helping. How did you befriend a woman like that?

And how was I going to work with her? Would she still want me in on this new investigation? Would she leave law enforcement altogether and drop me? My selfishness came galloping right over the edge of my concern. After all, I had stories for the paper to think about. I couldn't get close to the investigations without her. I pushed the button to hear the calls. The first was Jackson.

"Well," he began. "Despite the fact you made a very stupid decision—I mean, fishing instead of getting the good position I offered—I've arranged a meeting with Cecil Hawke and his wife, Lila Montrose-Hawke, tomorrow afternoon. Lila suggested we make it threeish, teatime. Cecil will have work ready for you. A test of your ability—to see if you're up to his standards. This isn't an insult, Emily—I know how touchy you can get. It's only good business. The man is a consummate professional, just as Noel

Coward was. One of those cool, but droll, Englishmen. I know you two will get along beautifully.

"I'll pick you up at two-thirty. That should give us plenty of time to get there. We wouldn't want to be exactly on time, would we? Puts people off. So, ta-ta. See you tomorrow."

The next call came on with a male voice, hesitant. No one I knew.

"Eh, Emily Kincaid. I read the news about the woman being murdered and might know something, or have an idea anyways. My name's George Sandini. Got a farm out west of Petoskey. There's a worker here who's been with me for years. He's a citizen even though he's a Mexican. I don't know for sure but it seems to me something's going on. This guy's really nervous. I asked him about … well … why don't you give me a call? If you come on out maybe he'll talk to you … eh …"

George Sandini left a number so I called him back. He picked up after a couple of rings and agreed to meet me at his place later. What I had to do then was call Dolly. It would be my way of getting around this big elephant in our friendship. I wouldn't say a thing, nor ask a question, unless she brought it up herself. She was right about one thing—none of my business. Her life was her life.

"Dolly's not available," Chief Barnard's wife, manning the switchboard at the police station, said. I asked Frances to send Dolly out to my house or over to Harry's by about three o'clock. "Tell her it's about the murder. Got another farmer who thinks he's got something for us."

Then it was finally time to call Madeleine Clark. I pulled her number off my computer and sat for just a minute with the phone in my hand. I made a list of questions I needed to ask, and then decided to forget the questions and be grateful she was willing to take me on, hopefully sell my book, and get me out of my financial mess so I could live a long and happy life back in my woods, on my little lake, with the crows in residence in the front oak trees, the fox under my deck, skunk under my shed, and Bob, the bear, visiting now and then to savage my garbage cans.

I already knew her voice when she picked up on her end, in New York.

"Emily Kincaid. Yes, I'm so excited. I'm having lunch with Bernard Long, an editor at Simon and Schuster, next week and plan to pitch your book to him. Do you have anything against Simon and Schuster? I mean, I want to sell your book, certainly, but I don't want to tread on any of your feelings about where you'd like to be placed."

I assured her that Simon and Schuster would be great but didn't get much more in.

"I love your work. What a quaint place you live in. I'm assuming you do live there ..."

"Yes, I live here," I said, swallowing hard at the thought of how she might be changing my life.

"Then I'll be in touch by the end of next week." She stopped, put her hand over the phone, and said something muffled to a person in her office. She came back on. "And keep in mind that whomever we sell your book to might want a series. That would be the way to go with this. Like Sue Grafton, you know, get people to meet your characters and like them."

"Paperback or hard cover?" I managed to get in.

"Oh, paperback, I imagine. The business is truly tough—what with the economic climate. You'll probably be on Kindle and whatever else they come up with. Such a volatile business, Emily. But paperback makes your work more accessible. Until you get known—maybe then. Let's take it one step at a time. I'll make the most advantageous sale I can—though, to be honest, the advance won't be large. We'll hope to make money on sales. That's what I want to get into your contract. Perhaps advertising dollars or something new and creative. Book tours have fizzled, even for the big writers, so I intend to be reasonable with any editor I deal with. Don't worry, Emily. You're in good hands."

She was gone and I had a week to wait. I knew better than to imagine things would happen that fast, still, as I got Sorrow corralled back on the screened porch and drove up my drive to get over to Harry's for my canning lesson, I hoped.

———

"Here's what ya do," Harry said, standing at his white enameled kitchen table with a large knife in his hands. The apron he wore over his funeral suit was bloody, but his hands were immaculate. "I skinned, boned, and filleted the fish. When you do it at home, ya skin it with a sharp knife. But don't scale it first. What ya do next is cut it into two-inch chunks. Then ya wash it good. See here?" He tipped a large bowl of fish chunks toward me. "That's what ya want. You go ahead get those jars cleaned and set here on this dish towel." He nodded to where the jars stood on the drain board. "I'll teach you the rest after that."

I washed the jars in hot soapy water, then rinsed them at his single, deep sink and set them upside down to dry as he instructed. When they were dry, Harry taught me how to pack in the fish, within two inches of the top. There wasn't much talk as we made a brine of water, salt, apple cider vinegar, and catsup.

"That's the secret ingredient," Harry told me, his voice lowered to a secret-sharing level. "Catsup makes it taste like salmon when you open the jar. Best thing you ever ate. Well, next to salmon itself."

I had my doubts but followed his instructions: packing jars, pouring in the boiling brine to within two inches of the top, then setting the jars into a low simmering canning pot and, finally, out of the hot water to sit on more dish cloths until the lids snapped down tight.

He was telling me to store the jars upside down in my pantry and how the fish could be eaten in about ten days or kept for the whole year, when his dogs, out in his makeshift kennel, began to bark their long, howling barks. We looked at each other. Harry didn't get much company—partially because of those fierce dogs—but something, or someone, was out there.

"What the heck's goin' on?" He untied his apron and grabbed up his shotgun from beside the door.

Dolly Wakowski was reaching for the door handle just as we burst out, bumping into her.

"Whatcha want, Deputy?" Harry pulled back, blocking her way in. All I could see of Dolly, behind Harry, was her hat. "No deer killed out of season around here, ya know. Got nothin' that would interest you ..."

"Yeah?" She pulled the door from his hand and walked in, eyeing me, backing toward the table filled with jars of our illicit fish. "Want to talk to Emily, there. Got a message…"

Dolly lifted her nose and took a sniff, then checked out the table behind me. "You and Emily been out fishing, Harry? Got yourself a license? Want to show it to me?"

Harry reared back uncomfortably and cleared his throat. "You see me or Emily standing in a river? You see us takin' any fish? Got some from a friend, is all. Invited Emily, here, over to learn how to can it, should she ever have a friend that drops some off to her house."

Dolly made a skeptical noise and glared at me.

"You picked the wrong way to learn how to live off the land, Emily. Harry hasn't had a hunting or fishing license his whole life long."

I shrugged and pulled off my dirty apron. "We better get out to talk to this George Sandini. I've got his address."

"Yeah. West of Petoskey?"

I nodded. "He said to come any time we wanted to this afternoon."

She nodded. "I got news too. Nothin' good. You know that Miguel we went to see? Over to Josh Sutter's farm? Mr. Sutter called me. Hasn't seen Miguel all day. Not usual since the man's a hard worker. Sutter said he's not the kinda' farmer you have to go out and round up. Went to his house and it's empty. Gone. The whole family. Said he's hearing it's happening to other farmers."

"I'm through here. Right, Harry?" I handed the apron to Harry and thanked him for the fishing and the canning.

"I'll bring over your jars when they cool, Emily," Harry said, frowned hard at me, and asked, "This about that dead dog you found over to Old Farm Road?"

"Hey! This is police ..." Dolly started but I jumped in over her.

"It is. You hear anything? I know how you love your dogs ..."

"Two found a month ago out at Tar Lake in Mancelona," he said. "What usually happens is that the dogs get old, owners get tired of taking care of 'em, and kill 'em off. Most of the time they bury them in their own yard, not dump the bodies like they done." He stopped to think a minute. "Or, could be one of those puppy mill things. Kill off old breeding stock. But I never heard of them killing people too." He shook his head. "Some awful folks in this world, but nobody I ever heard of killing people and dogs at the same time. Something going on. That's for sure."

"Did you hear about the gold cross the dead woman wore?" I asked, on the chance gossip had gotten around to Harry.

"Heard. Don't mean nothin' to me."

"You want to get moving?" Dolly was impatient. "We got an hour trip ahead of us."

On the way out to her car, I filled her in on what George Sandini had said.

"So, he thinks something's going on too. Good thing his worker's a citizen. Won't be runnin' back to Mexico. That's a break," she said, then leaved a deep sigh.

I looked sideways at her. She had the gray look of someone who was suddenly very tired. "You doing all right?"

She said nothing. Okay, I was back out of her twisted loop. Fine with me. I didn't need Dolly's kind of trouble. I'd help find a murderer. Break the story to cement my place at the *Northern Statesman*. That's what I had to think about.

But more than anything, Dolly or no Dolly, I wanted to find the guy who could so savagely kill a dog.

ELEVEN

DOLLY KEPT HER BELOVED siren off. The car was quiet. I sniffed and stared out my side window as she kept her eyes straight ahead. We got to Leetsville and she sped on up 131.

I took my reporter's notebook from my shoulder bag and began making notes. I wondered if immigration would have to be called in. What it sounded like to me was a dispute between the migrant workers coming in from Mexico. Maybe some kind of turf war. I didn't know enough about the process to make any guesses, but since that's all we had so far I was thinking the whole thing should be turned over to the government.

"ID the victim yet?" I turned to ask, keeping my face blank.

She shook her head. "Ran her through every site we know. Nothing. Lansing's got the body. They're asking the FBI to take a look at the prints. Who knows? This looks bigger than just what's happenin' here. Could be some kind of shakedown ring, getting money from Mexican workers, or from illegals. Maybe they're bringing illegals into the country and demanding money not to turn them in afterward." Her voice was the same stiff voice she used to talk to strangers. "You ever heard of 'coyotes'?"

"You mean the guys who bring illegals across the border for a price?"

"Yeah. Like that. I been looking it up. Those guys don't play around. If that's the problem ..." She hesitated. "Got a preliminary on the necropsy Lansing's doing."

I waited, figuring I shouldn't have to beg for information.

"Old injuries on the dogs," she said finally.

"What's that mean?"

Dolly shrugged. "I don't know. Just said old injuries."

"From what?"

She double shrugged. "Could be abuse, they said. Could be the dog was used in dog fights."

"Dog fights." I didn't buy that one. Not in my peaceful Northern Michigan—well—except for a murder or two.

"Had a dog-fighting group up here maybe twenty years ago. Townspeople turned those guys in. Can't see it happening again without folks putting a stop to it. Still, you never know."

That wasn't something I wanted to hear. Not up here. That kind of mindless evil didn't belong in my new world.

———

In Mancelona Dolly pulled up next to a state police car parked at the side of the road and exchanged how-ya-doings with the cop sitting inside, then we were off again.

I settled down for the ride. Fifteen miles or more, depending on where this farm was. The notes I continued making, head down, concentrating, were now notes on groceries I needed, body lotion, a box of dog bones, and anything else I could think of needing within the next month or so. Then I started listing home improvements I might one day make—if my book sold and I made any money. Things like adding a greenhouse off the porch. Like building a garage for the Jeep. Maybe I'd look into a sauna for me so I could run out through four feet of snow, sit in heat for a while, then run back in the house, steaming all the way. I crossed that one off. So, maybe someday I'd get a boat and fish in deeper water. Or maybe I'd get a kayak I could strap on top of the Jeep and kayak in any river I came across. Or go to the Upper Peninsula and get out on some of those perfectly clear lakes. Since I was making "someday" notes, I added a new car and a TV that wasn't twelve inches wide. Maybe ... since I was at it ... a trip to ...

"So, I can't talk about being pregnant to you. Since you seem kind of mad at me," Dolly said to the windshield.

"I'm not mad at you, Dolly. It's just that you're so ..." I sputtered, looking for a word that described her and how she made me feel. "You don't drop something like being pregnant on a friend and then pull away, not let them help. I mean, you acted like you were sorry you even mentioned ..."

She shrugged. "I'm not ... well ... good at needing people."

"Nobody is. But there are a lot of people who care about you, whether you want to see it or not."

"Not Cate. She wants out of here. Says she's not up to takin' care of a baby at her age. As if I'd even ask her. All my life I took care of me. Now I'll take care of me and a baby. Don't need no-body..." She was getting herself worked up again.

"See, that's what I mean." I sighed and settled back for a long ride.

Out of nowhere, stopping me in full throttle, Dolly asked, "You think I'll love it? I mean, you think I'll know how to be a mother? You know I didn't get much in the way of ... well ... of being loved from all those foster mothers."

I pulled in a deep breath. "I'm no expert, but I think it's built into us. Loving babies."

We were quiet. There was so much I didn't know about being a mother. Maybe even about being a woman. So much about the basics of everything. *Would she love it?* How did I know? After a while I asked, "What about the father? A child deserves a father."

"Lots of kids don't have fathers," she snapped back. "There's divorce. There's death. What's different about this?"

"With something like death and divorce, you deal with it. The mom, the kid, they're in it together. What if you have a boy, where's the role model?"

"That'll be me," she said. "More than I ever had."

"Your job's dangerous. I don't care that you're in a small town. There've been small-town cops killed in the line of duty before. What then? What about the baby? You think about a guardian?"

"What are you talkin' about? Anybody in town'd take my kid. Lots of good people in Leetsville. And what about you? Huh? You'd take my kid, wouldn't you? You'd be a good mother. You wouldn't let my baby go off to an orphanage or a lousy foster home."

I couldn't say a word, struck dumb at the thought of having a child. Anybody's child.

"Anyway, what I need now is for you to tell me if you think I got a problem or not."

"Yes, you've got a problem," I snapped back too quickly.

"I mean a medical problem. Kind of scared me."

I took a deep breath. One jump to the other.

"What kind of medical problem?"

"Blood in my drawers this morning."

"Blood? You mean in your pants?" I took a deep breath.

"Yeah."

"A lot?"

"No. Just some."

"That's spotting. Could be serious. Could be nothing. You call your doctor yet?"

"Don't have one."

"What! How do you know you're even pregnant?"

"No periods. Throwing up. I'd say I was pregnant."

"When are you due?"

She shrugged. "Don't know."

"Are you nuts? When in hell did you plan on seeing a doctor?"

"I was gonna go but I don't want to see nobody around here. Everybody in town would hear about it right away."

"Then go to a doctor in Traverse City."

"Who?"

"Why would I know an Ob-Gyn?"

"Don't you have one of them gynecologists? You're the type."

"What do you mean 'the type'?"

"Regular checkups. Pap smears. Mammographs. Stuff like that."

"Mammograms."

"Whatever."

"I'm that type, all right. I just don't have health insurance. But I'm going to when I get the money," I said.

"Yeah, well, me too."

"I think we should head for the hospital in Petoskey. Let them check you out."

"I'll go after we see these guys we're goin' out to see."

"I'll go with you. I mean to the hospital."

"You don't have to."

"Yes I do. You brought me into this and you're not going to shut me out now."

"Who says I'm tryin' to shut you out? That's just dumb."

"Yeah, well … at least I know how to take care of myself."

"Really? No doctor in … what … five years? When'd you get your last checkup?"

I sputtered, then sat glowering out my side window. She had me there. A long time ago now—since that dose of the chlamydia Jackson gave me for Christmas—like, seven years ago.

"Can't answer, can you?"

"I'm stopping this conversation," I said with the best huff I could muster. "I don't have the kind of patience it takes to be your friend."

"Who cares?" she said. "And you're not going to be the god-mother either."

"Fine," I said.

The rest of the drive was quiet, though I couldn't get Dolly's problem out of my head. Maybe I was mad, but I didn't want anything to happen to her. Being irresponsible shouldn't be a death sentence—for her or her baby. Then I wondered at the feeling I'd gotten when she said I could take the baby if anything happened to her. What was that lift inside of me? What was that extra heartbeat about? What biological trick was my body playing? The old ticking clock? More like a time bomb. I had no desire to raise a kid. None whatsoever. Not Dolly's and not one of my own.

————

This farm was a huge, going concern. Barns, silos, and a white, gabled farmhouse with extensions out the side and back. It was one of those lived-in farms that had settled in the midst of fields running back and off to the west, a farm set among rolling green hills with fields of corn in one direction, orchards in the other, and in between a fenced-in pasture where twenty or thirty cows ruminated and lowed in the hot afternoon sun. The ground in front of the biggest barn was bare, earth beaten down by the tractors and plows and trucks standing at all angles under two rows of huge oak trees.

I went off to find George Sandini while Dolly waited in the car. He was on the back porch of the sprawling, white farmhouse, sitting on an old kitchen chair reading the newspaper. We shook hands when he unfolded his long body. He nodded a few times, gave a kind of greeting, one long sentence about the weather, then we went back out to meet Dolly. The man was in his sixties. He wore faded overalls with a white undershirt beneath. His face was lined—too many years staring out at growing fields. His hair was mostly gray, with a few gray hairs sticking up from his undershirt, and even a few sticking out of his ears.

I introduced Dolly. They shook hands.

"My worker's name is Carlos Munoz. Right now he's doing a final spraying in the orchard," he explained to both of us, dragging his words. "Be back soon. Better you wait 'til he gets here. Don't either of you want to be out there with the spraying goin' on."

"Want to tell the deputy what you told me?" I said.

He nodded to Dolly, then nodded again. "Heard you're doin' a bang-up job there in Leetsville, Deputy. Be happy to help out anyway I can. What Carlos was sayin' was that he got wind of things—workers getting scared off and such. He says it's about something big that's either going on already or might go on. Couple of illegals got involved, then got scared and hightailed it outta here. Nobody knows what's happenin', but I'm thinking drugs. Something like that."

"What's with the dead dogs?" I asked. "Your guy have any idea?"

George Sandini shrugged, bringing his wide shoulders up to his ears and down again. "Heard about that, too. One man had a dead dog thrown up near his house. Kids found it in the morning. Maybe it's a Mexican thing. Like a warning they'd recognize right away."

"Any idea who the murdered woman is?"

He shook his head slowly. "Nobody went missing far as I heard. Maybe Carlos can tell you something. Doubt it though. I'll tell you one thing. This guy's usually real steady. He's with me permanently—long as I've got a farm. Carlos is a citizen. Been here over nineteen years. Good man. What he does is help the migrant workers when he can. I mean, helps them find places to shop, doctors when they need one. Things like that. But I never seen him as shook up as he is now. Already he sent his wife and kids to his brother in California. Says far as he can see, it's gettin' dangerous around here." He made a face, took off his cap and scratched his head. "You ever hear of anything like that, Dolly? Dangerous up here? But I'll tell you both, what I got to worry about is having help with the crops. Can't handle the harvest by myself. No way. So we're all hoping this thing gets resolved ..." He put a hand over his eyes and looked off behind where we were standing.

An old green army truck drove in and stopped. A small, dark man with a thick head of straight black hair, wearing a blue-striped shirt and old jeans, jumped out and hailed George.

"You finish the apples?" Sandini asked.

The man nodded, smiled, and walked to where we stood waiting under the trees. George Sandini made the introductions and the man's face closed down on itself. His eyes narrowed. All trust and friendliness got lost back in his head.

"Can you tell me what's going on, Carlos?" Dolly asked, toeing the bare dirt with her booted foot, then looking off across the road, to another farm.

"Only what I told George here." He shrugged his shoulders. "Workers are leaving when they shouldn't leave. Harvest time is ahead. This is what they come for but now, one after another, they're going away. Back to Mexico, I think. One whole family, the Diaz family, gone."

"Why are they leaving?" Dolly asked.

Again he shrugged and looked hard at his dusty shoe tops. "I heard some things. Just some things I don't know for sure. George asked me what I know and I told him not a lot. Just things I heard."

"What are those things, Carlos?" Dolly asked, glancing at George Sandini then back to Carlos. "It would help if you could tell us what's going on. One woman is already dead. You know who that could be?"

He shook his head. "I only heard one thing."

"What's that?" Dolly prodded.

"That the woman wasn't just nobody. I heard she might be official, with the Mexican government."

Dolly and I exchanged a look. *What now?* "Was she looking for somebody? Like a fugitive or something?"

Carlos shook his head again. "I don't know. Somebody said he heard a woman was around asking questions. They thought she was from immigration at first but she was Mexican. I mean, she came right from Mexico. She showed one man a badge."

"Badge? Like a police badge? Government badge?" Dolly asked.

"Don't know for sure. Just a badge."

"Can you give me the name of the person who talked to this government woman?"

"Yeah. But he left. He went out to where his cousin works, in California."

"Right after this woman talked to him?"

"Soon after, is what I heard. I asked a friend of mine what he thought was going on. My friend said it's something pretty bad."

"Can I talk to your friend?"

Carlos shook his head. "He's gone too."

Dolly thought a minute. "How many have been threatened, that you know of?"

He shrugged, looked up at George Sandini, then back down at his shoe tops. "All I heard was six or more. The ones who pulled out. Seems some of them got dead dogs thrown at their houses. Some just got scared because of what's going on." He squinted his black eyes at first Dolly then George. "Since we heard about this woman getting shot—with that dog there with her—well, I think more men want to leave."

"What about that Diaz family? You know them pretty good?"

He shook his head. "I knew of them, but..." Here he spread his hands to show he had nothing more to give.

"Are you afraid? I mean, now that you talked to us?" Dolly asked, voice low. "George here won't say anything. We're not going to bring you into it..."

Carlos shrugged. "I'm a citizen. Where can I go? I don't have anybody in Mexico any more. I don't know what this is all about. Maybe my brother, in California. But that would leave George, here, stranded right when he needs me the most."

George toed the ground. "If it comes to your safety, Carlos. Nothing is worth putting your life on the line."

We all fell silent.

———

On the way home we kept our talk to what we'd just learned and what we didn't learn. I had a lot more notes and many more questions.

Dolly said, "I'm gonna call Lieutenant Brent, see if we can get the government to find out who the dead woman is. Maybe immigration, I'm thinking. Or drugs. Those cartels down there are powerful. Could reach all the way back here, I guess. Not like we're near a border or anything. Only Canada. Drugs don't usually come in that way. More like down in Florida. But I heard even Atlanta's got some big drug problems going on." She talked almost to herself. "Still, I haven't heard of any new drugs, or even more drugs, up here. A few guys grow their own weed. That's about it. With the recession, nobody's got money for crap like that." She turned to face me. "Wha'd you think? Look like an agent to you? The dead woman?"

I shrugged. Never having seen a Mexican agent of any kind, I had no idea. "Had on shorts, not a uniform. Maybe she wasn't here officially."

"Wouldn't you think somebody in this country would've been alerted if a Mexican agent came in? 'Less she was undercover. Something like that."

"Wouldn't you think she'd have tried to fit in then? I mean, she looked like a middle-class woman. Not the kind of thing she'd wear undercover if her trouble was with the migrant population."

She shrugged. "People in different countries do different things. Could've been just the cover she needed."

I let that one go by me. We could beat it to death, but I had something else on my mind and I couldn't keep quiet.

"You going to get in to a doctor or a hospital now?" I asked, circling us back to where we'd been before.

She nodded. "Yup. Soon as I call Brent. Soon as I get this report turned in …"

"Soon as the moon turns purple …"

"Don't you worry about it."

"I won't," I answered.

She let me off at my mailbox. I slammed the car door behind me and she peeled off in a shower of stones. I was so pissed at her the stones felt good, hitting my bare legs. One more thing to be mad at Dolly Wakowski about.

TWELVE

JACKSON PICKED ME UP at exactly two-thirty, the immaculate white Jaguar sliding to a stop in front of my rose arbor in a cloud of dust and gravel pings. When he got out to hold the car door for me, he was resplendent in a white linen suit with a white tee shirt under the jacket. The guy would have been perfectly dressed for an afternoon soiree in colonial India, or maybe in Java. How about a pre-war plantation in South Carolina? Well—not the tee shirt and no socks with his loafers—but his air of *noblesse oblige* was firmly in place.

I, on the other hand, wasn't half bad either, despite needing a haircut and wearing old make-up I'd scraped out of the bottle. Although it was hot, and I'd been tempted to wear shorts and a tee shirt, I'd dressed in my best blue slacks and my next-to-best white tee shirt with only a little yellow staining under the arms. Because even I could be self-conscious about my appearance, I threw a yellow cotton jacket over my shoulders and gathered my blondish hair back into a ponytail tied with a white silk scarf over the red rubber band that held everything in place.

We made quite the pair as we drove past beautiful Torch Lake into the hills beyond.

———

At the guarded gate to the Hawke estate, where Jackson and I stopped and were cleared to proceed by a uniformed sentinel, we were sent on through a thick wood with snarled, dense underbrush. Ahead of us, as the road twisted and straightened, a low, dark-roofed house rose sinuously from the ground. The house was of stone, with the long, low sweep of Frank Lloyd Wright's Falling Waters. It was a house meant to become part of the landscape around it—a rock cliff built into the side of a rugged hill. The front of the house went on forever, curving at a far corner where a wall of mullioned windows looked into a thick copse of trees. The closer side curved back toward what must have been a garden. We parked beneath a low portico and climbed the wide stone steps to a door with stained glass panels that were oddly of doves and gargoyles. I thought I glimpsed Cecil Hawke's English background in small touches that would have been as much at home in the Lake Country of Great Britain, as here, in the woods of Northern Michigan. Above the door, a carved lintel read *All hope abandon ye who enter here.* I thought it a bit much—Dante's hell—but Jackson touched my arm and nodded at the devilish warning, smiling at the man's cleverness.

Off to the east of the house, set back a ways, I'd noticed a huge U-shaped barn, like the mews I remembered from an English trip early in my marriage. The center, surrounded by the wings of the two-story barn, was enclosed by a high wire fence. Inside the fence the ground was churned and muddy as if trampled by many animals, not visible today.

Further east of the barn were small outbuildings and even further off I could see a low, gray, bunker-like cement block building. There were no windows in the building, nor any in the dark, octagonal building beyond it. Low-cut pastures stretched as far as I could see, with what looked like a thousand sheep grazing—small white blobs set against the bright green of the grass and the bright blue of a clear sky. I caught the slightest tinge of manure on the hot breeze. The sound of baaing drifted faintly from the far fields.

Jackson pushed the doorbell and leaned back on the heels of his loafers. He crossed his hands in front of him and rocked, turning to beam down one of his best *wait 'til you see this* grins at me.

The door opened wide. Amid a blast of icy, air-conditioned air stood a man in a wine-colored smoking jacket tied with a fringed belt. He was barely taller than I was—which is only five-five—with a round face, like one of those upside-down puzzles. He smiled a wide congenial smile showing dull, small teeth. He looked to be the kind of overly hearty man who would want to hug us, and who would laugh a lot, and be merry and all of that.

Beside him, kept still by one of Hawke's hands on a nasty-looking, studded collar, stood a one-eyed, very big, yellow dog. The dog, which looked fairly old or used, cocked his one good eye at us. The skin over the empty eye socket had been sewn shut but fluid leaked from around the fixed skin. Not a pretty animal, but neither was my dog—beauty in the eye of the beholder and all of that.

Cecil Hawke threw his arms wide, as I expected. "Ah, yes, Jackson Rinaldi. My friend. How good to see you. Come in. Come in."

The accent was definitely British, but hard to place. Not Cockney, certainly, but also not the London accent I was familiar with. Cecil Hawke stood back, moved the yellow dog beside him with a kick, and motioned us into a wide front hall where the walls were white and covered floor to ceiling with what I judged to be a mass of bad paintings. Not a single sensibility here, not even good taste. Renaissance to Postmodern. Many were copies. Even these were washed out and badly done.

Cecil Hawke, himself, was astounding. His blond hair was an obvious toupee cut neatly to fit his head and curve around his long ears. He was clean shaven, almost hairless. His skin was pale, as if he hadn't left the house all summer. In his left ear shone a huge diamond stud. Over the paisley ascot he wore at his throat hung a heavy gold chain. He was straight out of a thirties romantic comedy. I smiled, trying not to laugh, thinking him funny and odd, as he clapped his hands together, then tented his fingers at his chin. Most of his left index finger was missing, leaving only a blunt stump. The other fingers were long and bent.

"And you must be Emily Kincaid, the astounding writer and editor Jackson speaks of so highly." He wobbled his head back and forth, then reached out and grabbed me in surprisingly strong arms. He pulled me close and hugged the breath out of me, finally giving a hearty pat to my back, then letting me go to step away while trying not to choke. The hug from the man was powerful. The smell of the man was even more powerful. I hadn't smelled that much cologne since a Mafia trial I'd covered for the *Ann Arbor Times*. The don, who had whispered in my ear that if he got off he'd give me a call; his two attorneys; and two rows of hefty male spectators all smelled like Macy's perfume aisle at Christmas. This guy smelled like that—musky and thick. I supposed it was expensive but it tasted cheap in my mouth. I could feel the cologne settling in my nose, certain to haunt me for the next few hours. Ever since I was a kid and passed out in church from the perfumes and colognes and lotions, I'd avoided all scents that weren't normal to the human body. I also avoided the normal ones, unless they came from me and it was a hot summer day and I was too tired, from working in my garden, to take a shower. But then, we all do have our standards.

Cecil talked on as he led us and the yellow dog, who tap-tap-tapped a limping tap along behind him into a room that looked like an English library. Books were everywhere: walls, cases, tables. Among the books were obvious collectibles. Most, when I got a glimpse of labels and titles, either had to do with Noel Coward or were his plays and ephemera: playbills from theatres where his work had appeared, small holiday editions of his plays. There was photo after framed photo, all standing around the large room on square tables, round tables, and long, library tables. The lamps, lighting the room to a soft, rosy glow, were dimmed by pink silk shades. Over the fireplace hung what had to be a painting of the man himself—not Cecil but Noel Coward, dressed, no doubt, for one of his plays in a smoking jacket, pipe in hand, seated on the arm of a tapestry-covered chair. Cecil Hawke's passion was evident and established his bonafide interest in Coward's life history. Maybe Hawke really could write, I thought, raising my expectations of the job ahead of me.

"They say I resemble him, you know. Noel Coward." He patted his small, round stomach. "Except in a few places."

"Isn't this a totally amazing room?" Jackson said, turning in circles, then pointing to one bit of Coward memorabilia after another. "Who else to write the definitive work on the man's life?"

"Please," Cecil preened beside me. "I'm sure this lovely creature doesn't want to hear my praises. Though, of course, I'm loath to stop you." He turned to me, grinning widely. "You would like a peek at the manuscript, am I right?"

Speechless at what I took to be an old British comedy I was caught up in, I only nodded.

"In due time. First, shall we draw up chairs and get to know each other? My wife, Lila, will be in shortly. She does love to make an entrance. Actress, you know. She'll see to tea."

"Freddy." He clicked his tongue at his dog and motioned hard with a bent finger to a place beside his chair. The dog, broad head puckered with old scars, settled to the parquet floor with a painful grunt.

Getting to know each other became a discourse on Coward's *Blithe Spirit* between Jack and Cecil. Then criticism of other writers, Hawke quoting Noel Coward on Gertrude Stein, "'*Literary diarrhea*', as Coward would say."

I smiled from time to time, then gave up and looked at my nails which hadn't been manicured in months. I picked at one obvious raw cuticle, making it especially interesting, then crossed my legs, recrossed them, and twisted in my chair. I scratched my neck, cleared my throat, blew out a bored sigh, and thought of a new mystery I might write, about a guy so in love with Noel Coward he took on his persona and then turned up dead; shot by a critic who hated Coward passionately. Would Cecil Hawke recognize himself? I decided that he would not. Not in the hands of a consummate professional like me.

After twenty minutes, Cecil struck the arms of his chair a solid whack, bringing the two of them back to the room and me. "But we've been neglecting you," Cecil leaned over and set his hand, with the missing knuckle, on my knee, softly kneading the cotton of my slacks, then thumping my leg twice. "I've seen your work in the local newspaper, haven't I? Something about a murder, wasn't it? Grisly business, as I remember. A woman? Migrant workers?" He gave a delicate shudder. "Hardly what you would expect in this Eden, is it? I mean, for heaven's sake, wouldn't you think farm workers could keep their battles to their own little places?"

I bristled. I was about to say something when Jackson, recognizing the signs, reached over and put his hand on mine, holding me still, warning me to keep quiet. I swallowed my comeback about one immigrant being much like another—since he was, after all, an Englishman—and settled for a blank, noncommittal, but reddening, face.

Cecil got up. "You two wait here. I'll see why Lila hasn't appeared with our tea and I'll get the manuscript, such as it is. I must say you'll soon know why I require an editor of your caliber, Emily. But I'll be back in just a ..."

The heavy, dark oak door to the hall opened with a solid bang against the wall behind it. A woman came in with a wide, Angelina Jolie stride, startling the dog. Tall and thin, with flowing, straight, white-blond hair, Lila Montrose-Hawke wore neatly pressed, wide-legged, white linen slacks with a red embroidered top. Gold, filigreed earrings hung to her shoulders, distending her earlobes. She was well tanned. Maybe a little too tanned, her skin having the leathery look to it that older, wealthy women get. Too many tennis games. Too many hours at the pool. Too many cocktails at the bar. Too many years living up to the trophy-wife image. I put her age at well over forty. Older than Cecil Hawke, but maybe not. Men like Cecil—the hearty, pink kind—didn't age as quickly.

Lila Montrose-Hawke hurried to where I sat, bent, and grabbed me before I could struggle up from my chair. I was given a quick, hard hug, and then a long, soulful look from a pair of clear, green eyes. "You must be Emily, Jackson's ex. He's told us so much about you." She planted a kiss on first one and then the other of my cheeks, holding me close and whispering, "Don't mind if Cecil has his hands all over you. It's just his way. Just his way, darling. He doesn't even like women."

I was dropped back to my chair as she turned to Jackson, who'd had enough time to stand for the onslaught of being hugged and kissed. Her strong hands held his shoulders so he couldn't get away. She held him just a moment too long, looking soulfully into his eyes, passing on a message I'd seen a lot of women transmit. She moved her body close to his, her knee pushing slightly between his legs. I glanced at Cecil but he was looking out the window. I had to be embarrassed for them all by myself.

Lila went to Cecil and turned her left cheek, offering this small target, then quickly pulling away and back toward the doorway. "I'll see to tea," she said over her shoulder and was gone; the whirlwind stilled.

I looked from Jackson to Cecil, who seemed to think nothing of the entrance and exit we'd just experienced. It had to be me, I told myself. Not used to city people any more. Certainly not used to English city people. But her warning... *hands all over me*? Oh God. I could have groaned aloud.

Cecil patted my knee again. This time I slowly pulled my legs back where he couldn't reach them. "I suppose that whisper of Lila's was to warn you about me and my... shall we say... predilections? She has this wild idea that I chase women. Only a pose, my dear. You have nothing to worry about. Not from me." He shrugged. "I think it makes me more valuable to her. I mean, as a catch. She likes to imagine every woman desires me. But look..." He indicated his rather wide body, straightened the toupee, and smiled so his little, clipped teeth showed. "All in her head. But if it pleases my darling wife, well..."

I looked hard at Jackson. He'd brought me into a terrible movie, somewhere between an early Cary Grant and a bad *Who's Afraid of Virginia Woolf.* What I was feeling—crawling up and down my spine—was the need to get out of there, leave this play with no ending, and go home to my dog and maybe a long shower, but Lila was back, pushing a rumbling and clinking tea cart, talking loudly as she parked the cart beside us, and began inquiring as to cream or lemon.

We sat, with lace-edged napkins in our laps, and sipped our tea, murmuring and nibbling at hard, dry cookies that didn't soften though I followed each bite with a big swig of tea. I was Alice at the Mad Hatter's party. At any minute the dormouse would fall into his cup and someone would shout "Clean Cup" and we'd all move around a place.

I smiled at the others and sipped, then sipped again. I patted at my lips with my dainty napkin. There was no game these people could come up with I wasn't ready to play. Time passed with the atonal ticktock of the large clocks standing around the walls. Freddy, on the floor beside Cecil, snored and shivered. I leaned toward Lila to tell her how good the tea was. She tossed her long blond hair back from her face with an almost tired gesture and gave me a wan smile. "Yes, Cecil will have only the very best of everything in his home."

I got a long stare from her—from the tips of my sneakers to my ponytail. She leaned close. "Do you think you're the best editor for Cecil's book, Emily? I mean ..." She looked me over again.

She'd caught me off guard. I wasn't used to bragging and honestly didn't know if I was the best editor for his project. I shrugged. "We'll see." I gave her one of my more gnarly smiles where I moved my lips up and down and kept the rest of my face stiff.

"Now, Lila." Cecil set his cup on the cart and shook his head at her. "Let's not make our guest uncomfortable. I'm certain that Emily shares my, and Noel Coward's, sentiment that '*work is much more fun than fun.*'"

"But that is exactly what I'm thinking of, my dear. Your work is so important. A New York editor is a necessity, wouldn't you say?"

He gave a light laugh. "Do I smell a selfish reason beneath your oh, so sweet love, dear? Is it that you want to be in New York to get discovered, to take your rightful place on the New York stage? My darling girl, you can't fool me. *Only thinking of me.* Really, are we so deep into farce?"

She pouted at him. "But, Cecil, is this woodsy creature really up to the job?"

Woodsy creature, indeed. My Irish ire sprang straight out of my brain and lit my face to a warm shade of something nearing Kelly green, I supposed. I could sit there like a rabbit frozen in the glare of a couple of coyotes, or I could get the hell out of there. I was close to making some real money, but getting even closer to a fine Irish snit. The snit won out over all good sense, as usual.

I sat a moment more, then rose, wordless, from my chair, set my empty tea cup precisely on an inlaid gold rose of the Italian teacart, napkin beside it, and turned to walk out of the room. None of them deserved the benefit of my goodbye but I stopped in the doorway to turn with what I thought was a nice, dramatic flounce.

"This 'woodsy' creature's got better things to do than waste time at a crazy tea party. You want to hire me, Mr. Hawke, give me a call. If I don't hear, you can bet I won't be losing sleep over it."

I sniffed and tossed my head, making my pony tail bounce like the white flag of our 'woodsy' deer. I walked off down the hall toward the front door. There was a nervous laugh from behind me in the library. Jackson, I thought. There was the satisfactory scrambling of chairs and feet. Someone got up and came scurrying behind me across the Italian tiles of the big hall.

Lila grabbed my arm as I neared the front door. She pulled forcefully, turning me to face her.

"I am a bitch." She leaned in close, red mouth stretched wide. The look she gave me was a near pout—long phony lashes blinking, face so very sorry. "You must learn that about me. But I promise to stay out of your way when you're working with Cecil."

She pulled harder at my arm. "When there is more than one man in a room and another woman is there, why I just get impossibly competitive. I want them all, you see. Men. Men. Men." She raised one hand in a wild gesture then put a finger to her lips and pulled me back to the library where Jackson and Cecil stood, looking equally uncomfortable.

The men relaxed back in their chairs, obviously happy that the female uproar was over. I took a deep breath. Was this crazy couple worth the fifteen hundred I'd get for ten chapters? Hmmm... yes, I thought. And maybe I could use them in a later book. I would kill off Lila—that was certain. Maybe him too. My mind was jogging in circles. I wanted the money. The work would be easy for me—I'd always been a good editor; even back at the paper I'd been known for almost perfect copy.

"I'd like to see the chapters you have so far," I said, looking directly at Cecil. He nodded at me and then at Lila, who leaped from her chair, ever the dutiful wife, and hurried from the room.

"Lila will bring the pages down from my study," Cecil said, smiling benignly at me. "We'll begin with five chapters. I'd like to see if we can truly work together; if you grasp the spirit of my book; if you, an American, have the intelligence to capture the deep and dramatic sensibilities of this consummate Englishman." He smiled his yellow-toothed smile. "I do, of course, have conditions for your employment. I will need you to sign a confidentiality agreement. You may not discuss my work with anyone but me. You may not show my work to anyone. You may not share my work at any time—under any circumstances." He smiled again. "And as to your criticism, as Coward once said …" He cleared his throat, leaned back in his chair and assumed a rigid pose, "'*I love criticism, just so long as it is unqualified praise.*'"

I was neither charmed nor bowled over by the man's wit. He was a creepy guy with a loony wife, in a big barn of a house, with a dog that looked as if he hated his master.

I took a deep breath and laid out conditions of my own. "Jackson's told me what you're doing. I hope the book lives up to the advance praise … from Jackson." I looked toward my ex, who showed his own uneasiness.

"And I, in turn, hope you can get beyond Lila's exhibition," Hawke said. "She sometimes … well … there are mental issues at work. Wouldn't you say so, Jackson? You've been with us both now for … what is it … over three weeks?"

Jackson, embarrassed, studied the palm of his right hand. He gave a fake laugh. "I'm hardly in a position to judge your lovely wife."

"Well," Cecil sat back, his face slowly turning the shade of a paperwhite. "It seems we've gotten through our first contretemps."

I took a deep breath. Not quite, I told myself. I hadn't been put through the afternoon's mania to leave without a clear understanding between us.

"Let's discuss how I work," I said, hurriedly making up a set of rules to lay down. "First, I charge fifteen hundred for the first five chapters. They're the hardest to deal with, the place where the book begins and announces its direction. The first chapters require more work than the entire book. If this is all right with you..." I stared hard at Cecil, who had relaxed back in his chair with his fingers twining on his chest.

He nodded.

"...then, it will be two hundred for each succeeding chapter. I will not work with your wife..."

"Agreed," Cecil laughed, sniffed, and pulled his lips in tight across barely exposed teeth.

"I'll work at home unless you need to consult with me face to face."

"I prefer face to face." His voice was cold. His eyes had narrowed. I figured this was the impasse. I had to give something.

"That's fine. We'll work it out." I took a deep breath. "I expect to be paid when I take the work. If you aren't satisfied, your money will be returned, but only if I agree that I haven't done the job you want done."

I ran out of steam and bravado. All I wanted then was to get out of there, check and manuscript in hand, or no check and manuscript in hand.

"Satisfactory," he said, fixing me with a guarded look. "Of course, the first consideration is if your work rises to my standards…"

"And that your writing rises to mine," I countered, pleased with myself.

We reached an uncomfortable agreement, a kind of line in the sand for each of us. For a moment I couldn't figure out why he'd taken any lip from me at all. He didn't need me as much as I needed him. It felt wrong, somehow. But financially right.

The man's eyes were very blue and very small and very cold when he fixed them on me. He made me uncomfortable, the specimen in a jar feeling. Usually I was smart enough to turn and run from people like Cecil Hawke. Not this time. I'd negotiated a darn good deal.

There was heel tapping from the hall and Lila flounced in again, large manila envelope in her hand.

"I've got it," she said louder than necessary. "Cecil, you ridiculous boy, you hide your work in a new place every day."

He smiled a Cheshire Cat smile. "The better to keep it from you, my dear. And, of course, from the maid."

I'd seen no maid. So far, on this whole big estate, in this enormous house, I'd seen no one but the Hawkes and their gatekeeper. There had to be others—all those barns and fields beyond the house—someone must be taking care of the sheep. Looking at Cecil Hawke, I wondered if he ever moved far from the chair he sat in, or from a tea cart, a whiskey bottle, or a mirror. This guy was no farmer, and he surely wasn't a shepherd.

I glanced at the sealed envelope dropped in my lap. It was thick. Maybe they were long chapters.

"When can I expect to hear from you, Emily?" We were back to being friends. Well, he was. I still felt a chill running through me.

I tucked the manuscript under my arm and stood. The men stood. Jackson stumbled over himself assuring Cecil Hawke that I would do a good job, that I was a little rough around the edges but that I was a good writer and a fine editor.

I asked for a check and got it, glancing down to make sure I really had fifteen hundred dollars. It was there, as requested: fifteen hundred, with a scribbled note at the bottom that it was a down payment on manuscript editing. Cecil produced a contract. I went over it fast. He was awfully worried that I'd give his idea away, or maybe peddle his precious words. The contract stated I agreed to read the whole manuscript and that I wouldn't talk about his work to anyone but Cecil Hawke, nor discuss it with anyone at all—not by written word and not in conversation. The guy was paranoid. To be honest, I couldn't figure out who would be interested in a study of a long dead guy who wasn't that well remembered. Maybe Jack and Cecil knew something I didn't know, but I doubted it.

I smiled at Cecil, who tossed his head, making his blond toupee slip slightly to the left. He waved his hand, dismissing us.

Lila took first my arm, then Jackson's, walking us both into the hall and toward the heavy front door. As she strode along, she pulled us close, though I sensed Jackson was pulled a lot closer than I. Something going on. Not the first time I'd had the feeling.

I sighed. At least he wasn't my husband to weep over any more. He could sleep with whomever he picked to sleep with. But with this one, this Lila Montrose-Hawke, he was probably in for a lot more than he could handle.

"You must forgive me, both of you, for my antics before," she said, throwing her head back to expose a perfect set of blindingly white teeth. "I'm an actress, you see. I left the stage for Cecil. He needed me; so you understand that at times I tend to indulge in a bit of drama. Rehearsal—all is rehearsal. And I do, after all, have to protect dear Cecil from an unfeeling world." She squeezed my arm hard enough to make me wince. "You've forgiven me already, haven't you, Emily?"

Jackson was the first to turn and smile happily at her. I grimaced behind her back.

"And now, for much nicer thoughts. You both must come to the party Cecil and I are planning. Next Saturday. A *Blithe Spirit* party." She turned to grin at us. "We are so excited. It will be our homage to Noel Coward, of course, but also our very first party here in the north country. We will follow the play as closely as possible. You know it, don't you?" This was for me. I nodded, hoping I remembered some of what I'd read at my father's insistence when I was ten or so. "There will be a séance and all. Just as in the play. You must, you really must, come. And if there are others—I mean of your ilk, of course—feel free to call if you'd like to invite them. We are eager to make a splash up here. To set an entirely new standard."

Thank God we were at the door. Parade over. I wanted to pull my arm from her grip. The woman gave off uncomfortable heat and I knew the heat wasn't for me.

"It will be costume, of course, the party. Who would expect anything different from a Coward production? Dress as a character in literature, a writer, or someone from history you most admire. Emily, you do have a favorite literary character, don't you? If not, call and I'll be happy to make suggestions." She turned to Jackson. "And you, my dear friend, you must be someone wonderful. Oh darling, I see you as D'Artagnan. A dashing Musketeer. Virile. Someone..." Her pointed pink tongue licked out, moved across her lips, then ever so slowly pulled back into her mouth.

"We'll be Jack and Jill." I tossed my ponytail. "Joined at the hip—that's what we are. If Jack goes down the hill can Jill be far behind?" I laughed a truly phony laugh.

She clucked at me. "Surely you can come up with something a little... well, shall we say... a little more creative? But you have plenty of time, Emily. And remember, if there are friends you would like to bring... well, all you have to do is whistle." She turned to Jackson and slowly puckered her lips at him. "You do know how to whistle, don't you, Jack?"

Her voice was low and sultry, a true Lauren Bacall imitation. "All you have to do is put your lips together, and blow."

I wanted out of there. I wanted to get home where I could take a bath or get in the lake and listen to the woodpeckers pound at my poor, bare trees. I wanted to forget how crazy human beings could get and how bills and life necessities were trapping me when all I'd come to Northern Michigan for was to be free.

I pulled the wide door open, hurrying, and ran into a dark man standing on the threshold.

"Excuse me..." I started.

The man, dressed in work clothes—blue shirt, baggy blue pants, and heavy boots—looked down at me and nodded. He had to be over six feet. Maybe two hundred pounds. Black hair. Black eyebrows. Cold eyes. His face was lined, but good looking in an early, cruel Clint Eastwood kind of way. His broad shoulders and thick, muscular body gave off the mixed message of strength and menace. He stood back to let us pass, looking off, away, not bothering to see us. He said nothing.

As we hurried down the front steps, I heard Lila, back in the open doorway, hissing at him. "What are you doing at the front door? Listen here, to me. Don't you ever enter my house this way. I don't..."

"It's not your house," the man answered in a deep, accented voice riddled with insolence.

"I'll have a talk with..." Lila sputtered, turned around, and slammed the door in his face.

I looked over my shoulder to see the man squeeze the door handle and push his way in. I turned to Jackson. "What the hell did you get me into this time?"

I shook his hand from my arm and stormed ahead of him to the car.

THIRTEEN

I HANDED MY CHECK reluctantly to the smiling teller at my bank in Kalkaska.

I went on to Leetsville where I drove by the police station. Dolly's car wasn't there. There were lots of other places I should have gone—like home to Sorrow. I could use the rest of the day to write, begin the new mystery about dead skeletons Dolly and I found out in Sandy Lake. I liked what happened in that investigation. I liked that we could bring a family together. I liked the way I came out looking. Still, I didn't know if I had a whole book there or not. What I needed to do was get started, make notes, fill out an outline as best I could, start gathering details, maybe even dare to ask Dolly how she remembered things—but probably not. She was still mad that I'd included her in my first book. I'd fight that battle when I got there. And if she was mad at me about the books, she was going to get a lot madder when I did what I'd decided to do—about her and her 'problem.'

I drove around the block a few times, asking myself: Did I really want to do this? And the answer kept coming back: *Somebody's got to.* I angle-parked in front of the police station and went in. Big, burly, Chief Lucky Barnard was at the front desk, completing a phone call. He made some notes, then turned his worn face up to me. In the few years I'd known him, Lucky had been through some bad health problems with his eight-year-old son. Charley's cancer had just about killed Lucky. The kid was better now, seemed to be cancer free though Lucky and his wife kept their fingers crossed from checkup to checkup. When I'd first met Lucky, about four years before, he'd looked younger than his forty-four years. Now he looked much older. His eyes were pouched, the corners of his mouth drooped; his chin sagged. He'd put on weight so that his stomach bulged over his thick, leather belt when he stood to shake my hand. He was a man who seemed to have the whole world on his shoulders. And here was Emily Kincaid, come to add a little more to his load.

"Hey, Emily. How're ya doin'. Haven't seen you around here since that cult thing. Good job you and Dolly did on that one."

"We had help."

"Yeah, well you stuck with it. That's what counts. Too bad about the reverend. He wasn't a fraud, ya know."

"I know," I said, shaking my head. "Just a man on a mission of his own."

"So, what brings you here today? Dolly's out. She said the two of you were working on this migrant murder. She really admires you, you know. Says you're one of the only people she knows she can trust."

116

I choked slightly at that one.

"Lucky," I started in then stopped to think again. No, I told myself. There was no way around it. If I was about to cut my own throat, then that's how it was going to be. Soon there'd be clouds of steam rising over Leetsville, but I didn't know what else to do. "Did Dolly tell you she's pregnant?"

He took in a swift, deep breath, then let it out. His red face got redder. His jowls and cheeks settled slowly into a blank look. He opened his mouth then snapped it closed. "You don't say."

I nodded. "She hasn't told anyone but me. She's having some problems, hasn't been to a doctor, and who knows how she expects to get all the way through without telling you."

He made a face and took in another deep and sorrowful breath. His voice dropped a note to two. "She'll probably take to wearing big sweaters and saying she's getting fat. You know Dolly. Her way or no way." He thought a while. "Don't know what I'll do without her. Got this migrant case. Got some bad checks passed at the IGA. Got stolen gas down at the Shell Station. Kid brought his dad's hunting knife to school. Got a suspected marijuana patch out on state land." He thought a while. "I could go on…"

"I wanted to tell you because she's got to look out for herself and she's not doing it. I figured you have every right to be in on this. You're here on the front lines."

"She'll be mad. I mean, that you told me." He thought a minute. "When's the baby due?"

I shrugged.

"So, who's the father?"

"Your guess is as good as mine."

"Never seen her with anybody since she was married to Chet. He's dead. You think she went to one of those clinics? Like that octo-mom?"

I shook my head.

The chief leaned back then sat down and crossed his arms over his chest. He was a man coming through a fog. Soon, he gave a short, amazed laugh. "Never saw Dolly as a mother. Always so, well, you know what I mean, kind of tough. Don't get me wrong. Good person and all. One of the best—Dolly Wakowski."

I agreed. I made a comment on how I'd seen many women changed by motherhood and hoped the miracle would hit Dolly too.

He laughed again. "Take a miracle, or she'll be hooking the kid to her gun belt and dragging it along with her."

I left feeling guilty and mad at Dolly for never handling things the way they should be handled. Her, and that holding everything tight to her chest, like she couldn't trust a single person in the world. So I'd jumped into her business. Probably get my ass kicked—figuratively, I hoped. Too late to worry about it now.

As my dad used to say—*in for a penny, in for a pound*. I drove over to Dolly's house. Her car wasn't there either but I thought I saw her grandmother inside. I was going to intrude in Dolly's business again. This took two more trips around the block and five minutes sitting at the curb before I got up my nerve to go to the door.

Dolly's potted geranium on the top step, planted in a red clay pot, was doing all right. At least it was still alive, which was a hopeful sign. Dolly didn't bother with flowers until she met me, saw my garden, and got the idea to dress up her house a little. This was the result. Purple geranium in a distinctly red pot. You could shudder when you looked at it, but at least Dolly had added color to what was a basic white saltbox, without the usual charm of a saltbox, with white trim, sitting on a small, bare lot, close to the street; this three-step, white-painted cement porch leading up to the front door, and pitted aluminum storm windows—open because, like me, she didn't have air conditioning. I knocked at the white door embellished with four fan lights and a dusty Christmas wreath, and listened, hearing footsteps cross the bare wood floor.

Catherine Thomas, Dolly's grandmother, stood there frowning at me. Catherine was an amazing woman, so completely who she was—a true original, or as meaner people might say, an oddity. She dressed the same no matter the season, no matter the occasion. Like come-down royalty. Like a bag lady who lived behind a Broadway theatre with access to their dumpster. Like a poor woman without a mirror.

Today she wore a black cotton skirt that fell to the tops of her truly broken-in Gucci shoes. Her white-lace, see-through blouse hung over a black, old-lady, sturdy brassiere. In her piled-high white hair a golden star bobbled back and forth, held up by nature, wiry hair, a stick drilled into her skull, or simply by Catherine's force of will.

"Emily," she moved her overly painted lips up and down, crinkling her eyes so that her false eyelashes had to bat a few times to get themselves untangled. "It's good to see you, but Dolly's not here."

I put a foot up into the house the way a salesman does, to stop the door from slamming. "I came to talk to you."

She made a coy face and waved me on inside. "Sounds ominous. Do you want to know where I buy my clothes? No? A more sinister reason for coming? Perhaps like somebody we both know and love getting herself stupidly pregnant because she thinks a child will make her life perfect instead…"

She closed the door and motioned me into the living room, then to a chair. "… of a living hell because no child guarantees happiness for the mother. It's the other way around, you know. A mother should guarantee happiness for the child, except it so rarely happens that way."

She sat on the plaid sofa across from me. "I mean, look at me, with my daughter over there in France with a terrible religious cult that's held her hostage for years, turning her against her mother and her own child, for heaven's sakes! What kind of thing is that? Well, I'm telling you, I'm giving Audrey one last chance. She's going to be a grandmother now and if she's ever going to live up to what she's done to Dolly and make things right, this is the time." She drew a breath but went right on talking. "I'm too old to go through all of this again. I just can't deal with another child that could be lost."

I interrupted when she took a breath. "Will Dolly's baby be lost?" I asked.

"Who knows what will happen?" She threw her hands in the air. "She is her mother's daughter after all, and a baby is not a doll. There's no changing your mind after you have it. Twenty years. That's what it takes. Twenty years, at least, of devotion. Well, I'm telling you, I just can't go through it. Not more shame and sadness."

"Would Dolly cause you shame and sadness?" I couldn't help myself.

She thought a while. "Maybe not Dolly. To tell the truth, she's not a bit like Audrey. The opposite I'd say. And nothing like her father. But I'm not up to looking after a child. Not at my age. Though, you know, I didn't exactly look after Dolly when she was a baby. I mean, not with Audrey never telling me what she did with the girl. All along I thought the baby was with Audrey, there in France. But no, my very own daughter deceived me and signed over all rights to Dolly to the State of Michigan. I never in my life heard of such a thing. Mother like that. Well, I'll tell you one thing, she didn't learn it at my knee. Maybe I never had much, with my husband, Ricardo leaving me when Audrey was born— dirty scumbag—flying off to Rio with a Spanish dancer named Florita, who he'd sworn was his sister when he first brought her home. Can you just imagine? I took that woman into my house…"

She stopped as if someone had hit her on the back of her head. She blinked a few times, bringing herself back to Leetsville, Michigan, back to Dolly's house, and back to this living room, and me. "But you didn't come to hear my long tale of woe, did you?"

"No," I said, clearing my throat because I'd forgotten for a minute that I could speak. "I mean, I came because Dolly told me she was pregnant and I wanted to talk to somebody because Dolly's impossible. She told me she's spotting a little, told me she has no doctor."

The woman clasped her hands together and thumped them up and down in her lap. "Were you going to suggest an abortion? You know Dolly would never be a party to…"

I shook my head. "No. I respect her choice. If she wants the baby… It's just that somehow I don't think she knows how to take care of herself, let alone a baby."

Catherine Thomas nodded. "Women. Women. Women." She sighed. "What a sorry bunch we are. That damned pull toward motherhood. If only women had a chance to get beyond it. I don't mean to speak against having children but, for heaven's sakes, at the right time, in the right circumstances, for the right reasons."

"There'd never be any kids if that was the way it worked," I said.

She shook her head at me. "It's just that nature doesn't respect a woman's right to a life of her own. Don't you think, Emily, that so much is stacked against us? I had so many friends with big dreams. My friend, Alice Trotter, for instance, wanted so badly to play the flute in a symphony orchestra but she got knocked up in high school and married Billy Comfort, who turned out to be the opposite of his name. Last time I talked to her, she said Billy never could stand to hear the flute and broke it into a million pieces. Well, now he's dead, but too late to do Alice any good. And then there was…"

I had to break in or I'd never get away. Cate Thomas, I could see, was spending way too much time alone in this house. "I don't know what I want Dolly to do. Not my call. I just wish she'd take care of herself."

Cate thought a minute then blew out a long, sorrowing breath. "Wish I could help out. Wish she'd listen to somebody. Last thing I want to see is Dolly losing that baby. I don't think anybody knows what a hurt soul she is. Baby'd be good for her. But still, I'm going, be gone from here in a week or so. Back to France one last time to see if I can find Audrey."

I frowned at that. Something stuck me as not right. Seemed, as Dolly said, too much a pattern in the Thomas family—leaving their kids when they needed them the most.

"I can see you're judging me." Cate shook a crooked finger near my nose. "I'm an old woman. I would have taken Dolly out of those awful foster care homes where they put her. I never even knew she was still in the States." She gave a mighty shrug. "I would have raised her but ... well ... now I just can't take on a job like that."

I said nothing but my gut was churning. If I opened my mouth I'd say something even worse than the stuff I'd already said.

"So, were you thinking she should put the baby up for adoption?" Cate said, then sat back and smiled.

The question made my stomach lurch. I couldn't imagine Dolly giving away family.

"That would never happen."

Cate blinked and smiled brightly. "Then what do you want her to do? I mean now that the deed is done?"

I shook my head, forcing myself to simmer down. "I don't want Dolly to do anything but look after herself and the baby. Later—I'll stand by whatever she wants to do. For right now, she's got to see a doctor ..."

"Oh, but she did. I should have told you. This morning. There's a doctor affiliated with the hospital in Kalkaska. They got her right in."

"Is she okay?"

"The spotting was nothing. Normal, for some women. Baby's doing fine."

"Does she know … what it is?"

"The baby?"

I nodded, getting a little frustrated chasing answers around the block and back.

"No, not yet. Too early, I think."

"How far along is she?

"About three months."

"Due?"

"Sometime in January."

I sat back, breath let out of me. So she did the responsible thing after all and here I was, busily discussing her business behind her back. I felt as if I was growing smaller, like Alice. Maybe it was because Alice stuck her nose into other people's business too—like following the White Rabbit down the rabbit hole, or demanding answers of queens and cats. A lesson I'd obviously missed in childhood.

I left after asking Cate not to mention I'd been by the house. She clucked and promised that not a single word would pass her lips, which didn't reassure me.

At home I was met with an angry puddle of pee right outside the door to the screened-in side porch. Of course I stepped in it with my bare foot, having kicked my sandals off as I'd entered the house. Sorrow sat in the far corner, behind a white wicker arm chair, and tried to look mad at me for being gone so long, right at the time of day when we usually went for our walk. All he could work up to was looking unhappy, and sad, now that he'd chosen to punish me by peeing on our floor, a method even dogs found degrading.

"Thanks a lot." Using sarcasm on a dog was a healthy way to purge anger.

His eyebrows went up and down, independently. He sneezed twice, obviously trying to garner sympathy for his faux malady. I hopped, on one foot, into the bathroom, then back out with a bucket and rag. Pee sopped up and forgotten, Sorrow came leaping at me for the joyous reunion we'd missed.

Our walk was short—because the day was hot and my shady woods didn't exist. I set the hoses in my flower beds and looked over the glorious, pink Queen Elizabeth bloom on one bush; propped up the last of the pink and white peonies; and checked for blossoms on the clematis I'd planted at the base of a tall stump where a maple had been bowled over by a wild, summer wind.

When I put on my gardening gloves I found a cocoon inside. I threw the gloves but had to go get them and pry the cocoon out with a stick. Instead of gardening I spent the next few hours pulling cocoons from my log pile, from the boards of my house, from my gardening bench ... just about everything inanimate that had a cocoon attached. Creepy. Like being trapped in a nightmare, the vampire creatures moving in on me, everywhere I looked—no getting away from them. I was afraid, if I stood still too long, I'd find one in my armpit, or behind my knee, in my ear ...

When the phone rang I had to put down my stick of death. Inside, I answered before checking the caller ID and got exactly what I deserved.

"Have a busy day, Emily?" Talk about angry, dripping, pointed sarcasm.

"Must be Dolly Wakowski."

"Been talking to Lucky?"

"Someone had to."

"And my grandmother?"

Ah, that woman was a true secret keeper. "I needed to, Dolly. You were scaring me. You weren't thinking straight."

"Yeah. Like it's your problem."

"It's everybody's problem."

She was quiet.

"Well, I'm sorry…" I began, knowing I didn't sound sorry at all. To sound sorry around Dolly was like offering your throat up for the knife.

"Nah, you're not sorry about anything." She was quiet. "I guess, if I was in your shoes I'd have done the same thing. I haven't been thinking right. Came as a big surprise. Still, it's not that I'm not happy about it. I am. And I don't care what anybody else thinks. My life, Emily. Nobody got me through anything before now. Not one single person. Anything I did, I did it myself. This too. So don't go on thinking you have to be my friend or anything. If you don't approve of me, see if I care."

"Dolly. I am your friend. I'm not judging you. I just got scared. It didn't seem as if you were taking care of yourself…" I hesitated. "Catherine told me you'd been to a doctor. That's all I wanted. I hear it's next January. Quiet time of year. Might as well have a baby and …"

She cut me off, in no mood to put up with my teasing. "Anyway, I called to tell you we could be close to ID-ing the dead woman."

My head wasn't up to the leap from Dolly being mad to Dolly being professional.

"… eh … fingerprints?"

"No. Got a phone call. Can't say anything else yet 'cause you'll write it up for the paper and we're not there yet."

I was back into professional mode too, wanting the story.

"Then when?"

"Somebody's coming to see me in the mornin'."

"You'll let me know?"

"Sure, me or Officer Winston."

"You mean that Omar? What a stick. I'm not working with that …"

"Don't jump to so many conclusions, Emily. Omar's a good man. Does his job."

"Can't stand him. I'll call Brent if you don't let me in on what's happening."

"I said I'd call you."

"Well … you better. I'm not talking to Omar Winston."

"You're just dumb."

"Yeah, well … and you're just …" I couldn't think of anything appropriate so I hung up and went out to tell Sorrow what a frustrating, pig-headed bully Deputy Dolly Wakowski was.

FOURTEEN

THE HOT SPELL WAS going to hang around for a few days, according to our stalwart weathermen, who took particular glee in announcing bad weather: *big storm coming; eighteen inches of snow or more by morning; conditions ripe for a tornado so stay tuned; thunder storm coming out of the west; sleet tonight; icy roads by morning.*

In the north country it wasn't like Florida where the weather, except in hurricane season, was bland. Our guys got to use their weather maps and projections and plots of fronts coming down from the north since Canada seemed to be at fault for almost all the bad weather we got.

The temperature didn't fall below seventy-five that night. My sheets felt like wet winding rags. I couldn't get them off my legs when I turned. Kicking and peeling them from my skin brought me wide awake. Sorrow was in bed with me, his large, warm, furry body laid out alongside mine. I gave him a push and he rolled to the floor with a huge complaint. So like Jackson in the latter days of our marriage, it made me wonder again why I'd ever thought a mangled-fur, ugly dog was the answer to all my problems.

I got out of bed at four a.m., got a cold diet Coke from the refrigerator, took a shower, and went to sit on the deck with my feet propped on the railing, praying I wasn't sitting atop a tent worm cocoon. Since I was naked, I was truly happy I didn't have any near neighbors. I figured any bear, or coyote, or fox who might be watching had nothing to compare me to and I wouldn't be judged. Skunks didn't care what we looked like. Raccoons had better things to think about. And chipmunks—well—they were probably still sleeping.

The sun wasn't up yet so the stars were a long, still curtain against the deep black night. Millions and millions of stars in shapes and forms I didn't have names for. One shot from east to west over the lake. Were you supposed to make a wish on a shooting star? I didn't know so figured I'd do it anyway—just in case. No sense missing a chance to have all my dreams come true. I threw my arms back, welcoming the earth dampness coming up between the floor boards. I yawned and thought again what a lucky woman I was. Maybe not forever. Maybe not even tomorrow. But right now, in this place where I so wanted to stay—I was the most fortunate of humans.

On the next shooting star I wished that Madeleine Clark would sell my book. Then I wished people would like it. Then I wished I would make tons of money. Then I wished that maybe, someday in the future, I'd find a wonderful, and funny, interesting and devoted, self-contained and humble guy who was into me, and Sorrow, and tent worms, and gardens, and finding dead bodies...

I had to go back and erase the last wishes. I was beyond my allotted one wish so I sat for the next hour hunting for shooting stars to carry all my dreams. No more shooting stars, and then the sun came up. I sat until I had deep ridges in my butt from the chair and my cheeks were almost numb. I sat until the eastern sky and the lake turned red, until the bare tree trunks were on fire. I sat until the cool damp disappeared and wet heat came from the lake; until the slightly moving ferns dripped a heavy dew.

No more shooting stars.

No more wishes.

I was tired. I went back into the house, drank another diet Coke, and lay down on my sofa with a fan trained directly on my body.

It was even hotter after the sun rose up. No sleeping. I took another shower, then faced the work I had waiting. Which manuscript should I start with? Cecil Hawke's in one hand, Jackson's in the other. Crass soul that I'd become, I weighed them both: *Canterbury Tales*? Noel Coward? *Tales*? Coward? Hmmm ... *Tales*? Coward?

Who was paying best for my attention?

I picked up Cecil Hawke's large manila envelope, went back out to the shady side of the deck—this time with clothes on—and sat in a half-reclined lounge chair. I unsealed the envelope, and prepared to be entertained with sparkling wit and light repartee.

I read:

The little boy crawled along the walls of the basement room where he was confined in the dark, small hands feeling their way across the rough cinder blocks, then over the wall where the peeling paint came off like dried skin. He moved his hands up the wall, hunting for the shelf where he'd seen her put a biscuit. In the dark he was disoriented, unsure of where he was in the room, he'd been around the walls so many times. If only the light beyond the door would come on. He sat on the rough cement floor and made a plan, the way he always did, eventually. What he would do was keep crawling and stand every few feet. He would search the walls with his hands until he found the shelf, and the biscuit. He was hungry. It was the only way he had of figuring how long he'd been locked in here and how much longer he'd have to wait until she let him out. If he was hungry it was past his lunch time. Once she'd left him until dinner time was over. He'd been very hungry then and cried. That was why she left him the biscuit on the shelf now. "Occupy yourself," she'd said. "Play find the biscuit. And I'll be back before you notice."

But he always noticed, because it was so dark. No light, she said, because he wasn't supposed to be there. Her new friend didn't know she was old enough to have a growing boy. And so—here she would laugh and put a finger to her dark lips—you must not 'be' for just a little while.

The boy was used to the dark. He would think about the biscuit and time would pass. When the man was gone, she would come and open the door. First he would see the light under the door and then hear the key in the lock and she would hug him and beg him to forgive her and cover his face with kisses as he pulled away from her and the smell of animals she would have on her. Not the smell of the *man's dog. He'd heard the click, click of the dog's nails on the floor above his head. He'd heard the man calling to his dog. "Freddy. Freddy, ya little bastard, ya peed on Freda's rug." The animal smell went deeper than that, all the way into her clothes, and on her skin so that when she pulled him close, he had to turn away from her or gag, and be smacked for gagging.*

I set the pages aside and picked up the envelope they'd come in to see if there was any identification, title, something, there. Nothing. I looked at the manuscript. No title page. No title on each sheet, as there should have been. Nothing to indicate that this was what it was supposed to be.

Obviously Lila gave me the wrong manuscript. But what was this? Something else he was working on? Certainly fiction. And very dark fiction. A completely different side of Cecil Hawke. Or maybe it wasn't his at all. Something he'd agree to look at for a friend. Or written years ago. It could even be one of Lila's little jokes. From a book of short stories. Stolen from the Internet. Certainly not light and funny. Certainly not Noel Coward.

I set the manuscript aside and went into the house to make a tuna sandwich and open a diet Coke. It was clear I'd have to call Cecil, tell him I'd been given the wrong work, and get it back to him. A lot of hassle when I least felt like facing chaos.

I went out to my dock to eat because the sun had disappeared behind a high bank of clouds and the water gave off little eddies of coolness. I set the sandwich and plate and Coke beside me and put my feet into the cool water.

I couldn't shake what I'd read. The ring of truth was there, almost of biography. I could feel what that boy was feeling, but even more, sensed something terrible to come.

Too much imagination, I chided myself, finished my sandwich, called to Sorrow who was busy chasing loons out in the lake, and went back to the house, glancing down at the manuscript as I passed the chair where I'd been sitting.

It was a thing calling to me. I should alert Cecil, but not until I found out if the boy got out of the locked room, and what happened to him after that. I was drawn back to my deck chair and the manuscript.

Eating the biscuit took as long as he could nibble, taking only tiny bites, then licking crumbs from his other hand, and chewing so slowly he fell asleep with the biscuit in his mouth and woke up, startled, with bits falling from his hand and on to the floor.

After the biscuit and the nap, he occupied himself by rocking back and forth and humming lullabies. He slept again and woke to noises overhead. There were heavy footfalls, and the scratching of the dog's nails against the bare floor. Words were spoken but he couldn't make out what they were saying. He lay back against the wall, rested his head, forgot the dirty floor and bugs and things and played word games in his mind. The first was thinking up as many words as he could to fill blanks he left in sentences:

'The little boy ... going to see his ... and receive a very nice ... He came up with 'was' 'grandmother' and 'present.'

Constructing sentences in his head impressed him. He could make pictures that way, make up nice things to do and nice places to go. If he kept his eyes shut against the dark and his ears closed against creaks and whispers he could be happy all by himself.

He fell asleep again, after making sentences that took him out into a green field where there were giraffes and rhinoceroses and they all came to him and though he really didn't want to, he yelled and ran at them with the big knife he held in his hand.

When he woke he didn't like that he'd dreamed of those dead giraffes and rhinoceroses and that he'd been stabbing them again and again and feeling happy about seeing them dead.

It was a very long time before a thin crack of light came on beneath the door. He crawled to it and lay flat on his stomach to fit his eye to the crack so he could see her shoes on the other side. Her shoes weren't there. He saw large paws instead; the big wide feet of a dog. Before he could remember a dog couldn't turn on lights, he stuck his fingers under the door, at least as far as his chubby hand could go. He wiggled his fingers to touch the dog, cooing nicely to it even as the dog stepped back and growled.

"Don't be afraid, Freddy," he soothed as the frightened animal licked the last of the biscuit crumbs from his fingers. "I won't hurt you."

There was another growl, and then pain that lasted as his hand was pulled and pulled and someone beyond the door laughed, and his mother's voice chided, "That's a mean joke, Murray. Ya didn't have to do that to the boy."

"What boy, Emily? Thought ya had no kids. Serves ya right for telling me lies."

The boy knew there was blood when he pulled his hand back from beneath the door. He tasted the blood when he stuck his fingers into his mouth. His middle finger was shorter than it should have been. He began to cry when he realized he'd never get that last knuckle back, that the dog on the other side of the door had bitten it off and was probably eating his finger right then because the dog was hungry, too.

What was I reading? I hoped not autobiography. Cecil Hawke had lost the knuckle of one finger—I couldn't remember which—the hand he'd put on my knee again and again. He hadn't hidden the fact that his hand was maimed. But what was this? And the dog ... Freddy? I thought hard back to meeting Cecil and his dog. Wasn't that dog's name Freddy too?

Writers had every right to use their own lives for material, I kept telling myself. But this wasn't supposed to be fiction and not supposed to be horror. I'd expected Noel Coward. Been led to believe I would be reading a life story of a very different sort.

There had to be a mistake. I had to call. We'd laugh and clear things up.

I'd have been more sure of a mistake if it hadn't been for that missing knuckle and 'Freddy.'

———

A woman answered the phone.

"Hawke residence." Not Lila but maybe that mysterious maid Cecil'd referred to.

I identified myself and asked to speak to Mr. Hawke.

The maid came back to tell me Mr. Hawke would be with me momentarily. As she said "momentarily" I got a hint of something, in the lift of that one word, that made me think I was talking to Lila, after all. Lila, the actress, playing so many roles in that house. There couldn't be a shortage of money—I'd seen the farm and the house and the furnishings. Though all that badly chosen art made me wonder. Probably a game she liked to play, like the other games they played: loving each other, making guests uncomfortable for their own amusement, using people.

"Hello." It was Cecil, hale and happy and not suspecting I'd been reading the wrong material, maybe very secret material. "Ah, yes, Emily. And have you made any headway with my book yet?"

I took a deep breath. It was like knowing something about somebody you shouldn't know and then having to face them. Maybe it was by phone, but still I felt that I'd been prying into his life.

"In a way."

"How on earth could you be reading my material 'in a way'? Either you're reading it or you're not."

"Yes, that's true, but…"

"My God, Emily! Spit it out. Do you find my writing so bad you can't speak its name aloud?"

"That's not it at all."

"Then, for heaven's sakes, my dear woman, would you please say whatever you've called to say."

"Lila gave me the wrong book. This isn't about Noel Coward. Not even a biography… well… I'm just guessing…"

"Oh, that." He covered the phone and had a conversation with someone nearby. I could hear laughter, a few more words, and then he was back. "But Emily. That was the point of our contract.

You aren't to tell anyone, certainly not Jackson, what you're editing. Let him believe what he wants to believe. What I've really written is fiction, you see. That was one of the reasons I agreed to have you do the edit. Jack said you wrote fiction. For a biography I would have had someone who was at least slightly familiar with Noel Coward. I should have thought you'd figure that out by yourself."

"This is fiction?"

"What on earth did you think you were reading? My life story?"

"No ... but ..."

"Oh, I see. You poor thing. It's because of my hand. You think I wrote about my own traumatic knuckle loss, don't you?" He laughed. Laughter came from behind him. "But let me tell you the banal story of my knuckle debacle, dear."

I settled back into my desk chair, feeling not stupid but angry, as if I'd been had by that pair—yet again. *Oh, let's shock the rube ...* They'd been waiting for my call: expecting me to be upset, to feel sorry for Cecil. All a big joke.

"It happened when I was seven," he went on, a touch of boredom in his voice. "My father bought a new car and I was eager to be taken for a ride. My mother was as excited as I. She pushed me into the car but closed the door too soon. The door took the end of my finger off, making it very difficult to impress people when I expose my middle digit."

He laughed. I was supposed to but didn't.

"So, is this what you want me to edit?" I kept my voice cool and business-like. "Is it a mystery? If so, I'll edit it with an eye to the conventions of the genre. If not, and you intend it to be something else, I've got to know before I continue."

"Oh, a horror novel, of course. And now that we've gotten all of that out of the way, what do you think of my effort so far?"

I hesitated. My first inclination was to tell him his writing stunk and his way of doing business stunk even worse.

"I haven't really read enough," I said. "Since you weren't honest with me, I stopped in the first chapter. I thought I had the wrong manuscript and that I had no business going any farther."

"Oh, no …" He chuckled again. "But that proves you're a person to be trusted. I don't want word of this novel getting out until it's ready to see the light of day. That's why the subterfuge. Now we'll be on solid ground. Please, continue to read my poor effort at fiction. Edit as you see fit. But you must not, under any circumstances, reveal the true nature of my work to anyone. Back in England, well, I do have a certain kind of reputation to protect. I have enemies who would love to get their hands on the manuscript, thinking it something they could use against me. A man as wealthy as I, Emily, doesn't get to where I've gotten without a few malcontents left along the road. Do you see what I'm saying? It's all part of a huge game, Emily. Certainly you know that by now. I play my game. You play yours. My enemies play theirs. And in the end, it comes to nothing but death. A game. You do see that, don't you?"

"I see fine," I said, still seething.

"Then you'll edit my novel."

I hesitated. The money was in my bank and I'd written a couple of checks on the account. I wasn't in a position to give him his fifteen hundred dollars back. And anyway—now that things were cleared up—what did it hurt me to finish the job? Maybe I'd have to tell a few lies to Jackson. Or I could simply say I couldn't discuss the project, he'd seen me sign the non-disclosure contract. What I was finding was that the poor didn't have room for a whole lot of moral reservations.

"Yes, I'll work with you. I should have these five done this afternoon. Could we meet tomorrow morning? You have more chapters for me?"

"Oh, my dear, not tomorrow morning. We have some very important guests here. I wouldn't be able to sit down for minute. How are you Sunday morning? About nine? I'll have another check ready."

Nine was fine. I'd get it out of the way early.

"And don't forget our party a week from tomorrow. Bring anyone you'd like to bring. Lila and I are so looking forward to it."

I promised I'd be there and that I was—at that very moment—choosing between costumes, and hung up.

By four, I was dripping sweat from the still heat. Sorrow sat beside me as I read and marked the manuscript. He leaped up at every move I made, hoping it was time to get on to something more interesting. Hot, feeling tired and dirty, and suffering from eye strain, I agreed with him. A short walk. Move the hose in the garden. A swim before dinner. Later, I'd call Dolly. See what happened to her. She was supposed to let me know about the dead woman out on Old Farm Road. But first there was doggy business to attend to.

The water was unruffled. Not a breeze. The willows along the shore hung unmoving, branches touching the surface of the lake. Mosquitoes didn't come to the middle of the lake where I floated, only a skating bug or two, and two curious crows overhead, looking down at me, commenting to each other. The beaver didn't bother to raise his head to see who disturbed his quiet. He swam in slow circles around his stick hut, ignoring me and ignoring Sorrow, who usually infuriated him.

I'd slipped on an old pink bikini, much washed out, maybe a little too small but Sorrow made no comment so I figured I was fine. I flipped over and out of the bra a few times, tucked myself back where I belonged, and took long slow strokes, stopping to drip cool water on my warm face. I put my tongue out and lapped at some of the drops. I asked myself, not for the first time, how had I ever lived anywhere but here? I was developing the contempt Henry David Thoreau had felt for civilization: for any occasion requiring new clothes. I could find my own food. I could live in solitude without ever feeling alone.

Maybe I wasn't like Thoreau. I had running water, an inside toilet, a writing studio, a fridge, a stove, a supermarket not too far away, and I wasn't planting acres of beans. Who cared? I rolled over, looked my wet and happy dog in the eye, and laughed.

"Hey!" A call came from the shore.

Dolly Wakowski, with a man beside her, stood on the end of my dock. She waved me in, an arm making frantic circles. I narrowed my eyes and wiped away the lake water so I could see. The guy was about my age. Taller than Dolly—but who wasn't? He stood with his hands in the pockets of his light summer slacks. Pretty good looking. Black hair. Trim, maybe even muscular. I turned around a time or two, paddling, then struck out for the dock. There was a towel there, at their feet; a raggedy old towel I used for swimming since I would never put it out for company. I felt around under the water, making sure the bikini covered all it was meant to cover, then relaxed, thinking, oh well, if it didn't, this guy was going to get a good look at what most men never got to see.

FIFTEEN

"Jeffrey Lo," Dolly introduced the man standing beside her. She kept her eyes down as she concentrated on not looking at me.

I scrambled up, as modestly as possible, onto the dock.

Jeffrey Lo stood against the sun, lowering in the western sky, getting lost among the treetops. He was Asian, a little taller than I, with warm skin, very dark eyes, and a nice smile. His blue summer suit didn't have a wrinkle. His tie was perfectly knotted. Maybe his white Nikes didn't go with the rest of him, but the guy might just be into comfort.

When I took the hand he held out to me, it was warm, the kind of hand that curves around yours and makes you feel enveloped. I grabbed the towel around my body as best I could, dripping lake water and feeling the blood rushing into my face. As he let go of my hand, I felt a sense of loss, as if I'd been tossed out into a lonely world again.

Jeffrey Lo was one of those guys who could make my knees go weak. A high school kind of thing I was never proud of, when a gangly boy would dip his head down to mine and kiss me ever so lightly on the cheek and I would look up and bat my eyelashes ... even back then I kind of made myself sick.

"Emily," he said, bowing slightly. "Nice to meet you."

I gave a half shrug. It would have been lovely to meet him too, if I weren't having the sexual spasms of a sixteen-year-old and if I knew what the two of them were doing standing on my dock.

"Mr. Lo's with the INS, out of Detroit," Dolly said.

I gave him a quizzical look. I didn't have a clue what INS was.

"Immigration and Naturalization Service," he explained.

I nodded, still very much in the dark.

"Could we go up to your house, Miss ... eh ... Kincaid ... ?"

"Emily."

"Emily. We need to talk about the murder you two have been investigating."

I motioned for them to go ahead of me. Better that than to think of him watching me from the back as I made my way through the bracken to my deck. Wet bikinis from behind aren't pretty no matter what size the butt they're covering.

Inside the house I told them to sit. Time to get shorts and a tee shirt on though I was already sweating and wishing I could have stayed in the wet bikini. When I got back to the living room Dolly and Jeffrey Lo were deep in conversation, heads bent close. They stopped as soon as I entered the room. I offered iced tea, made some, served it—with the last of the ice in the trays—and sat, looking expectantly at Mr. Lo.

Dolly began. "We've ID'd the dead woman. I'll let Agent Lo, here, explain it to you. And nothing for the paper, Emily. I told him about our special arrangement that you only put in what I say…"

"I choose what I put in." I snapped. I was no police flunky when I'd been a full-time journalist and wasn't about to become one now. I was smart enough not to blab things that could hurt a police case but that was all. Despite working with Dolly so closely, I was a good reporter and took pride in that. Every once in a while Dolly got the idea that withholding information from one of my stories was a good idea. So, every once in a while, I had to bring her back to earth.

"Yeah, well," she shrugged and rolled her eyes at Agent Lo. "Anyway, he understands you've been a big help and says he's okay with it."

Jeffrey Lo nodded, cleared his throat, and started:

"The woman's name is Maria Santos. She was an agent with the Secretaria de Gobernacion Instituto Nacional de Migracion." Impeccable Spanish. The guy was truly smooth. "That's the Mexican form of what I do: immigration, emigration, naturalization. Mexico City got in touch with our office in Washington when Agent Santos disappeared. My office in Detroit sent me up to look around. The first thing I came across was your unidentified woman who could be Mexican and was dead up here in Leetsville. Got a photo and prints. Sent them to Mexico and got a positive ID. So I'm here for as long as it takes. This is now a government problem and an international crime."

He waited as if I might have questions. I couldn't think of a thing or, rather, I had many questions but hadn't put them together.

"Agent Santos wasn't here on official business. A cousin of hers in Oaxaca called her about another of their cousins, Acalan Diaz. Acalan came to northwest Michigan with his wife and two children to work on a farm. The cousin told Maria Santos that Acalan was worried. He called and said there was bad trouble up here. What Maria learned from the Oaxacan cousin was that Diaz got threats after working on a particular farm. She was told the threats got so bad he was afraid for his life." Lo sat back and cleared his throat.

"Did he know which farm this Acalan was talking about?" I asked.

"I don't think even Agent Santos knew. When she got here Acalan Diaz was gone, along with his family. She found where Acalan last worked and went out there. That's what the officer and I learned today." He nodded toward Dolly. "We talked to the farmer this morning. I don't think the problem was with this particular farm, do you, Dolly?"

She shook her head at him. "Everybody knows Joe Swayze. Good man. Family's been up here a hundred years or more. Used to run the grange. I'd be very surprised if Joe was into anything bad."

Lo went on. "This Joe Swayze said a woman came to talk to him last week. She wanted to know what was going on with Diaz, but all Swayze could tell her was that Diaz never said where he'd worked before. Now he and his family are gone. He said the workers are all getting nervous. Oh, and he'd just heard from one of the men that a dead dog was found on Diaz's doorstep one morning."

145

I sat back, taking it all in: more dead dogs, threats. Drugs was the only thing I could come up with. Or that "coyote" revenge.

"Agent Santos wasn't here officially. We got that from her boss in Mexico City. They couldn't send her here for that kind of complaint. It would have been reported to us and we'd take it from there. What Agent Santos did was ask for time off to come on her own to investigate, and then she stayed in touch with her boss. I learned that while she was here she stayed in a motel in Kalkaska. We got the name and phone number from Mexico. I've been through her room and found nothing we didn't already know—except for a phone number, which I had traced, and that was this Swayze's farm."

"So Acalan Diaz went back to Mexico? Why?" I asked. "Didn't he know his cousin was coming?"

"The family's not in Mexico as far as anyone there knows. No one in Oaxaca has seen any of them. But he could have gone to another state to find work. He hasn't been heard from. They're all worried about him and his family, and sick about what's happened to Agent Santos."

I looked at Dolly, who made a weird face and shrugged her shoulders. International crime wasn't exactly her forte nor was it mine. We were in way over our heads.

"How can I help?" I asked, looking to Dolly to make sure I wasn't treading on any toes here. She nodded at me. '*In this together.*' I could hear her now. There were times the woman's Three Musketeers spirit was amazing.

"We're breaking the story and want you to contact your editor, get it in fast. Got her photo." He leaned over and handed me a picture of the woman I'd only seen dead on the littered floor of the Old Farm Road house.

"Actually INS protocol dictates that I conduct my own investigation, separate from yours. But, to tell you the truth, I need you and the deputy here because you know the people, the farmers. If I did this on my own I'd be starting so far back it would take me months to catch up. I need to talk to anybody who might have seen or heard something that could help. What I've learned so far is that the Mexican workers have been leaving the farms, and just a month before harvest starts. I've got to find where they're going and what's scared everybody so bad."

"Do you think the Diazes are dead?" I asked.

"No idea."

I looked over at Dolly. "Okay, let me get the story in first, I'll call Bill, give him a heads up." I sat down at the laptop on my living room desk and made quick notes of everything Lo could give me. Lots of huge, unanswered questions. What brought the agent here? What did she discover that led to her death? Where was her cousin and his family? Most of all: what was going on? I ended the article with a plea to anyone who could help and gave the phone number of the Leetsville police station and the INS office in Detroit.

I e-mailed the story to Bill, with the photograph, then called him, explaining what was happening. I said I was staying close to Dolly and the INS agent, and would be in touch.

My part was finished.

I thought.

Lo leaned forward, hands clasped together. "What I need from both of you now is your help. You guys could save me weeks of

147

interviews. You know, cut right to the chase. Dolly here's been looking into Agent Santos's death already. You've both been interviewing farmers. I've got all that, but what I need are the names of other farmers who might know something, who might still have workers on their places. I don't want to step on any toes here…" He looked meaningfully at Dolly, who dipped her head, agreeing. "I think we'll move along a lot faster if we work together. I guess that's all I'm saying. I'd like you to be a part of it, Emily."

This guy knew how to smile. He melted me right into line. It was to my benefit anyway, I told myself as I smiled back at him—a big, simple-minded grin like I sometimes caught on Sorrow's face when he was thrilled to pieces with the idea of a new toy.

Outside, in the driveway, standing next to Dolly's battered police car, we agreed to meet in the morning. EATS was decided on despite Dolly's objections and the drawbacks of everybody listening to our conversation.

"Hey, Dolly." I brought her up short. "You'll have to get over your snit sooner or later. The one thing I've learned about a place like EATS is how much help we can get there. You know as well as I do that if we need a farmer's name or ideas for places to contact migrant workers, EATS'll have somebody sitting in a booth right next to us who can help. And what nobody else knows, Eugenia will."

She agreed after a couple of grudging remarks about people who should mind their own business.

"If you didn't give people things to worry about they wouldn't be in your face," I said, then smiled at a puzzled Agent Lo.

"Dolly's got this thing…" I started.

"Watch it!" she warned me.

"She's got this thing about the people in Leetsville. Seems they try to take care of each other and worry about each other and help each other. Dolly doesn't like that."

Lo gave me an odd look, then turned it on Dolly.

"Let's just keep this to police business," Dolly growled at both of us.

I spread my hands, letting them know that was fine with me—business only.

I stood under the arbor waving as they backed up my driveway, through the birch trees, and out to Willow Lake Road.

SIXTEEN

FRIDAY NIGHTS ALWAYS SEEMED hotter than other nights. Maybe I was tired by Fridays. Or maybe it was because Fridays led to a weekend where I didn't have a whole lot planned. I don't know why Friday nights were different, but I was miserable. When I was married to Jackson there was always something to do—drinks with another professor and his wife; an appearance by one of the Hopwood authors and then taking her back to the Michigan League, to her room and maybe talking until dawn. Sometimes the writers stayed with us. If they had big egos and I was in for a four-hour drunken treatise on the depth of their work, their time at "Princeton" (always said with an affected air)—the evening was a chore. If the writer only got a little drunk and had stories to share—that was a good night. If the writer was British and wanted to sit, with fingers tented under his chin, pontificating on the terrible state of literature in America, I left him to Jackson. If the writer was interesting, actually liked people—and even let a few of Jack's best students come over for a dose of wisdom—those were my favorite times. Now I couldn't tell a Friday night from any other night—except that they were always hotter, or colder, or wetter, depending on the season, than other nights.

I watched Sorrow dig a hole in the dirt and lie down against the cool earth. I wished I were lucky enough to be a dog and could lie down against the earth. Instead I lay on a chaise on the deck, put a cold wet rag on my head, drank a lot of the iced tea I'd made earlier which wasn't too iced any more, stared out at Willow Lake, and thought about nothing much.

Until a voice beside the deck sent me leaping about three feet, straight up, out of my chaise.

"Didn't mean to scare you, Emily."

Harry stood down on the brick walk, his old, colorless eyes peering at me through the railing.

I invited him up, offered a glass of warm iced tea, and waited while he looked out at the lake, up at the sky, around at the woods—taking stock of where he was. "Came to talk to you about this dead dog thing what's goin' on."

"Words getting around?"

He nodded. "Lotsa folks worryin'. Don't know if you or Dolly heard but there's animals coming up missing. Heard it was happenin' from way north of here to down almost to Cadillac."

I relaxed back in my chair. "Dolly didn't say anything..."

"Well, mostly people thought their dog just ran off. You don't call the police about a thing like that. Even Old Mrs. Wilkie, up to Mancelona, was sayin'—when I ran into her at the feed store—that her cat just up and left."

He nodded a few times as if getting his mind going. "Then some of us started talkin' and it seems like there's way too many just to wander away. I mean, we was countin' there at the feed and seed and it was like ten animals we know of."

"What do you think's happening?"

He shrugged, his old suit jacket bunching way up behind his neck. "Can't say we came up with anything. Thought maybe you'd know. I mean, with this dead dog over on Old Farm Road. You and Dolly solve that one yet?"

I had to admit we didn't have a clue about the dog. But I told him about the dead woman being a Mexican agent and that the migrant workers up here were scared because dead dogs had been thrown in their yards.

Harry only shook his head. "What's this world comin' to, Emily? I ask you. All the farmer's want to do is get their crops in and get ready for next year. Now here's this awful thing goin' on." He gave me a sorrowful look. "If I knew one damned bit that would help, I'd even tell Dolly about it."

"Do you think these missing animals are connected in any way with the murdered Mexican agent?"

"Your guess is as good as mine. Sure hope the two of you women clear it up pretty soon."

I agreed as Sorrow pulled himself from his dirt hole and came up the steps to lay his head in Harry's lap.

Harry gave me a worried look. His grizzled face wrinkled so his eyebrows met his nose. His thin lips worked at each other. "You know, Emily. You got yerself mixed up in this stuff now. Stories are right there in the paper with your name attached to 'em."

I waited. There had to be more.

"You think about your dog, here? I mean, if there's something bad going on and they're stealin' animals, you ever think maybe they'd come for Sorrow?"

"I'm only a reporter."

He shook his head. "Folks up here know how you and the deputy work together. Word gets around."

"It seems like some kind of Mexican thing..."

He shook his head. "Doubt it. You know, evil's evil, no matter where you're from. I'd maybe think about it."

The thought chilled me. I still had the picture in my head of that dead dog laying out in that hot field and wasn't going to shake it anytime soon. My face must have told Harry how the thought frightened me.

"You want, I could take him over to my house. Keep him right there in the kennel with my dogs."

I thought a moment, picturing Harry's wire-fenced kennel with a pack of mean dogs he used as watch dogs. I shook my head and thanked him but said I'd get Sorrow away from there if I thought he was in danger. Harry stood, nodded a few times, walked down the steps, and was gone without a good-bye or any other word. He'd delivered his warning. His job was done. I could sense the relief he left behind him.

———

What I did have to do that evening—hot or not hot—was read the chapters of Hawke's work. I was getting together with Dolly and

153

Jeffrey the next day. Who knew where I'd end up with that pair, or how much of Saturday I'd have to read? Sunday morning at nine I was seeing Cecil. This evening was all the time I had to concentrate on that poor little kid locked in a basement while his mother entertained her boyfriend—who owned a dog named Freddy—upstairs.

For writing like Cecil Hawke's you had to steel your head against images people wouldn't want lodged there. I steeled myself—it was just a job. As they said in the Godfather movies: *it's business.* Nothing to do with me. Not like reading true crime. I could separate myself from a dark basement and a bleeding little boy.

I took the manuscript from the envelope. I got myself a yellow pad to write on. I got myself a red pen. I sat down in the living room—with two fans going—and began to read.

———

The manuscript said Chapter Two, but there was no connection to the chapter I'd read earlier. The boy—or who I thought had to be the same boy—was now a teenager. There was no basement, no dog, nothing from the first chapter.

He stepped into the street and waved at Mrs. O'Riley, out on the stoop watching for neighbors to complain about. The old woman waved back. Her face lighted with a broad smile when she saw him—her favorite among the teenage boys on the street. He knew because she told him so. "Yer my very favorite around here, Tommy," she would say to him and pinch his cheek. Then she would ask about

154

his mother, remarking she hadn't seen her lately and he would tell her again how his mother was in a sanitarium, getting over the TB she'd caught. "Could be years," he would tell Mrs. O'Riley again and shake his head. He knew how to look sorrowful, even force a tear from one eye. It was a neat trick that came in handy, especially with nosy, old ladies.

I wrote on my pad: connection between chapters? Transitions?

I read on. The boy walked to a fruit stand at the corner of the street where he filled his pockets with apples and ran off before anyone noticed. His next stop was the market where he stole an air freshener and candy bars. Then he was back home, eating a candy bar while sitting on the kitchen floor. He had to kick newspapers and empty cans away to find a place. When he finished the candy he tore the cover from the air freshener, opened the basement door while holding his nose, then slammed the door shut.

The good thing about the story was that I was catching on. He'd killed his mother or she'd died somehow and he didn't want to have to leave his house. The bad thing was that the story was making me sick. This boy, this 'Tommy,' was obviously deranged. I didn't like stories where kids were killers. I didn't think the public much liked stories where kids were killers. Maybe I was wrong. It wasn't what I would write, but there were all kinds of books out there. Still, I made a note to tell Cecil this could be a hard sell.

I went back to reading, going carefully over each sentence, marking misspellings and problems with grammar. I pointed out a couple of lapses in logic—where one sentence didn't quite connect to the sentence that came before. Then came the worst—I had to begin to think of something to say about the work—so far—as a whole.

I wrote down: great promise. I wrote: structure off a little but the writing is good.

I put that away and read the next chapter.

The boy had someone staying with him at the house, a girl he met after school one day. She came up to him with her hand out, a grimy mitten with dirty fingers clutching at him. Since he was lonely, he brought her home and explained about his sick mother and not wanting the social services taking him from the house. She was astonished that he kept such a secret but smiled and agreed that the two of them could do just fine without adults interfering with what they wanted to do.

"Won't this be fun fer the two of us?" Her small, freckled face *beamed at him. "Not like what I ran away from, my mum and her boyfriend treatin' me like junk. We'll be playing at keepin' house."* She stopped a minute and thought. *"But don't you go gettin' no funny ideas. I may be thirteen but I've seen more than you can ever guess."*

Robin fell back into what had been Tommy's mother's chair, let her legs hang out front and her arms clutch at the soft arms. "It ain't bad, ya know, Tommy. Maybe the smell in here. I think you should be takin' out the garbage. But the rest. I'm with you."

I read on. The two played loud music and tore up furniture when they felt like it. I wondered if I was reading a modern *Lord of the Flies*. Would these kids create a new world in this odd house of theirs? Would they sink to animal-like behavior? And where was his mother's body? I doubted very much that she was in a sanitarium. Dead. Walled up. But the smell—I wasn't born yester-day. Of course the mother had to be dead in that basement. If this new girl found out, would she turn on our Tommy? Probably not, I thought, and read on. If nothing else, Cecil had my interest.

Next chapter and Robin was gone. Tommy was alone in the house again, sweeping up the cans and papers and cardboard boxes. He scrubbed the floor. He picked up rugs and stuffed them into the washer. He washed dishes and scrubbed the stove, cleaned out the empty refrigerator. When the house was spotless, he set another air freshener on the top step of the basement stairs.

Now I was really creeped out, which was a good thing for Hawke's book, I supposed. He was getting to me. I had a morbid desire to keep going, figure out what the boy was doing and what was coming next. It wasn't the usual feeling I got reading a well-written book, more like I wanted to have my mind washed out and forget I'd put such things into it. I wouldn't be telling this to Cecil Hawke. I'd say I found his writing compelling and that while it wasn't the kind of thing I usually read, I still found it interesting.

Good enough. Enough of an ego stroke to keep the job. Not really a lie.

Next chapter: the boy was unlocking the door to his house. He seemed grown now. A young man named Nelson was with him on the front steps. Nelson was a nineteen-year-old from Australia, come to England to make his fortune. They stole beer together, were close pals when the chapter began, went into the house and sat at the kitchen table, drinking as they made plans to rob Mrs. O'Riley, Tommy's nosy, talkative neighbor. Tommy'd heard Mrs. O'Riley had gold jewelry her husband gave her years ago. Nelson said the old bitch didn't need it, not at her age. *Serves her right if we did her in.* And then he looked at Tommy slyly, watching to see his response to the idea of murder.

Wow, I thought. A murder per chapter. The guy'd overdone it. I'd have to tell him as much.

Our Tommy, now quite the criminal, knew a man who would take the gold off their hands. Nelson was excited by the prospect of cash in his pocket and went over and over the plans with Tommy. *"And if the old bitch finds us in there, she'll call the cops, ya know. I wouldn't like that. I've got a criminal record already. You think you can do what we'd have to do to shut her up?"*

Tommy laughs but Nelson wants a blood oath. They cut the palm of one hand, mingle their blood, and agree they're ready to take on the old woman and any other old women who get in their way.

Tommy thinks of the two of them as invincible. If a boy can kill, he tells himself in his bed that night, if he is afraid of nothing, he can rule the world.

I read on, hoping for a redeeming quality to surface before Mrs. O'Riley got murdered for her gold. I came across nothing. The robbery took place though Mrs. O'Riley was not home and so lived on. Not because of a change of heart in either of the boys, but because she was at the doctor's and the waiting room was full that day, which she came home complaining bitterly about to the neighbor who'd taken her, only to find her house ransacked and her precious jewelry gone.

Next chapter: Cecil and Nelson bought themselves new clothes with the money from the gold, and a fridge full of beer, and a pantry full of snacks. They were set for life, they assured each other. If they ran low on money, they'd steal something else. Life wasn't hard at all, Tommy observed at one point, as long as you have the courage to live the way you want to live. In a drunken moment, the two boys—probably both in their late teen years—talked about their dreams. Nelson wants only to go back to the land, but with money. He wasn't returning to Australia a pauper—not ever again. He'd show them all—the bastards back there. The ones who made fun of him 'cause his father was the village drunk. The "lousy bastards" who drove him from his homeland.

Tommy's dreams were even more grandiose. He would be famous. He didn't know for what yet, but he was sure of it, felt it in every bone in his body. The world would look up to him, admire him. Newspapers would write about him.

I got a little lost in Tommy's dream. As a reader, I wondered if what he was talking about was going to jail for the two bodies I assumed were tucked away in the basement of his house. I was jumping ahead at every character development and every plot twist. If I could see the end coming, Hawke had work to do. If I thought I could see the end coming—but was wrong—well, that would be a cheat. A very fine line, plotting a mystery. So far he was doing all right. But I thought the end of the novel must be buried here, in Tommy's plans. I wasn't sure Cecil Hawke knew enough about writing fiction to get that right.

Next chapter: There was a dog in the house with the two boys. A yellow dog with orange eyes that Nelson had stolen from a pet shop, breaking the glass and pulling the creature through the window, cutting it along its sides.

At least he was slowing the forward trajectory of the story. He was still in the same time period as the last chapter. Something other than murder was going on.

The dog was snuffling through the garbage. Here, in my head, he was connecting the dog to the boy in the basement in chapter one. And, also in my head, to that one-eyed creature Cecil Hawke kept beside him. *"Freddy," Tommy growled and bared his teeth at the animal. "Get yer fuckin' nose outta there."*

In this chapter, there's been trouble. Nelson's in jail, caught stealing cigarettes at a tobacco shop just down High Road from the house. Because of his record, he was being held overnight. When he's released, the two boys decide it was time to move on.

"Ya could sell this place," Nelson looks around, his cold blue eyes scanning the walls of the living room for saleable items.

"Can't," Tommy says, smiling oddly at his friend. "Got things … well … ya see Nelson … it would be a lot better if we didn't try to sell."

As if the young men inhabit one mind, Nelson leans forward, hands between his knees, conspiratorial smile on his lips. "Ya haven't! Not you. Ya mean she's down there?" He pointed toward the floor, and the basement.

Tommy nods and puts his shortened middle finger to his lips. "Got a couple of 'em. Bad luck for them. My mum, and a big-mouth girl who thought she was brighter than me."

Here was another connection to the boy in the first chapter. Cecil's book was chilling—with his references to reality and parts of his own life, then giving details from a conscienceless murderer. That finger, the dog named Freddy. It was all so difficult to read. I

160

kept picturing Cecil's benign, smiling face, and that mutilated finger on my knee.

I had only a few pages to finish . . .

The boys packed their things that night, split the money they'd stashed in an old teapot, and left the house. Behind them as they sprinted away, flames shot through the front windows, glass burst into the street as neighbors ran out their front doors to shout at each other and soon bring sirens to the place. They hid behind the half wall of a garden, shrouded in dark, as Mrs. O'Riley came running from her home shouting *"My God! There's a boy in that house. A poor, young boy."* The woman fell to her knees sobbing that she'd seen Tommy Mulligan, and maybe even a friend and his dog, going in there that very evening.

"Oh, poor thing. Lost his mother and now he's gone too . . ."

Tommy and Nelson run off laughing—alone. With no dog in tow.

SEVENTEEN

LUNCH WITH DOLLY AND Agent Lo was fast and busy. Two cups of tea straightened me out after a troubled night. When we asked around the restaurant for names of farmers we might talk to, Eugenia, Gloria, and the other customers in EATS, all had names of people to go see or a number for organizations that helped migrants. Jeffrey took names and telephone numbers and whatever else they had to offer. Dolly worked the phone book. Soon we were down to how we would handle all of it.

"Look, let's each take an area. Okay? I'll do Mancelona north—get the farms out there. Emily, you do these farms." Dolly held up a map that put me west of Leetsville. "And Agent Lo, you do the migrant service places in Traverse City. That all right with everybody?"

Agent Lo frowned. "I don't feel good about you women doing any of this alone. There's already been one woman murdered and a family missing. Whatever this is about and whoever's involved, they aren't playing games."

I kind of agreed. Nobody should be taking on any of the investigation alone.

To my surprise, Dolly went along. "Don't want them killing off a reporter," she said, gave a strained laugh, and grinned at Agent Lo. "Make me look bad."

"Nor a Leetsville deputy," I countered.

"What we'll do until we see how things go, is stay together," Lo said. "One car. Three people. Numbers rule. The INS is watching this closely. We don't take well to an agent being murdered. I'll give them one call and we'll have plenty of help, if we need it. You should put that in the paper, Emily. We want these guys to know who's coming after them. And the migrants too—let them know they aren't alone."

We agreed and we were off. First it was out to George Sandini's place, up by Petoskey, to see if that Carlos Munoz might have something for us. What we needed was a way into this mess; a path to follow. There was such a cloak of secrecy tying tongues among the migrant workers. We needed one break; one peephole into what was going on and what they were all afraid of.

———

At Sandini's place we found George with his head stuck under the hood of a huge John Deere tractor. He came out reluctantly, wiping grease from his hands with a large red rag. His gray hair stood up at the back as if it hadn't been combed that morning. The man didn't look thrilled to see a cop and a reporter, and even less thrilled to meet Agent Lo.

"INS? That's immigration." He gave Lo a suspicious look. Jeffrey nodded.

"So, something really is going on. You three got any ideas?"

"The woman who was murdered was an emigration agent from Mexico, worked for the Mexican government. Yeah, I'd say something was going on here, at least intimidation and death threats; murder."

"Whew." George Sandini ran a hand through his thick hair. "Wish I could help …"

"We wanna see Carlos again," Dolly said. "Maybe he remembered something."

George shook his head. "Gone. Just up and took off. Like so many of 'em …"

"When?" Jeffrey demanded, his face darkening.

George shrugged. "Yesterday. A couple guys came to see him and he left. His family went a few days ago. I think that was to Carlos's brother in Texas."

"You know where in Texas? Maybe we could call him …"

"Not a clue." George toed the churned earth at his feet. "This keeps up we ain't going to have a single worker here for harvest. Don't know what we'll do. Without those guys we're up the creek. Depend on 'em …"

"Only way to help yourself is to help us. We'll put a stop to whatever it is …"

"You think it's about some Mexican gang after them? That's what some of the other farmers have been saying. You know, like they owe money or something?"

We all shrugged.

"I don't think it's about drugs. Not these workers. Family men—all of them. Been coming up here for years. I don't think ..."

"We don't know anything, George," Dolly said. "It'll take help from you or other farmers who know or hear something."

He nodded, then nodded again. "Why don't you all come in the house? I'll make some phone calls. See what I can get for you."

Sounded like a good idea. We followed the man into a kitchen where he waved us to seats at a scrubbed oak table, excused himself, and went into another room to make phone calls.

"Better than nothing." Dolly leaned toward Jeffrey.

He kept his voice low. "You got any ideas, Emily?"

I shook my head. Out of ideas, but I had the feeling we were on the right path. At least some path.

George was back in a few minutes. He stood in the doorway looking from one to the other of us, making his mind up about something. He came over, pulled out a chair at the table, and sat down. We watched as George Sandini went through a few minutes of tortured soul searching. Obviously he knew something but wasn't sure he could trust us.

The man finally rubbed his rough hands. "Well, I called a couple of other farmers going through this. We didn't want to say anything to anybody ... but ... well, you see now, Carlos and some of the others didn't really take off."

We looked at each other, puzzled.

"You gotta understand. These men been with us a long time. Like friends, they are. We aren't about to let anything happen to 'em and we didn't think we could protect 'em the way things were."

We waited. This wasn't easy for the man.

"So, what we done is get 'em together. We're hiding them until whatever's going on is over. We need them and they need us. You get the picture?"

Jeffrey, voice low and encouraging, asked, "Hiding them? You mean they're still around?"

George made a face. "Not their families. They're gone where it's safe."

"Can we talk to them?"

"Guess you'd better."

"Where?"

"Right now they're out to Dick Crispin's orchard, the other side of Northport. We got together, we'll move 'em around if it's necessary."

"Is this Acalan Diaz family with the others?" I asked.

George thought a minute then shook his head. "Don't think so. Nobody's heard a word about them."

"I'd like to get out there," Dolly put in.

"'Course. That's who I called: Crispin. He says for you guys not to say a word." He looked hard at me. "Better be nothin' in the paper."

I agreed. Nothing.

"He'll be waiting at his house and take you to where they're hidin'."

We got up, thanked George, got an address, and were off again. A long, long trip around Lake Michigan, through Traverse City, and out the Leelanau Peninsula to Northport and beyond.

EIGHTEEN

WE DROVE THROUGH SUTTON'S BAY, a small town with a thriving arts center, with Brilliant Books and other stores strung along the main road, Lake Michigan in the background. It was a colorful place with the feel of real life underneath the touristy trappings. What I was learning about the part of Michigan I'd come to was that the arts thrived on long winters and cheaper homes off water. I'd learned that we had great writers like Doug Standon and Jim Harrison and Mardi Link among us—working easier up here than places where celebrity killed off lesser writers. I'd learned the rugged Lake Michigan coasts and lighthouses inspired painters of all kinds, and that photographers caught sunsets over vineyards as good or better than anywhere else in the world.

Once in Northport we passed my favorite used bookstore: Dog Ears Books on Waukazoo Street, where the owner, Pamela Grath, had a magic red chair you could sit in—if she liked you enough. Great places around Northern Michigan. It had taken me almost five years to find some of them, with a lot more to go.

We made the turn north at the center of town and headed out to miles of not much of anything. We turned in at the Crispin orchard. There was another long drive through rows of apple trees before we pulled up to a huge, gable-roofed red barn, and a low red-brick ranch home.

A big man, with big stomach, big chest, big head of brown hair, big suspenders, big round face, and a large German shepherd dog, stood in the middle of the driveway. Dolly parked carefully beside him since he wasn't going to move an inch, one way or the other. The dog barked, his head bouncing up and down, the hair on the back of his neck ruffled.

"I'm not getting out," Dolly said after rolling down her window. The big man ambled over, letting his dog go on barking and growling until a gangly teenage boy came from the barn, called to the dog, and took him off toward the house.

"You Deputy Wakowski?" the man demanded, sticking his chin out to emphasize her name.

"That's me. George Sandini said he called you about us coming out. You Dick Crispin?"

He nodded, then slowly bent forward to look inside the car. He nodded to Jeffrey in the back seat. "You with the INS?" he demanded.

Jeffrey nodded.

"Need to see your badge."

Jeffrey leaned forward, reached in his back pocket, brought out a brown leather folder and showed his badge over Dolly's shoulder.

"And you?" He lifted his chin in my direction.

I leaned across Dolly. "I'm with the *Northern Statesman*."

He stepped back and threw his hands into the air. "Un-uh. No reporters. What's going on here can't be public."

I assured him I would only use what was happening at his orchard when he was ready and the killer was caught. He thought a long while, long enough to make Dolly get out of the car to vouch for me. Finally he nodded.

"Guess I gotta trust you. Come on," he motioned the rest of us out of the car. "I'll take you to where the men are but don't go thinking you can take 'em in or anything. Once you talk to 'em, they're out of here. We got the next place lined up."

We piled into his big red truck and went out the drive we'd come in on to the main road, then north, then west, until we finally turned down a dirt two-track and bounced between rows of apple trees. We pulled into a clearing in the middle of a circle of brown tents, got out, and stood by a row of cars.

At first, the clearing was deserted. We waited a few minutes. Men emerged slowly from the tents. Ten of them. Carlos Munoz, from the Sandini farm, was first. Behind him Miguel Hernandez stepped out to join Carlos. Others walked out until there was a straight line of small, dark guys staring at us. I was guessing these were all the men who supposedly had gone back to Mexico, or most of them.

"That's all of them?" Dolly looked from one to the other of the men.

"Most. Some left when the trouble first started," he said.

"You farmers are putting your lives on the line, protecting them like this."

He shrugged. "Men been good workers a lot of years. Not going to turn our backs now."

"What if it's some Mexican feud thing?"

"They said it's not."

"Then what is it?" Dolly asked.

Jeffrey and I stood quietly, letting Dolly ask the questions on our minds.

"Don't know," Crispin said. "There's only one connection they've come up with—some guy one of them worked for. That's all I could get."

"Can we talk to them?" Jeffrey asked.

"Sure. They been waiting. Jose, he's the one got a name out of Acalan Diaz before he took off. Joe Swayze tell you Diaz found a dead dog on his porch? Diaz told Jose about it, and that he was afraid of some guy…"

We walked closer to where the men stood waiting, were introduced, and then vouched for.

"Any of you know Acalan Diaz?" Lo asked, looking from dark face to dark face.

Dick pointed to one of the six men. "Jose Rodriguez. He was Acalan's friend. Worked for Joe Swayze too."

"Jose." Jeffrey Lo held his hand out to the man. They shook.

Jose licked at his lips and looked around at the others. They were alone, these ten men, out here in this deep woods clearing. And for a good reason. A woman was already dead. I didn't sense fear around us so much as something different buried in every pair of watching eyes.

"He gave you a name. Is that true? Somebody threatening him. Maybe threatening others," Lo asked.

"'Toomey,'" the man said. "That's what he said the man's name was. And he was going to tell me other things—a kind of warning, but somebody came in then and told him to stop talking about the farm and what was going on there and that was the last time I saw Acalan."

"Anything to do with a dead dog?"

He nodded. "Before that day he told me he found a dog on his porch one morning. Later, I heard there was a man with binoculars watching Acalan when he was out in the fields."

"He know any reason he was singled out for threats?"

Jose shrugged. "From what I heard, it was because he talked too much about that place he worked. Maybe this Toomey man heard. I don't know. And I don't know what was going on. All I know is that Acalan was very ... eh ... scared."

"The family went back to Mexico?"

Jose thought a moment, his dark and angry face scowling with the effort. He shrugged hard.

"Doesn't matter. I'll call the agency in Mexico City," Lo said. "They'll get a hold of the family in Oaxaca, find out if they're there."

"Another man; another friend of Acalan's—he told me Acalan came to the United States. He worked on a farm where he wasn't happy. Something terrible going on there. Acalan was afraid he could be arrested, deported. Acalan talked too much."

"Is that other man here?" Jeffrey looked around the circle of blank faces with unwavering eyes.

"No," Jose said. "He's gone." He dropped his head and looked at his feet.

"Anything else you remember?" Dolly asked as she scribbled notes in her tiny notebook. "Something about this farm he worked on, or this guy 'Toomey'?"

"He just told me never to go work for this person. Acalan whispered, like he was … you know … afraid of the walls around us. He said the man was crazy and he saw things there …"

"You sure none of this has anything to do with drugs, right?" Lo put in.

All the men frowned, then shook their head.

"And you're all legals?" Lo looked down the line of men. "No coyote who brought you here and wants to be paid—nothing like that?"

They nodded.

"So, that's all you've got?" Dolly got to the end of one of her slowly written sentences, looked up, and demanded.

"'Toomey.' I don't know …" Jose shrugged and spread his hands. "I don't know—first name or last name. Americanos, sometimes your names are … eh … you know … funny. But—you won't say to anybody what I told you." The man moved close to Dolly as she kept writing.

"Not a word."

Miguel Hernandez stepped forward, cleared his throat, and said toward all of us, "Maybe dog fighting. That's what we think. Because of the dead dogs, you know. Or …" he shrugged "… something different. But if the police came to a farm … you know … and it was found out something so bad was going on, Acalan, well, he would have reason to be afraid."

"Anyone else hear anything like that?" Dolly called to all of them.

One by one the men shook their head. Some made faces. Others stared stoically straight ahead.

A few of the men began talking rapidly at Dick Crispin. Dick patted the air with his big hands, reassuring the frightened men. "We gotta trust somebody. This guy, and these ladies, they promised to help. Nobody's going to go around putting anything in the paper until this is all over. Right, Emily?"

He turned to me and I nodded.

"You'll be safe staying out here 'til we figure a better place to move you. Don't want you in one place too long."

Without more questions to ask, we thanked the wary men, got back in Crispin's truck, and headed out toward Dolly's car and home.

———

We were on the main road back to Northport in no time, agreeing we didn't get much from the hiding men.

"Think maybe dog fighting could be it?" Dolly said. "You'd think, if it was going on, somebody woulda been in to the station by now. People up here love their dogs."

She turned around to look at me and Lo. "That's the worst kind of cruelty you know? You ever see what happens at one of those things? Geez—enough to make you puke."

"Like that football player—had a fighting pit on his land," Lo said. "What I hear, they use other dogs and cats to train 'em. Use them as bait animals. Can't imagine grown men … oh, well … there's a lot about human beings I don't understand."

"And the name 'Toomey'—first or last, I wonder?" I asked.

"Could explain the dead dogs." Dolly worked at the idea.

"And maybe why Agent Santos was murdered," Lo added. "There's big money in dog fighting. Have these things where men come from all over the world. A million dollars bet on one fight."

"So what are we looking for?" Dolly asked. "A man? A farm?"

"Toomey," Lo said. "It's a place to start."

NINETEEN

SOMETHING WAS BOTHERING ME. A thing I couldn't put my finger on but nagged at me, like a word that wouldn't step to the front of my brain when I wrote my stories.

Off to the north, through my French doors, heat lightning flashed and pulsed over the lake, briefly outlining the willows, the starkly bare maples, and the craggy, worm-stripped oaks. Storms had the power to unsettle me. I thought maybe that was why I couldn't sit down, couldn't just open a can of soup for dinner and read a Sue Grafton I'd picked up at a used book sale a while ago.

It was one of those hot Michigan nights when not a single breath of air moved. I heard, not far off, an animal scream. Night forces were at work. I thought maybe I was nervous about facing Cecil Hawke in the morning. What did I say to the man? *I hate your main character. Why in hell did you want to write a piece of crap like this? How many more sadistic chapters will I have to read before you actually get to a story? How many before I grab a pen and kill off this 'Tommy' myself?*

I watched as sideways lightning cut directly above the lake. Closer.

So, I told myself, in the morning I'd get a check for a thousand dollars from Hawke.

I looked at the stack of bills on top of my refrigerator and asked myself, *What price my soul?*

The answer was easy—a thousand dollars.

———

The rain, when it came, blew sideways but was gone fast. Not a single tree came down. Nothing flew through my windows. A wimp as Michigan storms went.

What I needed, I decided, was to be in touch with another human being. I called Jackson.

"Emily! How...eh...nice." His bright voice signaled there was probably a woman with him. "Are you calling about my work? Have you gotten those pages done?"

"Not yet. I've been busy with Cecil's manuscript."

"Of course. And how are you finding his writing? Amazing, I'd imagine. Certainly it will be the absolute definitive work..."

"Interesting."

"That's all? Just 'interesting'?"

"I really can't say anything. Remember that confidentiality contract?"

"But this is me." He was hurt, then brought himself back to where he was and, maybe, who was with him. "But of course you wouldn't, would you? I'd hardly have recommended an editor who couldn't keep her word ..."

So. There I was. Not able to talk to him about evil and madness in literature and where the lines were drawn. I fumbled with words and was about to hang up.

"Do you have your costume yet?" he went on, making conversation though I could tell his heart wasn't in it.

"For what?"

"My God, Emily! The *Blithe Spirit* party this coming Saturday. Someone from fiction that you'd love to meet, a writer, even an historical figure. You haven't forgotten."

"Oh ... that. I'll come up with something."

"Lila's talking of nothing else ..."

"Is she there with you?"

A hesitation. "I hope you're joking ..."

"Please Jack. It's pretty obvious what's going on. The woman's not exactly subtle."

"Wouldn't I be an idiot ..." He stopped himself.

"Not for the first time."

"For heaven's sakes ..." He sounded much like Cecil Hawke. Probably his perfect ear for language.

"Do you think," he changed the subject, "that you could bring my work with you to the party next Saturday? I mean—a whole week more, Emily."

"I'll try."

"I'll pay you ..."

"Of course."

"Well, then, don't forget to find a costume. Wait until you see mine…"

"Someone from Chaucer?"

"Ah ha! That would be the expected choice, wouldn't it? But no. I'm out to surprise."

There are times when you just can't help but heave a big sigh. "Say good-night to Lila, Jack," I said and hung up.

———

Sleep wasn't easy. The air never cooled. I tried my bed but Sorrow thought that was an invitation to join me so I went back out to the sofa. All the doors and windows were open. A fan in the kitchen stirred dusty, damp air. I propped my feet on the sofa arm, closed my eyes, and drifted off.

A few hours later I sat up straight. My skin was clammy. A whippoorwill sang in the bare trees at the front of the house, and then moved off. Nothing stirred outside. That wasn't what had wakened me.

It was that thing going on in my head. At first I was afraid the uneasiness came from the manuscript, that I was having nightmares about a kid locked in a basement, but that didn't seem to be it. I ran everything quickly through my mind before it all disappeared.

An image.

A door.

Cecil Hawke's front door.

Well, no wonder—all those gargoyles and doves.

But something. Just beyond.

I lay down and drifted back to sleep.

When I next awoke, it was to voices in my head. Something was in there trying to come out. I hated nights like this. Dreams and voices and things I couldn't catch.

Gargoyles. Doves. A woman's voice. Gargoyles. Doves. A woman's angry face.

Lila.

That was what bothered me ...

Of course, no wonder she was in my head. I suspected she was with my ex-husband at that moment, laughing while Jackson tickled her as he sometimes did during sex. I'd hated being tickled but Jackson thought it part of his charm to be slightly sadistic.

Sadistic ...

No, something other than the manuscript.

A man's dark face.

A voice ... *What are you doing at the front door? Listen here, to me. Don't you ever enter my house this way. I don't ...*"

Listen here, to me.

Odd sentence construction.

Listen here, to me ...

... to me ...

Or was it something else and I'd heard it wrong.

To me.

To me.

Toomey.

TWENTY

"MY DEAR GIRL." CECIL Hawke, dressed in a Tom Wolfe white suit with white tie, white shirt, and—of all things—white buttoned spats over white shoes, grabbed me hard in his arms at the front door and hugged until I had to push him away to get a breath. His cologne burned the air I took in.

"And what do you think of my new image?" He did a twirl, ruffling his neatly trimmed toupee. The diamond at his ear sparkled in the hall light. "A bit startling, I hope. Does it work, do you think?"

I nodded as I entered the house. Maybe it worked. A trifle overdone. Could have been Mark Twain. No, not that rugged. Tom Wolfe. Good comparison.

"But ..." I thought a moment, trying to decide whether to open my mouth or not. "Weren't spats worn mostly by criminals? I mean, I think of old gangster movies. Prohibition, things like that. My dad loved those movies. George Raft? Wasn't that the guy?"

"Really? A movie gangster. Wonderful! More reason to wear them since I intend to be the best-known crime and mystery writer in this country."

"Ah ..." I widened my eyes but kept my mouth shut.

Freddy, the one-eyed, yellow dog ran up behind Cecil. I put my hand out to him then drew it back when he growled deep in his throat. Maybe he had a thing about journalists, or editors. Cecil hissed at the dog, and took a yellow ear in one hand, twisting until the dog fell over, to the floor, whining with pain.

Cecil laughed at my look. I was appalled.

"You didn't have to do ..." I sputtered.

"Yes, I did. It's all he's ever known. Bad home, you see. The only thing he understands is cruelty. Dominance." He shook his head sadly. "Terrible thing. But the truth."

I looked around as Freddy got up, slowly, and followed us to what Cecil called the 'morning room,' off the large front hall on the right. Paintings covered the walls here too, but again there was no theme, not even a sense of real thought behind them. More like a wholesale buy at an auction. More something to fill up space than a need to live with art.

And, again, I doubted they were originals. Probably for insurance purposes but still the house was beginning to impress me less than it had, as if it wasn't quite what it was meant to be.

A small, gate-legged table was set up in front of a pair of high, leaded windows on the far side of the room. Pens and writing pads were arranged on the table top. The tea tray stood beside the table, a delicate teapot and cups and saucers and creamer and sugar bowl waited. And, again, a plate of those inedible, and unsinkable, biscuits.

"Well, well," he took a chair beside me, rubbing his hands together. "And what do you think so far?"

I accepted a cup of tea and turned down the biscuits. "I've marked misspellings, places where more common usage is needed ..." I began talking as I pulled the papers from the envelope. I'd made a copy before bringing them back, but I wasn't going to tell Cecil. It was for continuity, I'd told myself, though something in me said I might need to cover my butt with this guy.

He threw his hands into the air, startling the nervous dog lying at his feet.

"I don't really want to know what you think about spelling and structure and all of that. At least, not at this point. Not even, really, what you think of the story. After all, what have you seen so far? Hardly enough to ..."

"There does seem to be an excessive amount of violence."

"Violence?" He snorted and looked out the bay window. When he turned back his face was bright red. "Did you think I was writing a cozy? That my work would be nothing but hearts and flowers?"

"No, I only meant ..."

"Violence," he repeated under his breath as he thumped his tea cup down on the cart.

"Do you want to know what I really think, or just flattery?" I asked, certain my face was as red as his. "I mean, I've done the spell check but any computer could do that for you. I've made notes for better sentence structure in a few places. I've made suggestions for additional description—more character development. What I think, personally, about your work doesn't have to come into it."

He sighed, then put his hands to his head. "No, no, no ... I mean, that's all wonderful, and of course I want to take advantage of your great editorial skills. But first and foremost there's something of higher importance here, isn't there? I mean, what I want most from you, Emily." He reached over to rub my knee, then pat it. I pulled my legs away. "What I want are your feelings as you read. I want to know when you feel sick and when you decide you want to kill my protagonist. After all, everyone has a breaking point." He stuck out a small pink tongue, licked at his bottom lip, then snaked it back into his mouth. "I need to know how my work provokes you."

His almost white eyebrows went up, blue eyes flew wide. At his chin, his fingers moved like little snakes. "Most of all, I want to know ... do I repulse you?"

Did I dare say: *Yes, you creep? You repulse me down to where I live.*

I didn't. I sat higher in my chair and moved my legs even further from his reach. "I don't censor things I edit, Cecil. My opinion of the work itself—if you mean a judgment, or if you are testing my morality—I don't think that's the issue."

He frowned. "So you refuse to have an opinion? Are you saying you can't put yourself in an acquisition editor's seat and judge whether the reading public can stomach my work?"

I was confused. Did he want an opinion of its chances in the marketplace?

He went on. "How can I know if I'm achieving what I set out to do if I can't rely on people I pay to tell me the truth?" He stressed the 'I pay' part hard enough to remind me I was doing a job here, not pleasing myself.

"In that case … I guess I'd say there's probably a market for this kind of psychological mystery …"

"Just 'a market'? Not best-seller material? People ate up Hannibal Lecter. Pun intended," he added, smiling. "But you haven't read enough yet, have you? I'm asking an impossible thing. Of course, you must read on. But this time, along with the edits, please take notes on what you feel as you read. I need that …" He cleared his throat. "And you've remembered to mention my work to no one. I really don't care to have your reactions watered down by the opinions of others. Nor to have my ideas stolen."

I was about to reassure him, once again, that I was a professional and didn't discuss a client's work when Lila swept into the room in a strapless red cotton dress that looked like it was held up by nothing but a prayer. She hurried to us, bent to gather me in her arms, hug me, and pull up a Queen Anne chair as she chattered about something I didn't catch because my mind was still on getting things straight with Cecil.

"Darling!" She leaned back to stare, open-mouthed, at Cecil, tea cup just below her bottom lip. "You look extraordinary this morning. Is this a new look you intend to keep?"

"I thought …" He patted at the front of his white suit.

"Ice cream vendor?" She looked at me to see if I found her remark funny.

"No, dear," Cecil smiled slowly. "World chic, I would call it."

She shook her head and snickered. "But my dear, dear Cecil. It's been done. Like wearing all black—done to death. Why not lime? Or red—now there's a color for you. And why bother? Who will care? You aren't exactly world reknowned, you know. Unless there were appearances to make, real people to impress ..." She smirked at me. "No slight to you intended, Emily.

"Why wear a costume at all?" Lila went on, sticking her chin out as if in challenge.

I watched as Cecil's eyes narrowed to empty slits. "We all have our costumes, don't we, dear?" He stressed the 'dear' and spoke through tight lips. "And our masks?"

Lila's face hardened. She looked her age as she set her cup carefully on the tea tray and got up. "All I meant is that if you're assuming a literary posture, please get yourself a cape to swing at book signings, or wear all purple. You could look pope-like—at least add a little gold. A look of your own, dear." She stood beside him, leaning down to give him a hug while pushing her breast briefly into his face. "Would you have people think your writing's only a cheap copy, like your outfit?"

She interrupted herself with a sigh. "I've got to be off."

"Hmmm ... Late for church?" Cecil asked, his narrow eyebrows raised.

She threw back her head and laughed. I could see the red inside of her mouth, not a pretty sight against her white skin, white teeth, and red, red lips. She turned to me.

"Emily, I hope you're as excited as I am about our party. You haven't forgotten, have you? This Saturday. Have you decided on a costume yet? Cecil and I are keeping our costumes a secret. We want to surprise our guests. And so many are coming—all corners

185

of the world. Cecil has friends everywhere." She flung a hand dramatically over her head. "Just everywhere."

"Mine's a secret too," I hedged since I had no costume.

"And remember, invite anyone you like. I'll leave it to you who might be an addition to our party. There will be a séance. Don't forget to mention that to your friends. A real séance. We will have our own Madame Arcati, just as in Coward's *Blithe Spirit*. Won't this be the most amazing event to ever happen here in your precious north country?"

She clasped her hands at her chest, turned, and flew out of the room.

Silence followed her. Lila was quite a show. The two of them were a play in themselves. I was outclassed here, out-thought, and left almost speechless.

Cecil offered more tea. I shook my head. He went back to his expectations of me as his editor. Maybe what he wanted wasn't unreasonable—I was to be a story editor as well as a copy editor. I could do that.

"Cecil," I leaned just a little toward him. "I have to ask you a question."

"You mean about my hand." He held the hand with the missing knuckle in the air. "You still think I'm the boy in the novel?" He laughed. "Of course not, Emily. All writers, as you well know, use their lives for grist; for color and background. I liked the idea of the boy losing part of a finger to a dog. Later in the book … well, you'll see why it was necessary to set this up early." He tapped the fingers of both his hands together.

I tried to find a way to sympathize with Cecil Hawke but I found him unsettling. When I was at the paper, in Ann Arbor, one crazy man with a nutty book he'd self-published demanded that I review his novel, even resorting to dire threats about my immortal soul when I explained it wasn't possible, that I wasn't a book reviewer. I sicced that one on our Arts and Entertainment editor and backed off.

With this guy there was no pulling away. I wasn't sure I even wanted to. If nothing else, the man was interesting. One of those: I'm dying to see what happens next, kind of things.

Back at the front door with a check for two thousand dollars in my purse and the next ten chapters in my hands, I stopped to make nice, figuring the man needed it. Freddy had followed along behind. When I turned I ran into his muzzle. I pulled away fast, not wanting to be the cause of more growling and more punishing. When I didn't try to touch him, he nuzzled my hand. At first I didn't move a finger, not wanting to come up with one or two fewer than I'd had before. He nuzzled my hand again and I patted his head. The dog stood there beside me, as if mesmerized. I patted him again, then left my hand there, on his wide head, until Cecil saw and ordered the dog away.

He gave me a reproving look. "I wouldn't do that, Emily. He's not a lap dog, you know."

I stepped out to the porch, looked him up and down, then smiled. "Personally, I like your white suit, Cecil," I said, causing his face to light up.

"I'm so glad, Emily. I knew we'd get along famously. You're really very intelligent, aren't you?"

I remembered then what I'd wanted to ask before I left. Just that nagging thing. Probably silly, but Dolly and Lo and I couldn't afford to pass up any idea at this point.

"There is one other thing…" I put my hand out to stop the door from closing in my face. "The last time I was here there was a man standing…" I pointed to the porch.

"Yes, and…?"

"Do you know who that was?"

He shrugged and looked at me oddly. "Could have been anyone."

"Lila didn't seem to like him."

He threw back his head and laughed. "Then he is one among many. Lila adores detesting her friends."

"He wasn't a guest, I don't think. A tall, dark man in what looked like work clothes. Maybe he takes care of your sheep. Don't you hire men for that?"

He hesitated a moment. "Of course I do. Can you really see me mucking out the barns or whatever they do out there?"

I agreed. I didn't see him as a shepherd. He stepped back, meaning to close the door.

"Lila called him 'Toomey.' I'm pretty sure that's what I heard…"

"Really?" His eyebrows shot up.

"It's just that an INS agent is here in town, looking into that murder I've been writing about…"

His hand fell from the door. His eyes narrowed.

"The name Toomey came up in connection with a man threatening a few of the migrant workers," I said.

Without hesitating he shook his head. "Never heard of him..."

"But, I thought she called that man..."

"You'll have to ask Lila then, won't you?" I got a tight smile and an impatient look. He stopped a minute. "Who is this agent? The one who mentioned the man's name? Is he still up here? I just...well...I hardly think anyone having something to do with a murder would be coming to my front door."

"Could you ask? It's important. The woman who was murdered was a Mexican emigration agent. Agent Lo—the guy here investigating—needs all the help..."

"I imagine he does." He stopped to think a moment then spread his hands. "But you see I employ so many."

"Would you ask Lila who the man was the other day? I mean, she'd know..."

The door closed in my face and I was left talking to myself.

TWENTY-ONE

EMILY, I SWEAR TO GOD, something awful's happened. I don't know what to do, where to turn. I'm gonna do something illegal. I got to. And I need you as a witness. Just to say why I did it, if it comes to that...

I was into the next book about me and Dolly. I figured I had every right, like Cecil Hawke, to use what I knew. We'd lived these things, after all. If she didn't like it she could sue me. I could just see that judge asking her if this really happened, if that really happened. All of it was true enough. I took a few liberties with any fact that made me look bad, but that was all.

I sat in my studio and dreamed the long dream that begins a book. Place: with colors and smells. Character: real people with faults and beauty. A plot that arcs and falls and curves in on itself, then out again until it ends and the threads make a whole. What I tried not to think about was the blood and pain it took to write a book; the pulling word by word from my head as if I were a spider, and the web had to be perfect or else I didn't catch flies and didn't get to eat. Then the greater pain ... when would I hear from Madeleine Clark? Was having her working for me in New York just another part of the delusion—that I would ever get published?

I got up because I'd depressed myself enough to shut down the writing for the day, and went to the window to check out a new spider web. Because it was daytime, she was hiding, I couldn't see my long-bodied spider, only her web. If I had to critique her work I'd say it looked a little ragged at the top, and some of her openings didn't match the openings below. Overall, it achieved what she'd set out to achieve but the symmetry was missing. A utilitarian web. Maybe only an impression of a real web. Overall I gave her a B. *This just isn't what I'm looking for, spider. Thanks for thinking of me ...*

Then, Dolly called to tell me they had some news on the case and they needed me to come into the police station immediately. I didn't argue. It wasn't as though I'd gotten deeply into anything productive.

———

At the station, Lo had gone out for a pizza and drinks by the time I got there. Dolly sat at the front desk since her little room, which used to be a closet, wouldn't hold all three of us.

"How are you feeling?" was the first thing I said since it seemed to be part of that big elephant hanging in the air between us.

"Fine."

"So, you're due in January."

"Who you been talking to now?"

"Your grandmother. She told me you'd been to a doctor, which I thought was smart."

"Thanks." She looked up at me. I couldn't see her stomach. Three months. She'd be showing soon.

"Are there maternity cop suits?" I asked.

Dolly frowned at me. "You mean uniforms?"

I nodded.

She shrugged. "I'll get bigger shirts, work out something with the pants."

"What about winter?"

"What do you mean?"

"You know, a coat. You'll be huge."

"I'll get a bigger coat is all. Got solid boots." She threw back her head, let out an exasperated breath of air, then slapped her hands on the desk. "You know how many years women been having babies, Emily? Every one of them got through it somehow. I'll bet they all didn't have new coats either. I'll bet they got on just fine with whatever they had ..."

"Yeah, and laid down behind the plow and delivered the baby right there in the field." I leaned toward her. "I'm here, Dolly. When the time comes ... anything."

Lo was back with the food. We ate, cleared the mess away, and got down to business.

"Dolly tell you the migrants have all left Crispin's farm?" Lo asked.

I shook my head.

Dolly muttered, "Didn't get around to it."

"Crispin called Dolly so we don't think they've just gone off to another farm. He said they'd cleared out completely. The farmers are getting worried that the rest will leave, once word gets around. He thought there might have been another threat. Something happened. Not a sign of any of them and even the worker he thought was a friend didn't come to say anything."

"So," Dolly said. "All we've got is this name, 'Toomey,' and that might not even be right."

"I remembered something." I got a couple of encouraging nods. "It's probably nothing but I'm working for a Cecil Hawke, editing a book he's writing." I explained what I was doing so Lo was up to speed. "Well, I thought I heard the name 'Toomey' when Jackson and I were leaving there, about a week ago."

They looked at each other and then back to me.

"What I mean is, I saw this guy at their front door. Hawke's wife said something to him about not coming in that way. Looked like a workman. I thought that was the reason she was so unfriendly. You know, mud on his boots. She said what I took to be 'Listen to me' or something like that. Can't quite remember. But I was thinking about it and I wondered later if she was saying the man's name instead: Toomey."

Dolly looked skeptical. Lo nodded.

"It was just that . . ." I didn't know how to describe an uneasy feeling.

"Not much to go on," Lo said.

"Yeah. Just a feeling. But the guy that owns the place is odd anyway. Nothing ordinary about him and then he's got this big Australian-type sheep ranch he doesn't really run and claims to know little about. Not even the names of the men who work for him. It just seemed…"

Agent Lo looked from Dolly to me. "We've got some information on that boot print at the crime scene. You might not be far off." He hesitated, deferring to Dolly.

"Don't put this in the paper, Emily. Could blow the whole thing," she warned.

I waited. Dolly was going for effect.

"Boot sole had imbedded matter."

"And?"

"Sheep dung."

That took my breath away. Cecil's wasn't the only sheep farm in the north country. Lots of mixed herds—cattle, sheep, goats, even a llama and a couple alpaca farms, but so far Hawke's was the only one with a guy named Toomey connected to it.

Dolly looked hard at Lo and then at me. "Maybe I should pay a call over there to talk to your friend. Couldn't hurt. We been seein' a lot of farmers anyway. Think he'd let me take a look at his place?"

All I could do was shrug. Who knew what Cecil, or even Lila, would allow?

"And I'll start looking into this Hawke," Lo said. 'Where he came from. Who he is."

"A writer," I said. "Rich. That's all I know."

"I'll check him out. Ask about his operation. Got to have men working for him, as you say."

"You know what?" I turned to look straight at Dolly. "If you want to go over there, take a look around without Cecil knowing, I've got a way to get you in."

"Sure."

"They're having a big costume party Saturday. Lila told me to bring anybody I wanted to bring." I had to smile. "You want to go to a party?"

She shrugged. "If it'll get me inside. I mean, without giving away why I'm there."

"Be a lot of people. Maybe that dark guy will show up. Or maybe you can get a look around outside. See what you think."

She frowned, making her nose twitch to one side as her lazy eye drifted off. "Costume? You mean like Halloween? I gotta wear one of those?"

"The party's based around one of Noel Coward's plays. Hawke's a Noel Coward expert. You've heard of Noel Coward?"

She shook her head, unhappy.

"Doesn't matter. Just remember the guy's got a big ego and he's a snob. When you meet him go along with everything he says. You don't have to know about Noel Coward, just pretend you do."

"Sounds like a prick, to me." She wasn't getting any happier, or any nicer.

'It's a *Blithe Spirit* party. The play's from the late thirties or early forties. I'm not sure, exactly. But I know there's a séance in it. A dead wife returns. Should be a fun party and you'll meet both the Hawkes without putting them on the defensive. If you get a chance, look around outside. If I see that guy I thought Lila called Toomey, I'll let you know."

She was still worried. "Costume, eh. You mean like going to K-Mart and …"

"I don't think so."

"Then what kind of costume?"

"You come as your favorite character from literature. Or your favorite writer."

Lo gave a whistle and then choked. His eyes got big but he didn't laugh. He knew Dolly already and waited to see what happened next.

"Sounds nuts, if you ask me," she said. "But I guess … if I gotta go undercover."

First she considered the idea. Then came a shake of her head. Then an 'Ah-ha' moment.

I nodded. "Some literary character. You know any?"

She ignored me. "Got one. All I need is an old raincoat. Maybe Eugenia's got one. Or my grandmother. Cate loves dressing up …"

"Who are you going to be?"

"Columbo. You know, the guy from that TV show. I watch reruns with my grandmother. I'll be him. Can wear the raincoat right over my uniform and …"

I threw up my hands and looked to Agent Lo for help but he wasn't talking. I gave Dolly a hard look. "What part of 'undercover' don't you get?"

She thought a while. "Guess not," she said. "I won't go as a cop. So, okay, you help me. But no damned Snow White or Rapunzel. Nothing like that."

I thought awhile, looked hard at her, and came up with the perfect costume.

TWENTY-TWO

DOLLY AND I PARKED behind rows of cars and walked up the driveway toward where the Hawkes's trees and shrubs sparkled with winking, white lights, and the front portico was draped with bare, marquis bulbs. Dolly tripped over her skirt again and again, swearing—inappropriately, considering her costume—every time she fell on her hem.

"Grab it and hold on," I said, tired of her grousing and carrying on about how the nun's habit she wore over her uniform was making her itch; how she was too hot—how the white wimple cut into her face, how the whole thing was way too large, and how the black veil kept falling over her eyes. One thing, then another, then another. All this after I thought I'd come up with the perfect costume. Plenty of room under all that black material, low-heeled, sturdy shoes, and veils to hide a burgeoning belly, a cop's uniform, and a gun belt. Perfect undercover outfit.

"A nun wouldn't do that. Prance around with her skirt in the air," she said. "They're more ... modest, I guess you could say."

"A nun wouldn't be pregnant either," I came back at her as we climbed the steps.

"What kind of nun did you say I am?" she hissed at me, peeking out from around the black veil.

"Any nun you want to be," I whispered back and rang the bell.

"Thought I was supposed to be something from literature."

"You are. If anybody asks tell them you're the nasty prioress from *The Canterbury Tales*. Jackson will love that one."

"He here? Hell! You didn't say nothing … for sure I don't want to be her."

"Okay. Try the ghostly nun from Charlotte Bronte's *Villette*."

"Never read it."

I sighed, adjusted my black straw hat with cherries on top, grabbed my parrot-headed umbrella by the middle, spread my feet wide, hoped I didn't have sweat circles under my arms, and waited to wow Cecil with my Mary Poppins.

Nobody answered. "How about Sister Fidelma," I said since she went on complaining that she had no idea who she was supposed to be. "She's a seventh-century nun who solved crimes. Or there's a pregnant nun in a book by one of our northern writers."

"No thanks. I'll be that singing nun. You know, from *The Sound of Music.* That's who I'll be."

"Then I guess we're both Julie Andrews."

We weren't going to win prizes for originality.

I rang the bell again and was about to walk in when the door opened with a blast of overly cooled air and a stout woman in a black and white maid's uniform—frilly apron, frilly hat—stood there, bent forward at the waist, feet splayed in overrun shoes.

"I'm Edith," she said. "Come on in now." She stepped back and motioned toward the front hall, filled with people.

"You'll jist have to take care of yerselves, I'd say," the young woman muttered, her face puckered into complaint. "Too many people. I wasn't expecting so many. Mrs. Hawke, well, she never said this many and I got to stay in the kitchen making those crumpled shrimp cakes what she wants me to be passing out. And I'd like to know how I'm supposed..."

She turned her back and scuttled off as fast as she could go leaving me and Dolly to close the door and find a place to stand, among the fifteen or twenty guests. We exchanged nods and smiles with other oddly dressed people, then hung to a side wall, under a faded copy of Georgia O'Keeffe's *My Last Door*. The people around us were already talking as fast as they could talk, as if they'd been at the champagne for a while.

"Would you look at this," Dolly said and had to repeat herself over the tinny, twenties music and the clipped voice of Noel Coward singing "Mad Dogs and Englishmen."

Cecil knew how to set a mood.

Around us, moving in and out of the hall and in and out of the library was a pantheon of literary characters. Cecil had said he had friends coming in from Europe but there was no picking them out in this crowd. There were writers. I recognized a grizzled Ernest Hemingway and a smug Gertrude Stein.

A writer's dream, I thought, looking around. Beside a small side table, on which a huge bouquet of white roses teetered, was the Hunchback of Notre Dame talking to Daisy, from *The Great Gatsby*. This Daisy had bee-stung lips puckered without the frozen

199

benefit of Botox. Her cigarette holder went high into the air as she laughed and blew smoke into the Hunchback's face, making the guy, one shoulder up to his left ear under a brown, rough wool cloak and cowl, choke. The Hunchback waved a hand and swore at Daisy to "cut that out" in what sounded like a flat midwestern accent.

The Mock Turtle from *Alice in Wonderland* walked by us, bowing and wringing his two top feet, crying out, "Soup! Soup! Beeyootiful soup! The Evening soup. Beeyootiful soup!" He dipped from side to side as he cut through the crowd and disappeared into the library.

Behind the Mock Turtle, a woman in a white mobcap and long black dress covered with a utilitarian apron sprinted to keep up. The woman carried a lighted lantern, holding it high as she called brightly to everyone she passed, "Good evening. Good evening. I'm off to the front. The boys are waiting. Poor Souls. Poor Souls."

If I had to guess, I would have said: Florence Nightingale. More history than literature.

The crowd in the hall shifted into the library or the morning room, and then out again. It was a kaleidoscope of changing books come to life.

"Did you ever?" Dolly, stunned and a little star struck, leaned close, talking from the side of her mouth the way wimple-constrained nuns learned to talk.

In a far corner, a stooped woman stood scribbling on a small pad of paper. Her hair was parted in the middle. From her long black dress and lace collar I put her in the mid-1800s. Again and again she looked around at the people gathered. She was afraid, very afraid. I bet on Emily Dickinson.

"Who's that?" Dolly pointed to a sheik in full robes.

I shrugged.

"You think he's real?"

"More likely Laurence of Arabia."

"See anything of that guy 'Toomey'?" She lowered her voice, stuck her hands up her sleeves, and leaned closer.

I looked around. He could be any of the men. Or none of them. But tall. That was one thing that couldn't be hidden.

We stepped along the hall, smiling at other partygoers, and mingling as best we could, though Dolly hung back, taking advantage of her nun's habit to stay anonymous—in case there were Leetsvillians there who could identify her.

A stout Mark Twain with a bristling mustache walked by us, arm in arm with a woman who might have been Virginia Woolf. I began to wish for nametags.

A couple stepped up to introduce themselves as Robert Browning and Elizabeth Barrett Browning.

"Robert is so kind," Elizabeth said, holding his arm tightly as she glanced lovingly up at him.

"*How do I love thee ...*'" she quoted, but Bob Browning had his eye fixed on a tray of martinis the flustered maid was trying to serve, hopping back and forth while nervously apologizing to a damp, furry mole and a stately Miss Haversham—more movie version than Dickens, with the piled-high white hair and wispy wedding gown.

I was up to three Lord Byrons (I guessed) when Lila came at us, flying down the center of the hall, crying my name so that everyone turned. She was dressed as a flapper from pink silk headband to chunk-heeled, buckled shoes. Her pink voile dress was low-waisted, the bodice pleated. A white feather boa was draped down one shoulder and crossed low over her well exposed breasts. Her make-up was bright, her blond hair short, with spit curls pasted across her forehead.

"Ah, Emily. And you've brought a friend, I see."

Dolly smiled and poked at her wimple.

"Delores Walker. Lila Hawke." I introduced them—sort of, keeping to the fake name we'd come up with. Lila put out her hand and shook Dolly's.

"And which nun are you, dear? No, no, no. Let me guess... from Shakespeare. Now what was that nun's name?" Lila puckered her lips and forehead and thought. "Isabella, I think. Wasn't that her name? A postulant nun. *As You Like It.* No, no, no: *Measure for Measure.*" She threw her head back, arms out, staggered a little, then blinked hard as she quoted, "*With the measure you see, it will be measured of you...*"

Lila, well along into the booze, closed one eye and smiled tipsily at Dolly. "That's it, isn't it? You're Isabella."

Dolly shook her head and was about to come out with her singing nun thing but Lila stepped back, not interested, and ready to fly. "Never mind," she said. "Cecil will guess who you are. He's simply loving all of this. I'll tell him you're here, Emily. And Jackson too. They're in the library showing off Cecil's Noel Coward collection to everyone. And, Emily, Jackson is divine as Romeo.

Wait until you see him ..." Her eyes shone as she said his name, almost tasting it. I'd seen that look before and wished I didn't know what it meant.

"And here I thought he'd be the fat monk from *The Canterbury Tales*," I said, but Lila wasn't listening. She waved and blew kisses to those around us. She twirled in place for one couple who stopped to comment on her flapper costume. She did it all so prettily, and with such charm. And with a red-hot blast of whiskey breath that had almost seared my eyebrows.

Lila brought her face close to mine. "I rather like your ... is it Mary Poppins? Droll. Quaint. I was thinking of coming as Scheherazade. You know, body suit and veils and all of that, but Cecil frowned on it. He's such a prude. He said I had to be Ruth, the wife in *Blithe Spirit*. He is, after all, Charles, the husband in the play. Or maybe he's Noel himself. I never know with Cecil."

She sailed back up the hall, stopping to talk to Macbeth and then to a short man in small, round glasses dressed as Harry Potter. She got past Humpty Dumpty with only an air kiss and punched playfully at a tall and bearded Julia Child, I guessed, in curly brown wig and flowered dress, cinched at the waist with a wide belt, and holding a large spatula in her hand.

"I'm going to find Cecil and Jackson," I said, wanting to get my part in this charade over.

"I'll take a look around, talk to some people," Dolly said. "If you see that guy, Toomey, come find me. In case I run into any tall, dark men I'll just say the name and see what happens."

She shrugged, wimple and veil going up and down. "Can't hurt. And I'd like to talk to that screwy maid. If the guy works here, I'll bet you anything a maid would know his name."

"You mean Edith?" I laughed, watching the scurrying woman spill a drink on the Cat in the Hat. "She's an actress. There's a nutty maid in *Blithe Spirit*. I think her name was Edith, too. This is getting interesting. I wonder what else they've got planned?"

I cut through the crowd, toward the library. The music was louder. I heard "Mad Dogs and Englishmen" for the fourth time.

Edith, the maid, bumped into me going through the high, carved library doorway. She juggled a tray of rather sad-looking appetizers, holding the tray out to me, then pulling it away and hurrying off before I could take one.

The two men stood at the fireplace. Though it was the middle of July and hot outside, a fire burned in the grate. Great air conditioning, I thought. The room was cold enough to grow icicles.

Cecil saw me first. He was dressed in yet another smoking jacket with a puffy white silk ascot at his throat. His toupee tonight was sparser than his others, and combed tightly to each side in distinct rows. He gestured with the unlit pipe he held in his left hand. "And here's our girl now," he cried and put his arms out to hug me, kiss both of my cheeks, then push me back for a slow once-over. "Perfect costume. Mary Poppins. Ah yes, the Mary Poppins who came to the Bankses' home to fix things and has come to mine to fix my poor book."

He laughed. I laughed. Jackson laughed and stepped up to take me from Cecil, hug me, and whisper, "Have you ever seen anything like this in your life? I think I recognize some of the guests. At least one writer I've seen before. Who knows what else?"

He held on longer. "Did you bring my chapters with you? I'm so ready to move ahead..."

I stepped away from him, made my face show sorrow, and spread my hands. "I forgot, Jack. Beginning of the week... I promise."

"I hope so. After all, I was the one who got you this job. At least a little gratitude..."

I didn't get a chance to answer. Cecil called for attention, announcing that a big surprise lay ahead and he had, sadly, to leave us to go prepare.

He was gone and Jackson, looking surprisingly good in his black Romeo tights with white doublet, was off to gather everyone and move them to the hall, as Cecil asked him to do.

Amid the crush of characters, I made my way out of the library and searched for Dolly. Being the only nun there, she wasn't difficult to find. I could see the black figure moving across a bay window at the back of the hall, approaching a tall man with his back turned. The man, maybe an Abraham Lincoln from the stovepipe hat, stood near the door leading to the kitchen. Edith, the maid, made another foray past him, a tray of appetizers clutched in her white-knuckled hands, just as Dolly tapped the man on the back.

The tall man whipped around to face Dolly. His head went down toward her for a minute and then he was gone. He'd turned enough so I could see him, and recognize the face. The man from the front porch. The dark, angry looking man I thought had to be Toomey.

Salman Rushdie stopped in front of me and by the time I got around him Dolly and the tall man were gone. I hurried in the direction of the kitchen, pushing at people who got in my way. When I looked again, Dolly was standing alone, frowning around her as if searching for someone. I put my hand into the air and was about to call out when the candelabras along the walls and the overhead chandeliers went dark and I was caught in place, unable to see.

At the central staircase, a floodlight came up slowly, focused on a woman posing dramatically at the top of the steps. The crowd below was hushed by the spectacle.

The slightly rotund woman held still for effect, drawing her wide and flowing gown of jeweled damask around her. Over her hair and across her face, she'd wrapped a jeweled scarf, the gems catching the floodlight and blinding us as she turned from side to side.

Other scarves flew about the woman's shoulders. At her ears and wrists, diamonds caught the light and sent out bright sparks.

One step down and then another. She held her skirt in a white-gloved hand as she slowly descended.

At the base of the steps, near the edge of the floodlight, Lila Hawke stepped out to point dramatically toward the woman. "Ladies and gentlemen," she cried out. "May I introduce our psychic for this evening, Madame Arcati. The séance is about to begin."

Around me, guests oohed and ahhed as Madame Arcati—straight out of *Blithe Spirit*—descended the rest of the way, waving her scarves from side to side, then drawing them over her face—one after another—until she was at the base of the stairs, pulling the last of the scarves away to reveal herself, and her little diamond-studded ears, to the stunned crowd.

There was a collective gasp and then nervous laughter. I laughed along with the others.

Cecil posed, with smudged make-up on his round face, gown and scarves draped prettily over his wide body, wig askew atop his head. He bowed and threw kisses from left to right. Finally, he grabbed on to his wig and scarves, threw back his head, and began to laugh.

Cecil Hawke in drag, made an amazing woman.

TWENTY-THREE

DOLLY WHISPERED FROM THE corner of her mouth. She smiled and nodded to people around us as Cecil Hawke made his way through the clapping crowd.

"The guy was dark and tall, like you said," Dolly hissed. "A real Abraham Lincoln. All I did was say Toomey to him and he was outta there. Think he's the one?"

Partygoers, with the lights now turned back on, unfolded chairs in front of a makeshift platform that had been hastily set up at the middle of the hall. A table and tall chairs were lifted up to the stage. Madame Arcati, with a queenly wave to all his friends, took his seat in the highest chair, at the center of the table.

I shrugged and shushed Dolly, afraid people around us might hear. In a place like this, with so many strangers, and all of those strangers in disguise … well … I didn't think it was a good idea to take chances on Dolly being ratted out.

Madame Arcati fussed with her flowing gown—getting settled in her chair—and then was joined by Jackson, who waved to the crowd. He bowed and was probably about to break into one of Romeo's speeches when Madame Arcati stopped him.

"Let's get on with it," Madame Arcati growled. Jackson sat down and Madame Arcati leaned up as tall as he could get, looked out over the assembly, spotted me, and motioned me to the stage.

I kept my head down, pushing through the crowd.

"Lucky you." Voices followed me, the comments sour.

"Mary Poppins! Criminey, Madame Arcati. She'll bollox the whole thing," someone yelled and the crowd laughed.

Jackson helped me up to the platform. I took the chair next to him. Three other people I didn't know were invited to the table and then Madame Arcati put up her hands for quiet.

"I will need total silence in the room. If spirits are to be called to us, you must stay as still as you possibly can stay. I hope for a glorious séance. A séance to end all séances. A memorable séance. The lights will be very, very dim, to encourage the spirit world to join us."

There was a titter of laughter from the middle of the crowd, quickly shushed by others. The lights went down again. I was surprised that Lila hadn't joined us and then realized she was probably a part of whatever ghostly manifestation we were in for.

"Everyone here at the table must join hands," Madame Arcati, in a high falsetto voice, instructed us. "And those in the room, please take the hand of the person next to you on either side and don't break the link while I am in trance. I could get hurt, you see ... "

Around me, people laughed nervously and Madame Arcati clucked at them.

With the room quiet and dark, holding Jackson's hand on one side and the White Rabbit's on the other, I could feel the smallest chill work up and down my spine. I'd never been into séances and Ouija boards. Part of that came out of fear. Some things were better left alone, I'd always felt. If anything real happened here, I didn't want to have a whole new set of rules for living to believe in. If a Ouija board or spirits from another world could tell me my future, or bring me messages, then how the heck could I ever trust my own choices? Nope. I had to believe that my life was my own. That I could run it or ruin it—all by myself.

Still … sitting there with only the sound of clocks ticking and twenty or thirty people breathing in the darkness, holding one sweaty paw and one cool hand in mine, waiting for something to happen … Who knew?

Madame Arcati's breath deepened. She began to moan, then mumble. After a few minutes of the mumbling, Cecil Hawke, in his own voice, called out, "Spirits! If anyone is here, let us know now!"

A deep, waiting silence settled over the room. The floor creaked. A noise came from the kitchen. A few nervous coughs were quickly quieted. I was perspiring and wishing I were anywhere but there.

Knock. Knock. Knock. Knock.

The sound was startling. People gasped. I found myself holding my breath.

Knock. Knock. The sound came again.

"Spirit. Are you in this room?" Madame Arcati called out.

We waited. I figured if there was an answer I would connect the two hands I was holding, slip off the platform, and head for the front door. The only spirit I was interested in right then was a glass of wine, preferably in my own home, with my brave dog keeping watch beside me.

There came a low moan. The voice behind the moan was high. Female. The moan came again, louder. A heartbreaking sound. My sensible self told me it had to be Lila, doing a little acting. My old brain—flight or fight response—told me to get the hell out of there as fast as I could or the zombies would come after me, or a ghost would appear right where I was sitting and tell everybody all my sins and why I should be condemned to hell. I couldn't have said when I'd become the center of that particular universe; all I knew was that childhood learning went deep, and old stories about dragons and ogres my mother used to read to me were shaking their roots like tambourines in my head.

"Ahh," Madame Arcati, now back into her high womanly voice, said. "We have a spirit. And do you have a message for someone in this room, kind spirit?"

A gasp made its way around the hall as a quivering light near the library door showed in the darkness. Only a weak, candle-like flicker, it moved quickly, side to side, as if hunting for something or someone. People fell back from it.

The moaning grew louder and then a deep voice, coming from everywhere, said simply, "Why?"

"Ah, a spirit with a question of its own. Can you tell us, spirit, who your message is for? Can you, by indication, or name, or something, identify the one you are here to speak to?"

211

Madame Arcati hissed for quiet as a low current of conversation buzzed through the partygoers. Probably, like me, no one wanted to be the target of the disembodied voice.

The moaning began again. There was a brightening of the flitting light though it seemed attached to nothing. The spirit voice said, "Cecil Hawke..."

"Ah, but he's not among us this evening, spirit. Perhaps someone else? Don't you have a message for Jackson Rinaldi?" Cecil's voice was hard and insistent. It sounded as if someone wasn't playing by the rules in a new Hawke game.

"Perhaps," Cecil went on in his own voice, "your message was to be about not bedding the wives of new friends? Don't you imagine that's what you wanted to say?"

Now the low buzz became a gasp. I felt Jack's hand tighten hard against mine and then pull away completely. I was left with a very cold, very wet empty hand.

"This isn't funny, Cecil." Jack, still in darkness, pushed his chair back violently. He stood beside me.

"Ah, but all is funny, my friend," Madame Arcati said. "All the world's a stage, don't you agree? And we are simply players? Isn't that right? And your part has been to bed the queen. A little out of your league. But time to stop, I'd say. Oh yes, time to stop."

Knowing Jackson, I was sure he wanted to find a way to go along with this terrible joke and come out of it looking all right. He tried for a shaky laugh then gave up. There was a thud when he jumped off the platform. Comments followed him as he made his way through the crowd. I figured he was heading for the front door.

When quiet fell again, Madame Arcati went on as if nothing had happened.

"Spirit? Are you still here?" His voice filled with choking laughter.

I decided to escape too. This wasn't just creepy, it had taken on a cruel edge. Between them, Cecil and Lila probably had plans to decimate others here at the party. What a miserable pair, I thought, as I felt my way off the back of the platform. They weren't just a little nuts, but something much worse.

The spirit didn't answer him this time. I figured she'd done as instructed, been there to humiliate Jackson, and was now entering the hall from another door, ready to take her place among the partygoers as if nothing had happened.

Cecil Hawke called out louder, in an insistent voice. Oh-oh, I thought as I edged around seated people. Cecil fully expected her to answer. Somebody else was in for it. Could even be me, the one who dared to criticize his work. Oh God, what next! I felt my way along the wall.

The spirit moaned again.

"Ah, you're back, spirit. And now, have you another message for someone in this room? Maybe for a woman named ... oh, let me see ... could it be ... ?"

More moaning and flickering of the light.

"No," the quavering voice of the spirit answered.

"Spirit ... you must know the woman I'm speaking of ..."

The spirit's voice came back stronger, but different. "Ah yes. Cecil." Again the moaning began. "Ah, Cecil. It's Amanda. You murdered me. Will Lila be next?"

213

Madame Arcati was up and out of her chair, struggling with her gown, and swearing hard in Cecil Hawke's clear voice.

I didn't know where to look first, at the flickering light, or at the shadowed figure disappearing back toward the kitchen. Around me people yelled for someone to put on the lights. The séance was over. The party was certainly finished. When the lights came on, we blinked bleary-eyed at each other. It didn't take long for someone to yell, "Let's get the hell outta here." I agreed and looked around for Dolly, lost among turtles and moles and a startled Gertrude Stein. Before I could get anywhere close to the front door there came the loud and echoing sound of thunder close by. A loud crack. Then silence.

A gunshot.

"Down. Everybody. Hit the deck. NOW!" Deputy Dolly's voice yelled before the echo faded from the room. People screamed. There was a panicked rush for the front door as chairs flew and bodies careened into each other.

I saw the nun with a .38 in her hand standing in the doorway to the library. As fast as I could, I got over to her. She put out one arm, holding me away.

"Stay back," she yelled. People stopped in their tracks, curiosity overtaking fear. It crossed my mind that this was just another part of the whole crazy night.

"Close the front door," Dolly yelled. "And stay back," she ordered again as she ripped at her habit, tugging at the wimple tied up under the veil. I got to her side and helped her, tossing the habit aside to expose the official uniform beneath. No one said a word about the cop the nun had become.

A man yelled for someone to call 911. I heard maybe a dozen voices soon shouting into phones even though Dolly was screaming at the top of her lungs that the police were on the way.

No sound came from the library. Behind us, Cecil Hawke edged his way back through the crowd. He got to the library and tried to ease Dolly out of the doorway. She put up her hand, stopping him. "Can't go in there. That was a gunshot. We don't know …"

"But I will go in," Cecil insisted, his made-up, androgynous face twisting with outrage. "My entire collection of Noel Coward works is in there. They are invaluable! I have a fortune tied up …"

"I don't think we're looking at a robbery," Dolly shushed him, her voice calm and low.

"But you don't know. Out of my way," Cecil ordered, voice shrill, pushing hard against her. Dolly pushed back, the two of them ending up inside the room. Cecil flicked on the lights, took a few more steps and stumbled over the body of a woman lying atop a scattered pile of books. Beneath the body a heavy black, hooded cape lay spread open. Beside it an incandescent tube glowed faintly. Blood pulsed from the woman's chest, the dark stain widening slowly across the finely pleated bodice of a pink voile dress and the feathers of a white boa. Freddy stood above her, looking down into her face with his one good eye. He gave one of her cheeks a brief lick, then backed off when Cecil screamed.

TWENTY-FOUR

LILA MONTROSE-HAWKE WENT OUT the tall, polished front doors in a dull, gray body bag she would have hated. Cecil didn't watch. He'd taken himself off to the morning room where we'd had tea on my second visit. He sat in the bay window with twinkling lights from outside silhouetting him in the half-dark, a picture of misery, made more miserable looking by streams of mascara running down his cheeks, with lipstick smeared onto his chin, with his wig at an odd angle, and his embroidered gown twisted around his rotund body so the place where a breast should be was caught up under his armpit.

He sobbed on and on. His shoulders shook. Tears flowed as he threw back his head and keened the way old Irish and Italian women keened at death. I'd helped him into the room, then sat next to him, talking low, trying to be comforting. Each time I attempted to get up he put his maimed hand on my arm, keeping me in place beside him. I sat straight, embarrassed in my Mary Poppins costume, long blue-serge skirt to my ankles, lisle stockings in prim black shoes, a bunch of plastic flowers at my throat, hair pinned back and up, and a straw pork-pie hat atop my head. The parrot-handled umbrella was lost somewhere in the stampede of the crowd after the shot rang out.

I heard the police, one by one, opening and closing the front doors. Drifts of hot air found their way into the room, little touches of warmth amid the icy air conditioning. Dolly came in from time to time to tell me who'd arrived and who was doing what. Lucky Barnard pulled out all the stops. Every cop I knew from the area was there. Even Lieutenant Brent from Gaylord, and that annoying little automaton, Omar Winston. There were officers from Mancelona and Kalkaska, men I'd talked to for stories

"We've got a lot of interviewing to do," Dolly came in to inform us. She kept her voice low, glancing at Cecil's bent head. "Hope you don't mind, Mr. Hawke. Something we've got to get to. Statements have to be taken from every single one of 'em here."

Cecil lifted one shoulder. I wasn't sure he'd heard her. "They won't know anything."

"Got to get a statement from you too," she added, pulling a straight-backed chair over and sitting, notebook out, pencil in hand.

"About what? You don't think I had anything to do with this, do you?" Cecil's face, when he looked up at her, was bright red from weeping. His eyes were puffed to almost closed. Freddy found him in all the confusion and sat next to his chair, on guard. Cecil reached out absentmindedly and pinched Freddy's head. At first the dog flinched, then sat totally still.

"I need to talk to everybody. Even Emily."

Cecil sniffed at Dolly, then fished around in the bodice of his dress for a handkerchief, found none, and sniffed again. You couldn't help but feel sorry for the man. "I won't be able ... I don't know when ... Oh, dear. Oh, dear ..." He was off into sobbing, eyes closed, hands wringing in front of him.

"It would be better to take care of things tonight," Dolly said, her voice steady. "You want us to get whoever did this, don't you?"

Cecil's body stilled. He opened his eyes wide. "Did what? Lila committed suicide. I've been afraid of such a thing for a while now. Her depressions ... Oh, my dear, such depressions."

Dolly gave him a confused look. "No gun in the room. This was no suicide."

Cecil's mouth dropped open. He hesitated only a moment, got control of himself, then scoffed at Dolly. "You didn't know Lila. Of course she would take herself out with high drama. You'll find it—the gun. She came up with something ... I don't know what. You have to believe me."

"It's murder, the way it looks now."

Cecil sat back, took a few deep breaths, then spoke hesitantly, as if reluctant to say anything. "Then I know who did it." He gave me a long look, reached over the arm of his chair and snapped Freddy hard on top of the head. "Check Lila's room. You'll find her packed suitcase there. She was leaving me right after the party. Probably the reason for what happened. Though I think she'd ... misread the person she was leaving me for."

"Leaving?" Dolly knew how to look skeptical.

"Yes, running off. Just the kind of thing that would appeal to Lila."

"Who with?"

"Jackson Rinaldi."

How did I know that name was coming? *Oh, Jackson.* I wanted to groan, but somehow felt it best to show no emotion in from of Cecil Hawke.

"You know him, don't you?" he asked Dolly, who half nodded. "Why do you think I accused him during the séance? Fool. Lila and I'd been fighting all day over that man, you see. I didn't know what to do. It was all I could think of. Of course she was angry with me." Here he spread his hands wide. "But what's a man to do? That Rinaldi fellow posed as my friend while secretly having an affair with my wife. And then, I learned he was plotting to steal her away..."

The drama was getting to be too much. I could see Jackson going after a famous man's wife. Good for his ego. But not running off. Not him.

"Or perhaps not," Cecil looked from me to Dolly. "Maybe Jackson had no idea she was planning this escape. In that case, I'd say talk to the man. Get his side of it. But remember..." He put a finger up beside his nose. "A woman is dead. Test his hands for gun powder residue, or whatever you do in such cases."

"That's crazy," I said.

Dolly gave me a hard look, signaling me to shut my mouth while she conducted her interview.

"Did she admit to the affair?" she asked.

"Admit! She threw it in my face. I couldn't believe it. The man's a fool. A snob and a wannabe—but dangerous around women. A very dangerous man. Just ask Emily, here." He nodded in my direction. "I'm sure she can tell you a thing or two."

Cecil waved a flaccid hand at me and went on. "Who knows? Maybe because she was insisting on this running off thing. Maybe because she threatened to tell me and he'd lose an influential friend. I couldn't begin to read the inferior mind of someone like Jackson Rinaldi."

"And this other thing…" Dolly leaned in a little closer, notebook resting on her knee.

"What other thing?" He was impatient now, ready to be done with Deputy Dolly.

"Eh, when your wife pretended to be the ghost…"

He raised his eyebrows and waited.

"She asked you if you murdered someone named Amanda, and if you would murder her too. Who's Amanda?"

I'd heard the same thing coming from the ghost but I didn't think it was Amanda. More like Armando. Something like that. I said as much to Dolly.

She gave me one of her disgusted looks. "You heard wrong, Emily. It was Amanda. A woman. Not Armando. A man."

I shook my head. "I don't think you heard right…"

"Yeah? Well, I'm the professional here. I know what I heard and I'm trained to listen."

"Not this time," I insisted, more into showing her up than the truth.

She blew her lips out and rolled her eyes. "I already asked the other guests. They said 'Amanda.'"

"You know how unreliable eye, or ear, witnesses are."

She gave up and turned back to Cecil. "Okay. Why did your wife ask if you'd murdered somebody named Amanda or Armando?"

"I thought it was a joke. I've never known an Amanda, or even an Armando, in my entire life—that I'm aware of." He shook his head. "Typical of Lila's cruel humor."

Dolly sat back, then looked hard at Cecil Hawke.

"About those friends," she said, then stopped a minute.

"Yes?"

"Something's coming up over and over while we've been talking to your guests."

We waited to hear her out.

"Except for a couple of neighbors, the rest said they were hired, down in Grand Rapids. Supposed to be here for some kind of dress-up party. So, almost nobody here is a friend of yours or your wife's."

Cecil took a deep breath. "Another illusion. Lila was so set on a party. She was used to city life, night clubs, openings. Here, we live quietly. Really there was no one to invite. I have friends…"

"You said European friends would be here." I frowned. "The ones who came for shooting, and riding to hounds—or whatever it is you all do."

"Well, yes. But those are business friends. Lots of those. Sheiks. Even minor Scandinavian royalty. They'll be here for the hunt this fall." He thought a while. "I hope this doesn't put a dent in those plans…"

"So this party was for Lila? Because she was bored?" Dolly said.

"She didn't know the people I invited weren't really…" He sighed and sat back. "That's why I encouraged her to invite you, Emily. And then your friends. I told her it would be droll, having some of the locals attend. You must know Lila was a snob. She so wanted you to see the kind of life she was used to. I think she said it might open your eyes to what you were missing." He shrugged. "Just her way of helping you out."

I sat back in my chair. This was a real murder, not another of their endless, silly games. Actually it was a second murder, if my tenuous 'Toomey' link between them proved to be true. What I had to do, to keep my tightrope walk going between Hawke, Jackson, the police, and my duty to the newspaper, was stay neutral, keep any feeling I had about all of them out of it.

Cecil reached over and set his hand firmly on my leg, fingers digging into me. "You will stay the night, won't you, Emily?" His voice pleaded as his eyes insisted. "I have no one else and I couldn't stand to be alone…"

I opened my mouth to speak as Agent Lo came into the room, hesitated in the doorway, then took a few steps toward me. He stopped and looked hard at Cecil Hawke.

TWENTY-FIVE

"INS?" Cecil made a face after the introductions were made. "Emily mentioned you were here. But isn't that about immigration? What's your business in the death of my wife? She was an American citizen, you know."

Lo patted the air between them, calming him. "I'm very sorry about your wife," he said and pulled a straight-backed chair up next to Dolly. "It's just that I'm investigating the death of a Mexican national. She was killed up here recently. The only name we've come up with in connection to that killing is a name that Emily, here," he nodded toward me, "thought she heard your wife call a man who was standing at your front door."

Cecil shook his head. "Oh, that. Yes, Emily mentioned it. Ridiculous. I didn't recognize the name, didn't know who she was talking about ..."

Dolly spoke up. "Emily saw him here tonight. He got out before I could get my hands on him."

"You saw this man, Emily? At my party?" The question from Cecil had disappointment buried at its heart.

I nodded.

"In the middle of everything going on here? With all my guests in costume? And you still think it was the man you saw once before, on my front porch? Maybe a salesman? Maybe some down-and-outer needing a job?"

"I'm pretty sure it was the man Lila called 'Toomey.'"

"And I'm pretty sure it wasn't. Besides that, can you tell me just what's going on? I thought you worked for me. I didn't know I was harboring a spy at my bosom. And, on top of everything, you bring your friend, a policewoman, to my party. Really, Emily." He clucked his tongue at me. "I'm disappointed, though I suppose you did what you thought you had to do."

Jeffrey jumped in. "Sorry to bother you with this right now," he said to Cecil, "but this means there could be a connection between the two murders."

"So far-fetched." Cecil shook his head at me.

I tried to look truly sorry, but wasn't. Murder was murder.

"Could this Toomey have come to call on your wife?" Jeffrey asked.

"Many come." Cecil wiped hard at his eyes. He deflated in front of me. "She is … was a very social woman, as Emily well knows."

"Would you have any idea why a man named Toomey, who Emily said looked like a worker here on the farm, would be calling on her?"

Cecil shook his head.

"Maybe a family member ..."

"She has no family."

"Do you know all the men who work for you?"

"No. Just the ones who report to me."

"No one named Toomey."

"Not that I recall."

"Could I nose around the farm? With your permission, of course. I'd like to talk to the guys who take care of your sheep. Maybe they'd know ..."

Cecil sat up straight. His body was stiff. The smell he gave off now was oddly not of his thick cologne but a mixture of dying flowers and sweat. His hands gripped then ungripped the chair arms. For a moment he closed his eyes. When he opened them they flamed with annoyance.

"This is outrageous!" He threw one hand into the air, waking Freddy, who got up and ambled out of the room. "I lost my wife this evening. The love of my life. And you badger me about my farm hands? You have to leave. Now! All of you. In fact, I want you off my property. And no, it isn't all right to bother my workers. They have their hands full with our flocks." He tried to stand but fell back in his chair. "Go! Go!"

"I wouldn't bother anyone." Jeffrey kept his voice low. "I don't want to have to get a search warrant ..."

"On what grounds?" Cecil demanded, half out of his chair.

Jeffrey looked hard at the man. "I can see you're upset ..."

"You can, can you? How astute of you! And now you want to bother my workers? You just wait and see if I don't put up a fight. I'll call my lawyers immediately ..." He was blustering, trying to stand again. "Now, would you please go? The house is overrun with policemen as it is. You're not needed, nor wanted here."

Jeffrey got up, pushed his chair back to the wall, nodded to me and Dolly, turned, and left.

Cecil had worked himself into a manic state of mourning. He stood and held his arms out to me, child-like and needy. "You must help me to my room, Emily. Here I thought you were my friend, and now look at what you've done. Sicced a federal agent on me. I would never have believed it."

I took his arm with no clue as to what was expected next.

"Please—up to my room," he whispered as I guided him carefully into the hall. "You must stay the night. You simply have to. I need you. There's no one left to me now. If you're my friend, please, let me rest and then we can talk…"

Dolly, coming out of the room behind us, said, "I'll call somebody if you need a nurse…"

"Absolutely not! You've done enough, Officer. I want Emily here. She knows more about me than anyone." He waved his hand with the missing knuckle in her face. "My life has been one of eternal strife. Tonight, is the worst of any. Emily must stay."

I looked hard at Dolly, begging her to get me out of what he was planning. Staying in that house of mirth, in that house where a murder had just been committed—with Cecil Hawke—was like asking me to spend the night alone in a morgue. Maybe worse.

"We'll all be here, Mr. Hawke. I have to interview Jackson Rinaldi."

"That evil man's still in my house?" Cecil was outraged.

"And Emily's had a rough night…"

"Brought on herself. She's the cause of some of this misery. You owe me, Emily." The eyes he turned on me weren't friendly. "As for Mr. Rinaldi, the sooner he's taken off to jail the better. He's the most obvious suspect. You won't miss the obvious? Will you, officer?"

Dolly puffed her chest out to amazing proportions. She was ready to come down hard. I got in between them.

"I'll stay for a little while," I said.

"We have to talk." He took my hand and pulled me toward the hall. "After I've rested. Maybe later . . ."

"You know what, Emily?" Dolly called after me. "This is like one of those crazy English mysteries. You know—we got all the suspects in the library . . ." She shook her head and went back to her interrogations.

———

Cecil's bedroom was exactly as I would have pictured it. Mostly feminine. Ruffles. Canopy bed with red bed hangings. White carpeting. Lila's dressing table was strewn with fancy spray bottles, make-up, and creams for every part of her body. The room looked not just overdone, but silly.

Cecil collapsed on the bed and motioned for me to cover him with the sheet. As I did, his head popped up. "May I say one thing about your friend, down there? The police officer. You put entirely too much trust in her. As Noel Coward was heard to say about a person who looked much like your Dolly—well, I'm paraphrasing now: *Never trust a woman with short legs. Brain's too near their bottoms.*"

He snickered, threw his arm over his eyes, and asked me, in a weak voice, to dim the lights.

"Don't leave," he begged from the bed. "When I'm stronger, we'll talk. There are things about Lila, well, I want you to understand."

He waved a limp hand in the direction of a fussy boudoir chair against the wall.

I looked at the silk-covered, uncomfortable-looking chair and shook my head. No way. I wasn't Freddy, already stretched out on the floor beside the bed.

"I'll be downstairs," I said. "Whenever you feel like coming down..."

"Only what I expected." He made a broken sound halfway between disgust and agony; then wiggled his fingers at me, motioning me out of there.

I was dismissed.

TWENTY-SIX

THEY WERE ALL COMING to my house the next morning: Agent Lo, Dolly, Lucky, Brent, and Omar Winston. We didn't want to be seen together at the police station in town. Radar, built into Leets-villians, would track us and blow our summit meeting into a crime spree everybody had to prepare for; or a terrorist threat: *Ya hear? They're tryin' to poison our water.*

Whatever they came up with, it would be good for days of phone calls to Lucky and Dolly, sightings of strangers lurking about town, suspicious wrong numbers, shadows behind buildings.

I slouched out of bed at seven-thirty, immediately fell over Sorrow and hit my head against the door, opening a cut up in my hair. I stood in my washed-out nightgown, blood curling down my forehead, with a bunch of people due to arrive any moment. The most I could do was jump in the shower, get rid of the blood, hold a wash cloth on my head until the bleeding stopped, then get dressed, towel-dry my hair—avoiding the place where a good-sized lump would be—and glance at the mirror, telling myself I looked just fine. I am a woman of low and convenient standards. If lies were needed to get me through the day, then it was lies I told myself.

I still had time, before the others got there, to pick up my dirty underwear off the bathroom floor and stick it in the washer. I thought about maybe cooking everybody breakfast but I had no eggs and no bread so I got over it. I could have served canned fish from my new supply but … for breakfast? No. Anyway, I was saving the fish for winter. For that dark day in February when I opened my fridge and found only old pasta with a scrim of mold on top. Or a day when a blizzard pounded the house. A day my drive was blocked by ice and snow and I wasn't going anywhere. A day my plowman got the flu. A day when I really, really, really wanted to have a jar of long-dead fish to open and dig into.

Jeffrey Lo arrived first. He stopped in the doorway to squat and look into Sorrow's happy eyes as he rubbed the dog's neck and ears. I gave him a cup of coffee. He laid a clipboard on the counter, took a notebook from a jacket pocket, and settled on a stool. If he was tired from our long, terrible night, it didn't show. He was as languid, cool, and in control as usual. His "Good Morning, Emily" was warm, making me feel good about myself, my coffee, and the day ahead of all of us. I took my cup of tea out of the microwave and leaned on the counter, across from him, slowly lifting the hot cup to my lips.

He smiled one of those friendly smiles I wasn't good at interpreting. Did it mean we were making a connection? Or maybe that the coffee was good? Or did he mean it was a new day, we were both alive, and let's leave it at that. No, I told myself as I dug some not-too-white-anymore paper napkins from the pantry and set them on the counter, it was more than that and I'd have to watch myself. I didn't come to the north country to fall for anybody. Too easy, that knee-jerk response to a good-looking man. Too easy, and dishonest. What I wanted out of life wasn't another guy to screw things up for me. What I wanted was to live free, to make my own money, to chop my own wood, to rototill my own garden. I wanted to live as just a human being, not some thirty-something looking for love.

The napkins I set out were my stab at being a good hostess. My mother—as much as I could remember—was a stickler for place mats and cloth napkins and a sugar bowl and creamer, not the sugar box and milk carton. Maybe if she'd stuck around a little longer, hadn't died, at least until I'd gotten into my teens, some of that would have rubbed off on me. As it was, I just didn't get it.

"You know something, Emily?" Lo looked up. "I'd like to come back up here sometime when I'm not working. And you're not working . . ."

Okay. I got it. I hadn't been wrong.

"That would be nice," I said and colored a bright pink. "Trouble is, Jeffrey, I'm really working hard at the writing. I don't have a lot of time . . ."

I could see the disappointment in his eyes. Too bad, I told myself. They all start like that—needy, hoping you're the one who will love them and pick up their ugly underwear and cook their meals. What I planned for the rest of my life didn't include being anybody's mommy.

"Got it," he said. "I just thought . . ."

I am a sucker for sadness. Lo was sad. Maybe more at the fact of a rejection than at losing any hope he had with me.

"I know …" I began. "I've only been divorced a while. Not enough time to heal."

"And he seems to hang around," he said. "This Jackson Rinaldi. Can't be helping you get over him."

I nodded and got angry because I had tears in my eyes. He understood. He really understood. *Yeah,* that buried part of my brain called out. *Sucker.*

Lo was off his stool. He came to where I stood. His hand was out to touch my shoulder. I didn't know if I wanted that warm hand on me or not; all I knew was that I saw him coming and smiled at him.

"Hey! Anybody home?" Dolly burst through the side door. Behind her came Lucky. Lo was back on the other side of the counter. Before they'd all settled at the kitchen table, coffee cups in hand, Brent and Omar Winston came clunking in.

With everybody assembled, Dolly began. "I got a nurse in to stay with Cecil Hawke last night," she said to me. "Couldn't see you stayin' at the house, the way he wanted. The guy's nuts. That whole awful party. Wouldn't stay there myself."

Lieutenant Brent drew his single, long, black eyebrow together and nodded toward me. "What's your relationship with the man?" he asked.

I explained the editing job I was doing; the visits to his home. "I don't know if that'll continue now. Maybe he won't want to stay here in the United States. Lila was American. Used to be an actress, or wanted to be one. Seemed like, according to her, Cecil stood in her way. I think that's what was behind their fighting and baiting each other. I'm just giving you my impression, but that wasn't a happy marriage."

"Two murders here," Jeffrey put in. "They don't seem to have any connection between them but this 'Toomey' guy. The migrants gave us the name, and you think you saw him at Hawke's farm. Not much but it's a link."

"I got pretty close to him at the party," Dolly said. "When I said the name to the dark guy by the kitchen he ran like a skunk with his tail on fire."

"Hawke says he doesn't know anybody named 'Toomey,'" Brent said. "I interviewed him later. Got the same things he told Dolly."

We were at an impasse.

"So, what do we have?" Lo asked.

"I been checking anywhere I can think to check," Lucky put in. "Dolly's been doing the usual—license, birth, census, police records. Hunting for a 'Toomey.'"

Omar Winston cleared his throat. "Emily might have gotten information we can't get any other way if she'd stayed there at the house last night. You know, something about the wife's family, people to contact."

"Yeah, put her in with a guy who could be a murderer. Real smart, Omar," Dolly came back fast.

Omar looked to Dolly, his face reddening as that place beneath his left eye ticked.

"Hawke said she didn't have any family. Maybe a cousin out in Oregon. That's all," Dolly went on.

She looked over at Brent. "Think the bullet they got out of the body will help?"

Brent shrugged. "Who knows? Didn't find a gun. Killer took off with it. A big window was open. Big enough for a guy to get through. But no footprints under the window. No fingerprints anywhere. Nothing. Guy had to be wearing gloves. Nobody saw anything…"

"It was dark in the room," Dolly said.

"We know it wasn't Hawke who shot his wife," Jeffrey said. "He was out in plain sight when the shot was heard. Everybody agrees on that. Toomey was at the party and Toomey's the one the migrant workers said was threatening them. Why was he threatening them? Somebody's got to know something. When we find out what Toomey's afraid of, why he has to keep people quiet, then we'll know what this whole thing's about."

"So," Dolly said, "what we've got here are two murders with one single link: Toomey. If you ask me, the next thing is to find those workers. Somebody knows something and I'll bet anything it's that Carlos Munoz."

Dolly turned to Brent and the others. "I want to know about the dead dogs. What in hell's that all about? Can't stand this case. Feels dirty, just talking about it. We got that first murder—the one Lo here is most interested in. Not robbery. Not rape. She wasn't killed where we found her. And she's related to one of the workers, a guy whose whole family has disappeared. So what we've got is this Toomey, who's connected to both the migrant workers and the Hawke farm or ranch or whatever it is. We've got one dead woman connected to the migrants and another connected to the Hawke place. One connection between the women—Toomey."

"I gotta get a look at that farm of Hawke's," Jeffrey said, rising from his chair, picking up his coffee cup and taking it to the sink. "I asked Hawke but he refused to have me on the property. Either there's something to hide or he's just that kind of guy. The way he seems, I'm betting he's just that kind of guy. I don't have the authority... not up here." He shrugged. "I'm going to get an order but he says he'll fight it. Don't know what's next..."

"How about the funeral," I offered. "I'll be going to that."

"We can't intrude on a man's grief," Omar smacked his straight-line lips together as he chided me.

"Emily's right," Dolly countered. "She can be there. She's the guy's friend, or employee—or something. I'd say that was next. See who turns up. We'll all be somewhere out there. You won't be alone," she turned to me.

I thanked her, shot Omar a gotcha look, and was about to pick up the remains of the coffee when the door opened and a frayed and startled Jackson Rinaldi walked in.

TWENTY-SEVEN

I'D NEVER SEEN JACKSON so rumpled. He wore a tee shirt with sweat stains under the arms, bed hair, no socks, wrinkled pants. You couldn't help but feel sorry for the guy. This wasn't something he would ever have asked for. A romp in the hay, to him, was like another man's game of golf. He didn't expect much to come of any of his flings, certainly not murder.

"I didn't mean ..." Jackson backed toward the door when he saw the police power gathered in my kitchen.

I waved him in, explaining we were just trying to figure where to go next with the investigation.

Everyone nodded to him as he entered hesitantly and sat down on my desk chair, in a far corner of the living room. He nodded back, tried to smile, but ordinary good manners were beyond him.

Dolly gave him a long look. "You weren't in the hall when we heard the gunshot."

"I told you I got out of there after he started in on me."

"Out to your car, right?" The color was slowly draining from Dolly's face, her pale eyes were big. Something going on with her that had nothing to do with Jack. I thought I knew what was happening but, for her sake, hoped I was wrong. After all, it was morning. She was pregnant. And turning pretty green at the moment.

"That's as far as I got. When I heard the gunshot I went back in. I wasn't sure that's what it was, but it was loud. I was worried about ... well, about Emily. After what he did to me, I wouldn't put anything past that man."

"You didn't see nobody coming out the front door or from around the side of the house, right?" Dolly licked at her bottom lip.

He shook his head at her. "I was parked down the drive. Anyone could have run into the woods. I wouldn't see them unless they went right past me."

Dolly nodded, hesitated, and took a deep breath. "You don't own a gun, do you?"

Jackson agreed. No gun.

"I'll find out if you're lying, ya know." Her heart wasn't into threats. Her voice was weak. She stopped to take a few deep breaths.

They all made ruminative sounds. A lot of hard thinking was going on as Dolly edged out of the living room, toward the hall leading back to my two bedrooms. And the bathroom—which was where she went, double-time, slamming the door behind her.

There was an embarrassed silence in the room of all men, and me.

Dolly was in there throwing up. I tried to think of something to say to cover the sound of her morning sickness but nothing would have done it. The men listened and gave each other sick looks.

"She okay?" Omar finally asked but she was back, out of the bathroom, wiping her mouth with one of my towels, and looking around as if she dared one person to say a word. Nobody did.

Soon, everybody but my sorrowful ex left. He stayed to share his misery.

"I'm leaving here," he said. "This country isn't safe for civilized people. Even this man, whom I thought was an intellectual, why, you saw how he turned on me." Jackson's face folded into creases. He looked tired, and much older, as if he'd learned a terrible lesson and would maybe change.

"Back to Ann Arbor?" I asked, hoping he meant to return to teaching Medieval Studies or English Literature at the University of Michigan.

"Of course." He gave me an impatient look. "I can write there as well as here. I won't have you to help me ..."

I smiled a sad and benign smile. *Woe is me ...* I was making fun but inside I felt a hole opening. He wasn't much, but he was all I had up here, where I would probably always be a stranger. Jackson had been my one touch with home—or as much of a home as I had anywhere before coming to my cabin in the woods.

He moved to where I sat and took my hand. I expected something along the lines of what I'd been thinking. That we were finally at that place where our marriage was over, the emotional divorce final. All he said was, "The police don't actually suspect me, do they? You know I'd never have anything to do with such a thing. Murder! My God! I'm not a savage, after all. You don't believe I was actually going to run away with her, do you, Emily? I mean..."

"Maybe she thought so. That could have put something into motion."

He blew that off. "I could see suicide. But the woman was murdered. There had to be someone else. Maybe another lover." He thought a minute, then seemed to like that thought. "I'll bet you anything that's it. Another lover. Another man she was running off with. Get them to look, will you? I mean, you're all I have, Emily. You could help..."

Of course I would help, I assured him. I knew him better than anyone. He might be weak. He might be a snob. He might be a lot of unpleasant things, but Jackson wasn't a murderer.

My offer to help relieved him of a lot of worry. He became more like the old, self-assured Jack.

"Maybe I should call Cecil," he said. "Tell him what I've come up with. Maybe we could still be friends, after all."

He was beyond help. I took a last shot at reality. "I don't think that's a good idea, Jack. If you ask me, I'd call this one dead in the water."

He looked disappointed but kissed my cheek and went off in his white Jaguar to find solace someplace else.

———

I spent the rest of the morning writing a story for the paper. When the phone rang, close to noon, I knew who it was going to be and hesitated to answer.

Cecil Hawke.

"Why did you leave me, Emily?" His normally high voice was deep and accusing. "I told you I needed you. We have work to do."

"Cecil. I don't think…"

"Actually, I have been working on my book. It calms my nerves. But that's not what I need you for right now. It's about Lila. I need your help."

"And … what can I do … ?" I asked, hoping the answer was 'nothing at all.'

"Why, the funeral, of course. I have to make arrangements. There has to be a funeral. As the writer said: *Attention must be paid*. I can't possibly do it alone. I thought you'd know that immediately. Very simple. Lila has no real family and this was her home. So it will be up here. You're a native. You can advise me."

"Cecil. I'm not a native. I'm your editor. I don't think it's my place to…"

"Of course it is. You're a woman. You knew Lila. You understand. Women always understand death. Isn't that what you all deal in? I mean, caring for babies and old people and such."

I hesitated, thinking of my nonexistent babies and my father's lingering death from which I was absent, living in Ann Arbor, married to Jackson, who didn't want me away from him for more than a day at a time.

The ever-negligent, ever-guilty daughter.

Cecil went on. "And, I'll give you more chapters of my book. I worked all morning. I think you'll be happily surprised with the quality..."

His wife murdered not twenty-four hours ago and he was able to write fiction. A better writer than I, I told myself. Maybe not much of a human being, but a dedicated writer.

Out of a mixture of old guilt and curiosity, I agreed to help him make funeral arrangements.

TWENTY-EIGHT

TUESDAY MORNING, THE DAY of Lila's funeral, was one of those cool summer days when the air is fresh, the sunshine pure gold, and the north country turns back to brilliant green. Except in my woods, where the trees were struggling to put out a single leaf and I still picked little green cocoons from my log pile and my house and my garden bench.

Dolly called first thing. She wanted to go with me to the funeral but wasn't sure she was up to it.

"Puking all morning. Hate to get out there and be running behind some tree," she said.

"Then stay home."

"Can't. This being pregnant thing is getting in my way. I'm a cop first."

"Not anymore."

"I need to be there. What if this Toomey guy shows up? Maybe somebody else. We got a couple of murders on our hands. I need to see what's going on."

"I'll keep my eyes open."

"Yeah, like you're a trained police officer," she scoffed.

"What in heck did you think having a baby was going to be like?"

"Wasn't my idea."

"Then whose was it?"

"Nobody's. Just happened." She cleared her throat. "From what you said, women drop kids all the time and keep right on going. Hardly notice a thing's changed."

"Women weren't cops back then, Dolly."

"Yeah, well, there's got to be a way to get through this. After it's born I'll bet I can take it right along with me."

"On shoot-outs?"

"You know what I mean. Hell, how many shoot-outs I been in? Kid can stay in the car ..."

"Oh, no you don't."

"Anyway, I'm feelin' a little better now that you made me mad again. Might as well come by and get me."

I let Sorrow out, then called Jeffrey to see if he was going to be at the funeral. I didn't really see Toomey showing up if he was involved in Lila's murder but I'd feel better, just knowing Jeffrey was there somewhere. Behind a tree. In his car. Just there.

He was coming, he said. "Don't want to get in too close and scare off anybody." He paused. "But I'll have your back, Emily. You can count on me."

Good enough. It was a funeral, after all. Not the place most killers would pick to knock off a witness—which I supposed I was. Of a sort.

We agreed to meet for coffee in Leetsville after the funeral. There were still some things to get going on.

"You heard the bullet they took out of Lila was the same caliber as the bullet that killed the dog in the Maria Santos murder? We need that gun."

"How much of this can I put in the paper?"

"Nothing right now. Lieutenant Brent said the lab found stippling around the wound, and scorch marks. You know what that means?"

I thought so, but let him talk.

"That's from where the flame exits the barrel. It burns the hair and tissues around the site. Found gunpowder residue, too. That's expected. From the wound track it's clear the woman was kneeling when she was shot. Looks like, from that wound track, and the place the bullet entered, that the shooter was pretty tall. Seems to fit. If it's this Toomey guy."

"But nothing in the paper."

"Let's keep it simple, okay? We've got little enough going for us. I don't want to send up any signals, like what we've got. I'm going out to that sheep ranch. It doesn't matter what the guy says, this is a murder." I could hear the frustration in his voice. "Hawke's got lawyers fighting—unnecessary invasion of privacy, harassment, interfering with his ability to conduct his business—everything you can think of to obstruct our investigation but I'm going in there anyway. Christ, you'd think the guy would want to find who killed his wife." He sighed. "Doesn't much matter how rich the guy is. The law's the law."

———

Lila's casket was white with bright gold handles. The top was carved, a smiling angel incised about where Lila's head must be. Dolly and I parked behind the hearse, a limousine, and a couple of other cars drawn up off the road. I saw Jeffrey's car parked farther ahead and thought I saw him standing in a copse of trees across from where the green funeral tent stood. There was a blue state police car up around a bend in the road. Two men in overalls sat on the back of a red pickup, leaning on their shovels. They waited to close the grave after the service. That was everyone who came to see Lila Montrose-Hawke out of this world.

Walking up to the gravesite, I put my arms out to a grieving Cecil Hawke dressed in a dark summer suit, the blond toupee firmly on his head, diamond winking at his ear, and a large white handkerchief raised to wipe his eyes.

"Oh, my dear," he said to me. "I'm so happy you've come." He gestured around us. "As you see, there's no one here to grieve for Lila. Poor Lila..."

A group of men who, from their blue shirts and unpressed pants and heavy shoes, must have been workers from the sheep ranch, stood off to one side, not moving to occupy the rows of folding chairs set up for mourners. No tall, dark man.

Henry Watson, Leetsville's new funeral director, came over to lead Cecil to a seat in the front row, nodded me and Dolly to chairs beside him, and went to stand at one end of the coffin, open Bible in his hands.

Henry began to speak, thanking all of the mourners for coming—as he nodded to the three of us. He read a passage from the Bible before closing the book and speaking of death in general and unexpected deaths in particular.

I listened with half an ear. It was embarrassing to sit there, with the grave diggers waiting, the workers standing off a ways. A funeral without friends and close family, without real tears and real regret, is depressing. Almost as if Lila hadn't lived, she was being ushered out by strangers—and a husband who couldn't have really loved her.

As Henry Watson moved on to a woman's life, the meaning of the word "wife," and a few extraneous things, I thought about the way I was living. Not even the word 'wife' could apply to me. No kids. Few friends. If they threw my funeral tomorrow, who would come? Jackson. Dolly. A few people from Ann Arbor. A few people from Leetsville. Maybe Bill Corcoran from the newspaper. Not enough to fill the rows of chairs behind me. And not enough flowers to add color to what I hoped would be a dreary occasion.

Henry was up to "Poor Mr. Hawke. My condolences…"

I planned my funeral and then axed it all in favor of cremation and a quick sail on the wind, probably out over Willow Lake. Oh, but what about poor Sorrow? Dolly would just have to get over her aversion to animals and take him…

Back to the current funeral. Henry gestured for us to stand, then make our slow procession past the coffin.

I took the rose Henry Watson held out and was laying it across the white coffin as a black Ford Fusion made its slow way down the narrow cemetery road to stop and park behind my yellow

Jeep. I couldn't see who was in the car. Maybe a relative, after all, I thought. They could have seen the notice in the newspaper, or maybe Cecil had called someone.

I stepped back from the coffin, tripping slightly over Dolly, who had her rose in hand but was staring hard toward that black car too.

The door opened and a woman got out from behind the wheel. She stood in the open door, put a hand over her eyes, and looked hard toward where we were gathered by the grave.

The door closed and the woman, in a staid black dress and black hat with a veil pulled over her eyes, walked slowly toward us. Cecil didn't notice her. His face was buried in one hand. The other hand lay open against the closed casket. His back heaved with awful sobs.

As the woman got close to us, I left our little coffin-side group and walked toward her. I wanted to make sure she was in the right place and not about to blunder into the wrong funeral. I moved quietly, so as not to intrude on Cecil's grief.

She was very young, much younger than she'd seemed at first. It was the prim black dress, and that squashed-down black hat with a veil hiding her eyes, that gave her the look of an older woman, or a woman dressed in a costume. No kid her age—maybe twenty-one or twenty-two—went around in that outfit. Not on purpose. Or not unless there was a good reason for it.

Since I was standing in her way, she looked up at me through the veil. Bright eyes. Almost no make-up. She gave me a tentative, half-frightened smile.

"This is the funeral of Lila Hawke," I whispered toward the woman. She nodded. "I know," she said, face stiff, voice small.

She began to tremble in her short-sleeved dress and bare legs. "I'm here to see my stepfather."

The accent was definitely British. The face, when she lifted her veil, was one of those fresh English faces with pink cheeks and perfect skin.

Cecil's head snapped up at the sound of the girl's voice. He turned toward where we stood, eyes and mouth popping open, then took a clumsy step backward, away from her. His pale face turned a wine red, blood climbing into his cheeks then disappearing up under the blond wig.

"What are you doing here?" he demanded, his voice as much a snake hiss as real words.

"Hello, Father." The young woman stiffened her back. "You must have known I'd come. Aren't I always with you when one of your wives dies?"

TWENTY-NINE

CECIL HAWKE LOOKED FROM one to the other of those who had gathered around him. He was a man caught in a trap, searching for a way out. When he looked back to the young woman standing firmly in front of him, he was more in control. His face relaxed, but not completely. He began to nod his head slowly, then clasp his hands and shake them a few times, as if in despair.

"This isn't the place, Courtney. Nor the time. I'm very sorry you lost your mother, but that had nothing to do with me. It never did…"

The young woman smiled. "Aren't you happy to see me? I've been hunting for you…"

"Oh, I'm certain you have. But you don't belong here, my dear. I've begun a new life…" He cleared his throat and glanced at those of us gathered close by.

"With a new wife." She nodded toward the coffin.

"…a new life far from England. Tragedy follows me…"

"Oh, yes, I'm certain something follows you, Father." The girl smiled an almost angelic smile as she put a long stress on the word 'Father.'

"You can't continue to stalk me." He made a slight motion of his hand toward the men from the ranch, signaling for them to move closer.

"Is that what you call it? Stalking? I only want to know. That's all. What have you done with all of our money? I need to hear you say it aloud."

One of the men, a thick-bodied guy with almost no neck, inserted his body between Cecil and the woman. He put a hand up as if to push her back.

I looked at Dolly, raising my eyebrows. We couldn't let this girl leave. I searched the trees for Jeffrey Lo. I could just make him out, moving through swaying blue spruce branches.

I nodded to him, then to Dolly, hoping he got what was happening.

The thick man took the girl by one elbow and roughly pulled her back from the grave and away from Cecil. She resisted at first, elbow sticking out at an uncomfortable, even painful-looking angle. She stumbled over a tree root, then stood straight, and followed where the man pulled. She looked back hard at Cecil Hawke, digging her heels into the soft earth and pulling against the big man's grasp. At the road, she stopped just a second to stare at Cecil. She got into her car, started the motor, and drove off.

I looked around for Jeffrey. He wasn't where I'd last seen him, among the trees, but as the woman drove slowly off, I spotted his green Element as it fell in behind hers. I figured he'd be in touch later, or meet us at EATS with the woman in tow.

When I turned to Cecil he raised his eyes heavenward as if pleading for strength. He looked around, at those of us still gathered, and shrugged expressively "The price of being wealthy," he said, sighing. "The insane are always with us."

Henry Watson hurriedly motioned for Dolly to place her rose, and then for the workmen behind her to hurry right along. Poor Henry was flustered. His perfectly planned funeral for the first rich guy who'd come his way was in shambles. He urged everyone to walk faster past the coffin and spoke a couple of hurried words—as eager as we were to have it done with and be out of there. He shook hands, indicated the way down to the street, and murmured a few last unintelligible words.

Cecil was off to the limousine as Dolly and I scurried down the wide slope to my car.

"What're you thinking?" she asked in a stage whisper while opening the door on her side.

"I'm thinking we should head for EATS. That's where we're supposed to meet Jeffrey. Let's hope he didn't lose that girl."

"Could be some nut, like your friend said." Dolly slammed the door behind her as I started the car. "I guess rich people get 'em all the time. The funeral was in the paper. No knowing..."

"From that accent, she's not from around Leetsville."

"Yeah, well, we got all kinds here. Have to admit, though, she sounds like Hawke."

"Not quite. I've always thought he sounded more Australian than English. But what do I know...?"

I drove off slowly behind the limo though it didn't take long for it to pick up speed and get out to the main road, where it turned not toward Leetsville, not even toward Torch Lake, but south, toward Traverse City.

"Think Jeffrey'll bring her to EATS?"

Dolly shrugged. "We gotta go see."

"What if he can't get her to stop her car?"

"Possible. I wouldn't stop for some guy waving me over, would you?"

"Wish we could call Agent Lo," I said. "Maybe he needs help."

She pushed her gun around to a better angle, settled far down in her seat, then up again to pull her handcuffs out of her backside. "If you had a cell phone like normal people, we'd be okay."

"I'll be happy to get one if you pay the bill." I looked over at her.

"Yeah, like I've got money to throw away."

"Me either," I said.

———

We drove into EATS's unpaved parking lot and checked out the cars. No Elements. Jeffrey wasn't there yet. Maybe he hadn't been able to stop the woman. Maybe he was still following her. We figured we'd go in and hang around until he got there but we didn't have to wait. Inside, Eugenia, behind her glass-topped counter, waved a slip of white paper at us.

We nodded to the farmers and women shoppers in for a late morning piece of apple pie and coffee, said 'Mornin' to most of them, then turned our backs as we approached Eugenia, dipping her fluffy blond head toward us. "Your friend, that Asian guy, called and left a message. Says to come on over to the station. He's got somebody there he wants you to talk to. See…"

She held on tight to the scrap of paper she waved toward us, then frowned myopically and read it.

"Says: Please tell Deputy Dolly Wakowski or Emily Kincaid to come over to the station. We have the woman they should talk to here."

Eugenia read slowly from her paper as if trying hard to get every word right. When she put the paper down on the cracked counter top and looked up, she was quick to ask, "What's he mean? What's going on? Is it about that rich guy over by Torch Lake? I read his wife got murdered at some party he was throwing. Sounds like quite the party. Still, if somebody got murdered…"

Dolly gave her a look, lifted her hand to the brim of her hat in a kind of salute, and we were on our way out the door as Eugenia called after me, "Hey, Emily. You got something going with this guy? This agent? Kinda looked like it the other day. Good luck to ya…"

At the car Dolly gave me a sour face. "All I can say is, he's sure better than your last one."

THIRTY

I GOT A WARM look from Jeffrey when we walked in. He smiled, which sent me thinking of other things besides dead bodies and dead dogs and a young woman who just might be totally insane though she looked sane enough, sitting there in Lucky's office, in a high-backed wicker chair, hands set primly in her lap.

She was much prettier than I'd thought, with the hat and veil gone. She had almost translucent skin, and bright, shining, blue eyes. She could have been a high school kid. The chair she sat in dwarfed her. Her back was straight—the black dress too large, pouching around her neck, short sleeves hanging wide over her arms. She held her hands tightly together in her lap, bitten fingernails picking at one hand and then the other. The nails were ragged, red around the cuticles. Her feet were set firmly against the worn linoleum as if planted there permanently in her Minnie Mouse shoes.

"Courtney James," she said, getting up clumsily from the wicker chair to take first Dolly's hand and then mine.

She looked at Jeffrey and smiled the kind of womanly smile you don't want to see other women give a man you just might be thinking could be special. "I had a difficult time stopping when Agent Lo motioned me to the roadside. Part of me thought he might be someone in Cecil's employ." She lifted and dropped her shoulders, then put a hand up to brush a stray honey-colored hair back from her face. "With all that money... well... I'm very afraid..."

"Of whom?" I asked.

"Cecil. What he might do..."

"Where you from?" Dolly asked.

"Bristol. England. I had to come. I'd been following—through an American private investigator—Cecil's movements. I owe my mum at least that much. To find out for certain what he did..."

"If we call England...," Lucky broke in. "This 'Bristol.' They won't tell me you're a known stalker, will they?"

"Please call. I'm really just a girl. I guess you could say that. Second year at university. I have many friends who will vouch for me. They might tell you I've been obsessed with Cecil Hawke, but for good reason."

"And that reason is?" Jeffrey pushed her.

"As I said," she turned first to him and then to both Dolly and me. "Because of my mum."

"Your 'mum'?" Dolly asked. "What's that?"

"My mother. She was Cecil's first wife. Or, at least, that's what I think. That's what she believed, that she was the first. I don't really know."

255

"And?" Dolly pressed. "Your mother's where now?"

"She's dead. Three years." The girl stopped to wipe quickly at her eyes. "I've been looking for him ever since."

"You called him your stepfather out there at the cemetery. Do you think of him as that—a kind of father?" I asked.

She made a quick, unhappy face. "A father? Heavens no. The man's a terrible human being. I know he murdered my mother."

That sucked the air out of the room. Nobody moved.

"She was a diabetic for most of her life," the girl went on. "Mum was so sweet about it, didn't want anybody burdened. She always took care of herself—with the insulin, I mean. Never a problem—well, maybe once in a while, if she'd exercised too hard, or had forgotten to take one of her shots. But never a serious reaction. Until one night, three years ago, she slipped into a coma. The doctor said it was brought on by taking too much insulin. Way too much insulin. As if she would do such a thing." Anger showed. Her quiet voice hardened.

"Was it called a murder by the coroner—or whatever you have over there?"

She shook her head. "She stayed in the coma for three months. And then, suddenly, she died. They said it was the diabetes that killed her. I know it wasn't."

"Was Cecil Hawke at the hospital the day she died?" Jeffrey asked, stopping his note taking to look up and watch as she answered.

She dropped her head, then shook it. "No. As far as I could learn, Cecil wasn't there all that day."

"Then how … ?"

She looked up, young eyes tortured. "You have to understand, Cecil has … for want of a better word … friends."

"Friends?" Dolly was beginning to lose patience. We were going too far afield for her. She liked things much simpler and more direct. English cities and English girls and English women who'd died three years before didn't compute. What Dolly was looking for was an answer to a dead Mexican immigration agent, a dead wife, and a few dead dogs.

Courtney nodded. "Friends. How I hated them, but Mother said to just ignore their presence. She said all men had friends. But not like these men. Crude, they were. Like something from out of a pub, and I mean a very low pub. Please don't think me a snob. You would have to meet them … then you'd know. First one male friend and then another. More like acolytes, I guess you could call them. The men had come from Australia, Cecil told Mother. But they didn't begin to show up until after he and Mother were married and they began gathering earlier and earlier in the day until even Mother couldn't stand having them in the house. I think that's when the problems began." She stopped to think a while. "But maybe not. Maybe whatever was going on was already worked out between them—those men. I really can't say. I just know as Mother began to put her foot down Cecil grew petulant, at times even surly—snapping at her. I know she was considering divorce just before she slipped into that terrible coma."

"In this country," I said, "a long time ago, there was a wealthy woman who had that same thing happen to her. Have you ever heard of Sunny Von Bulow?"

She thought a while, then shook her head.

"Same kind of thing." I was a little suspicious of the girl's story. Something more she wasn't telling us. "You're not ... eh ... making any of this up, are you, Courtney? That woman's husband was suspected of giving her an overdose of insulin. Coma—the whole thing. She didn't die right away, though. Took her years. If the husband was after the money, he didn't get any."

"Cecil got Mother's money. All of it." She sat back. Here it was, I thought, the reason for her single-mindedness and inability to accept that her mother was dead, and probably had cut her out of the will.

"Most of Mother's money came from my real father. His father, my grandfather, had been in the House of Lords; he was a barrister. Quite famous. Father came into the money—all of it—because he was an only son. When he and Mother married he left everything to Mother, except a small trust fund for me. She'd always said it would all come to me, eventually. That it wasn't hers to give to anyone else. In fact, she led me to believe there was a prenuptial agreement when she married Cecil. If that ever existed, it wasn't anywhere to be found after her death."

"Cecil Hawke isn't exactly ..." Dolly was searching for the right words. "Well, not exactly young and good looking."

"Mother thought he was funny. And terribly talented. He wanted so badly to write. You see, he'd grown up poor. His university education was gotten through the kindness of others. After they married he made it a point to give parties for writers, and attend poetry readings. All that sort of thing. He visualized a salon where writers gathered. Mother wasn't against it—it was just those other men, those friends, that she detested."

"Ever anybody hanging around named 'Toomey'?" Dolly asked.

The girl turned to face her directly. Her eyes opened wide, the blue irises large. "Nelson Toomey?" she asked. "Is he here too? Worst of all of them. How Mother hated Toomey. Simply detested the man."

THIRTY-ONE

Now we had the problem of Courtney James on our hands. If what she was saying about Cecil Hawke and Nelson Toomey turned out to be true, she was in danger. You didn't just turn a kid like Courtney out on unfamiliar streets, in unfamiliar towns, and ask her to take care of herself. I doubted, at this point, that returning to England was even the right thing to do. Courtney was ours until this investigation was over.

I had a bad headache. With a bad headache nothing else seems as important as the pain. What I wasn't letting into my brain was something that was scaring the hell out of me—if I even thought about it. I was the only one who had read Cecil's manuscript. Now that Lila was dead, I was the only one, other than Cecil, who even knew it existed. I was glad I'd made copies. Not to show to anyone, but to protect myself. The book was about a serial murderer, and his good friend. With two totally real murders on our hands here, I was beyond feeling uncomfortable about Cecil's book. I was moving into a place where I wondered if I was intended as a target too—in this biography that wasn't a biography, in this story of two men who lived to kill.

Jeffrey signaled he wanted to talk outside of the chief's office. I knew what had to be coming. We gathered at the front of the police station. Jeffrey leaned back against one of the scarred tables and looked from me to Dolly. "You know we can't let her go," he said. "If this Toomey hears that she's in Leetsville, she'll be dead in twenty-four hours."

Dolly nodded. "She's the only witness to anything that we've got."

"And she can identify this guy," I said. "Cecil told me he never heard of Toomey. Big lie. I don't know what kind of an awful game they're playing..."

Jeffrey nodded. "Don't get carried away." He gave me a hard look. "We don't know for sure what the guy's done, as yet. Or even this Toomey. Let's take it slow. I'm going out to that sheep ranch and take a look around. That's what's holding us up."

"Maybe Cecil Hawke's not even involved," I said, wanting to believe the man I worked for wasn't as evil as I suspected. "Maybe it's all Toomey and he's only protecting him because they're old friends."

"Yeah." Dolly looked disgusted. "So he lets this Toomey kill his wife, maybe two wives now, and a Mexican agent here looking into threats against her cousin, and denies knowing him."

"I'm checking with Australia—see if there's a criminal record. On either one of them," Jeffrey said.

"What about Bristol?"

Jeffrey nodded. "Got that already. Nothing. As far as they're concerned Courtney's mother died of natural causes."

"They say anything about Courtney?"

"Said they know what she believes, but there's no proof. Cecil was out of the country when his wife first went into shock from the insulin. They had nothing on him."

"What about Toomey? They ever hear of him?" I asked.

"Only that the daughter said he was involved. They like the girl, but all she's got are suspicions. And, according to the officer I spoke to, there is the matter of her mother willing all her money to Hawke instead of to her. Makes for a bad grudge that could get in the way of the kid's judgment."

We stopped talking to think.

After a while, Dolly offered, "I believe her. Maybe I wouldn't if it weren't for our own two murders."

"We know Hawke didn't kill his wife," Jeffrey said. "You two are his best witnesses. He was in plain sight when the shots from the library were heard."

"And it wasn't Jackson," I put in quickly. "Ballistics showed the same gun was used to kill the dog. And the Mexican agent.

"But there's Toomey," I went on, knowing we were going around in circles. "And there are things about Hawke that worry me..."

"Like what?" Jeffrey lifted his chin, challenging me.

"Like, well, I think you could call Cecil a game player. I saw it with Lila. I read..."

"Read?" Jeffrey was fast.

Not yet. I wasn't ready to give up Cecil's book. What was it, after all, but fiction? And I'd agreed, in writing, not to divulge anything about it to anyone. It was a bind I didn't appreciate. Depending on how bad things got, did I have a breaking point? A place where I'd be forced to show the book to Jeffrey or Dolly? I could be sued by Cecil Hawke. At some point I was going to have to face my fear—of maybe losing the only thing I had in a lawsuit: my house on Willow Lake—and do what I knew I had to do.

That point wasn't yet. I couldn't take the chance until I was sure...

"Books I've read about psychopaths."

He nodded then got right back to Courtney James.

"That leaves you and Dolly to keep this kid safe," he said, wiping his hands together. "Here's what I propose. You two take an hour, go off somewhere, and come up with a plan between you. The chief and I will take her statement, have Courtney sign it, and use that as a way to get moving on this. I'm taking on the sheep ranch. Don't know how, but I'm getting in there to have a look around, maybe talk to men who work there. Lucky's following up with the farmers. You two stick tight to Courtney, and, Emily, we'd like you to keep seeing Hawke, if you think you can handle it. You're editing for him? What's that book about?"

I shrugged and said, "You know, about Noel Coward."

That satisfied Jeffrey. My first lie to him—a big one. But maybe not for long. If we found proof linking Cecil to any of the murders, I'd drag that manuscript out in a flash and face the rest later.

———

Dolly and I had an hour to come up with a plan to keep the girl alive and have her around as a witness when we caught up with Toomey. EATS was out of the question. They'd know the whole story before we drank a single cup of Eugenia's strong coffee or, in my case, a cup of weak, generic tea.

Dolly said we could talk at her house, since she was still off duty. "We'll work out how I can help you—having her there with you," she added.

"With me?" I wasn't sure I'd heard that right.

That set us off, arguing over who was best set up to protect a young woman who some creep nobody could find was after.

Cate Thomas, Dolly's grandmother, was sitting at Dolly's kitchen table when we got there, a cup of hot tea in front of her. She stared off, out across Dolly's backyard toward a stand of tall fir trees. Her greeting was halfhearted, though she offered tea, which I knew would be hot and dark and good.

"So, you don't want to take her in?" Dolly said.

We sat at Dolly's white, wooden table. I remembered coming here before Cate arrived and having to carve a place to sit at the table, clearing off cereal boxes, newspapers, and books on forensics. Then there were dirty mugs, plates with dried chili stuck to them, and small blue pots with food burned at the bottom. Cate, with not much of a place to call home herself, got busy when she moved in. Now it was a pleasure to sit at Dolly's kitchen table without the fear of a bug carrying off your cup.

"You got a dog," Dolly went on.

"And you've got Cate, here," I said with perfect logic. "When you're on patrol, Cate can keep an eye on her."

Dolly made a noise, expressing her disagreement. "You think this is some runaway kid we got on our hands? You think all she needs is watchin'? You're nuttier than ever."

"And you think me and Sorrow can keep away some killer bent on getting to her?"

"Better than here, in town. How about Harry's house? Think he'd keep an eye on her?"

"Yeah. The house is big enough for about a half of a human being, and you're going to put this young Englishwoman there."

"Got a better idea?" Dolly asked.

Cate Thomas, dressed in her usual getup of green scarves twisted around her neck, a long pink cotton skirt, a lacy blouse, and tons of make-up, cleared her throat. "Don't count on me." She shook her head vehemently. "I'm going. I'll be in France, looking for my daughter. It's time she stepped right up to the plate..." She sipped her tea and stole a look at Dolly. "Now that this one's gone and got herself pregnant. I'm not a young woman. I can't take on a baby. No sirree."

Cate turned to me. "I told her, dumb thing to get yourself pregnant."

"Didn't get myself any way at all."

"Well, this mysterious immaculate conception of yours," Cate turned to me. "She tell you a father's name?"

I shook my head.

"Me either. Could at least get some support..."

"Don't put on, Cate," Dolly growled across the table at her. "You're doin' what all the women in our family do. You're runnin'. So, what's new? Guess you can't break a cycle like ours. Only thing

I know is, I'm not runnin'. This kid is going to have a great mother. Best ever, if I have anything to say about it."

Dolly's hat was off, that short, dirty-blond hair sticking up like a teenage boy's buzz cut. Nothing beautiful about Deputy Dolly, but I had to admit there was something new there. If this was the glow of pregnancy, maybe she was right. She was already improving.

Dolly slumped down in her chair, staring at her hands. Cate kept her eyes turned from both of us. I sipped my tea and stayed out of this ongoing battle.

"So, what are we doin' about this Courtney James?" When Dolly got back to the subject at hand her voice was strong and unemotional. We were on the work track again and off babies, mothers, and traitorous grandmothers.

THIRTY-TWO

WHAT WE CAME UP with was that it was best to get Courtney James out of the Leetsville area. That's where Toomey would be looking for her. I could only think of two places to take her. Jackson's or Bill's.

Unfortunately, or maybe not so unfortunately, Jack wasn't home when I called. Bill Corcoran was.

"You understand she might be the target of a really crazy killer," I said, wanting to make sure Bill didn't go into anything with his eyes closed.

"I get it, Emily," he said. "I'll get somebody to stay with her when I can't be here. Otherwise, she'll come to the office with me. I'll put her on your old job—doing obits or that garden column you dropped. Whatever you need."

He stopped a minute. "To tell you the truth, I almost wish you'd come and stay too. I don't know what's happening, but two people are dead. That's something to worry about. You're there alone..."

"Got Sorrow."

"Yeah, that's what I mean. Nothing like a dog kissing a killer to death."

"And I've got Dolly. And Jeffrey Lo is here."

There was a long pause before he went right on. "I'm glad of that. Hope he stays close…"

I drove Courtney into Traverse City. Since Lucky thought a yellow Jeep wasn't exactly the right car, I borrowed Eugenia's old Buick. Dolly followed us in Courtney's rental. We took care of that first, turning it in, then drove together over to Bill's. He and Courtney got on right away. Bill put a big arm around her shoulders and promised to take good care of her. I watched the two of them and kept telling myself he was twenty years older than the young woman, that he was not like Jackson, that he was a good man…

I wasn't into trust yet. Old scars cut deep.

———

Back in Leetsville, I dropped Dolly off at the police station. It was a relief to be rid of all of them. Courtney to Traverse City. Dolly in Leetsville. Jeffrey Lo off doing his thing. I got Eugenia's car back to her and picked up mine from the parking lot. All I had left to do was get home and maybe read some more of Cecil's book, or put time into the new book I was writing. I voted for me and began working in my head: me and Dolly and what happened out at Sandy Lake where that poor Native American girl was killed and left floating on a raft. Then the brave brother and sister avenging her death.

How good it was to clear my head of Cecil and his work; of a dead Mexican agent who had tried to help her cousin; of a silly woman who wanted to be a Broadway star; and of a girl who, rightly or wrongly, thought her dead mother had been murdered.

I could think clearly as I drove home. My head was empty of all the stuff tying me into knots. I purred, raising my shoulders to my ears, and holding them there. I let myself be happy. If I got down to my writing studio. If I got in there and shut the door ...

———

I planned to unplug the phone and light a bunch of candles and put on ani diFranco, whose voice could break your heart, and move back into a place where nothing came close to touching me, except a story that was over and was safe and I could step right back into and relive any way I liked.

I drove with all the windows down and Eric Satie, after ani, blaring at me like he was the latest rock star. The end of July up in Michigan could be hot—in the nineties; or cold—down into the fifties. Today was a compromise—low seventies, breeze so soft it almost wasn't there. Sun so thick you could stick your tongue out and taste it. The last of the wild daisies made flashes of sparkling white on the hillsides. I passed a field of sunflowers—tall and bright yellow—turned toward the sun so their faces and spiked hats lined like watchers along the road.

It was one of those days I'd come to Northern Michigan for. Almost no one on the roads. Woods—where the tent worms hadn't gotten—lush and dark with beauty and mystery. And then blue water and blinding shots of light skipping across the surface; hidden roofs, crows watching me from telephone wires, and hawks sitting high on poles scanning the ground for an unsuspecting mouse to kill. All of it was there. A single afternoon of beauty and death.

What I'd first come to northwest lower Michigan for wasn't what I'd been getting lately. I was getting something else; filling a lot of gaps in my life I hadn't known were there when I first left Jackson Rinaldi and Ann Arbor. There were people up here who knew me on sight now and seemed happy about that fact. A dog that loved me unconditionally, and that I loved in return. A book written and out there somewhere in the world—maybe sitting on an editor's desk as I drove. What else? My poor, nude trees . . . a small fox that had moved in under my deck . . . turkeys that came down my drive to see if there was anything worth eating and getting the shock of their lives when Sorrow drove them off . . . deer that used to come into my garden but didn't now because they'd learned I wouldn't scare them away if they waited and came in September to eat all they liked while saving me winter cleanup. Maybe it wasn't much—what I had—but there was magic to it. I wondered if Lila Hawke had found any of that magic here. Or if she'd only lived inside her head, with dead dreams for company. Funny, that I could feel sorry for anybody who didn't find what they were looking for, somebody with that much money, that much opportunity. But so very blind.

The first thing I noticed, driving along Willow Lake Road toward my drive and the long curve down to my house, was Harry's slapped-together car—part old car, part old truck, and some other parts I couldn't put a name to. It was parked at the very top of my drive, almost blocking my way in. I had to edge around the front of the mostly red truck with rust holding it together. I stopped, got out, and called to Harry, standing just a ways down the gravel. I figured he was out on one of his roadkill hunts, or maybe about to go into the woods for puffballs, if there were any this year. He turned, looking back over his shoulder at me, then waved his hands in the air, motioning for me to stay where I was, not come any closer. He walked up toward me at a rate I didn't often see Harry achieve. I parked there on the verge of the road and got out, figuring I could go down to meet him halfway. He yelled, stopping me where I stood. Harry's face was never emotional. He took life at a pretty even pace. But now his face was working, mouth going in and out, old teeth I rarely saw biting at his lip.

"Stay where you are, Emily," he yelled as he patted the air. Out of breath, he ran toward me. "You wait right there."

"What's going on, Harry?" I called down at him. This wasn't the man I knew—old jacket flying out behind him, feet slapping along the gravel at a great rate.

"Nothin'. Nothin' at all. I'm takin' care of it. No need fer you to go on down there ... "

That was enough to send me flying toward Harry and whatever it was I could see lying on the ground.

Harry put out his arms, catching me as I drew even with him.

"What is it?" I pushed against him, then looked into his old faded, very worried eyes. I was scared to death.

He shook his head. "Nothin' for you to see, Emily. Just ... well ... nothin' you'd ever want to see in your whole life."

THIRTY-THREE

THE DOG LAID OUT on my gravel drive was very big, very bloody, mutilated, and dead. I stood beside the animal, looking down, and wrapped my arms around myself, trying to stop the shaking. I bowed my head. Murder—again. Cruelty. This damned, horrible evil set loose around me.

"Told ya not to look." Harry was unhappy. Still trying to protect me, he tugged at my arm, pulling me away.

He was right. It wasn't something I ever wanted to see—except that I'd already seen one, laid out dead in that hot field. This was just as bad. The only thing good about it being that it wasn't Sorrow.

The dog was yellow. It was huge. It would have been frightening, if I'd run into it when it was alive. Somehow, dead, unable to hurt me, all I could think was: *poor thing*.

I held on to Harry, clutching at him, scared I was going to pull a Dolly and barf on his shoes.

My turn to be warned. There was no mistaking what this gutted dog meant. It was a message to me. Good thing Courtney James didn't come home with me.

"Think I saw who dumped it here," Harry turned me carefully away from the dead animal. "A guy parked an old blue car right there at the top. He was coming up the driveway when I spotted him. Got inside his car and took off 'fore I could ask him what he was doin'."

He didn't get a license number. "Didn't know anythin' was wrong then."

I thought I knew what the man he'd seen looked like. "Big guy? Kind of dark?"

Harry scowled. "That's him. Kinda crazy lookin'. How come you know 'im? You mixed up in something you shouldn't be mixed up in again?"

Toomey, the ghost. The chimera haunting my imagination. He was more real now than before. Harry—my down-to-earth, steady-as-you-go friend—had seen him.

I shook my head in answer to Harry's question. I hadn't chosen to be brought into this any more than Dolly or Jeffrey had.

Harry clucked and shook his head at a great rate. "Could be bad, ya know. Heard of this kind of thing before. Leave a dead animal to warn people. Anybody doing that means business. Not real human beings at all, you see, 'cause real human beings got somethin' in their head that makes 'em know better. Hate to see you gettin' into anything..."

"I don't have much of a choice."

"Heard about them others. Dead dogs and migrant workers out to some of the farms. They was talkin' about it in EATS the other morning. Then that rich guy's wife. Think it's one of us?"

Since I wasn't thinking much of anything, all I could do was shrug and make a face.

"Somebody from around here? Hate to think such a thing."

"Don't know, yet," was all I could give him.

"People's pets comin' up missin'. Told you about that. Keep my shotgun right next to my back door in case I hear anybody at the kennel, trying to get one of mine to bait those killer dogs of theirs."

I shook my head.

I put up a hand. I'd had enough for one day; all the evil I could stand sloshing around in my brain.

"Can you help me bury him?" I asked finally.

Harry nodded. "Got a shovel in the back of the truck."

"Could you make a kind of cross? I'll pay you. Just something... I don't know. I don't think this dog ever knew much kindness."

Harry looked hard at me then nodded. "Got it," he said. "No need to pay me anything. Feel just the way you're feelin'. Only thing is, if I ever get a hold a that guy what did this—well, he ain't gonna get no cross when I'm done, unless I drive it straight through his heart."

———

We buried the dog under maple trees that were covered with a soft, green fuzz—slowly coming back to life. The tent worms had gone from that first awful stage of eating everything they came on to the small brown moths, to the green, sticky cocoons I waged war on.

Harry got two white-painted boards from his house, sawed them to size, nailed them together and planted the cross at the head of the animal's grave. I asked him in for a sandwich when we were done but he said he was worn out. "Don't have many days this bad. Pickin' up dead stuff all the time but when it comes to a dog... well... now there you reach my limit."

What I had to do was call Dolly and Jeffrey—fast.

Dolly was mad, because I'd already buried the dog. Lo was madder that Toomey had turned his attention to me.

"Got to get you out of there, Emily," was his first reaction. "This has gone way beyond some migrant worker grudge. Where the hell are the dogs coming from? Nobody notices... I don't get it."

He took a long breath, maybe to clear his mind of the dead animal I'd described. "Listen, why don't you come into Kalkaska and stay at the motel where I'm staying."

"Can't leave Sorrow."

He thought a while. "Then why don't I come stay there until this is over? You shouldn't be alone. This Toomey guy's heard about Courtney James being at the funeral. He's letting you know he's around."

All kinds of things flew through my head. "If you don't mind... just until... I mean, I like the idea of you coming out here."

There was a slight pause from his end. "Tonight. I've got some things to take care of first. That ranch really bothers me. Where the hell else would Toomey be holing up? It's like he doesn't exist unless somebody's dead. Think I'll start with Hawke. See if he'll talk to me, explain why in hell he's lying about knowing Toomey?"

"Be careful," I warned. "They're both crazy. If what Courtney told us is true, that's maybe three people Cecil or Toomey's murdered. Nothing's going to stop them from killing you."

"Yes, there is. Me. I gotta be there tonight to keep an eye on you, remember? Think I'd miss that? Could be the best part of this whole mess."

When I hung up I took a look at the house around me. The only live thing there was Sorrow, sitting up, pink tongue hanging from his jowls, waiting for something exciting to happen—like a long walk where he could run and sniff the grass.

I told myself I wasn't going to be spooked by anyone, but I was lying. I wasn't only spooked, I started figuring places where I could hide if he got in my house. I planned on the best window to leap from, should I hear a noise. A window where I wouldn't break a leg and be a sitting duck.

I checked the locks on all the doors and pulled the curtains across the front windows, even though it was still light. I didn't want anyone standing between the house and the lake and looking in at me. Or anyone getting in a boat and spying on me. Or hiding down in the tall reeds, then sneaking up the path at me. Or anyone coming at me from any direction.

I worked myself up into such a state I thought about going into Traverse City, and buying a gun. Then I thought how much I didn't know about firing a gun and decided I would wait until I'd gotten a few pointers, maybe found a range where I could learn to shoot, and then I'd bring a gun into my house ... or not.

When the phone rang I fell over myself getting to the desk. I hoped it was Jeffrey and he was on his way. I had a list of groceries for him to pick up in town so I didn't have to go out to my car and get on the road. I was thinking of a salad with chicken and a nice pinot grigio—or whatever he wanted to drink—and maybe some eggs for breakfast. But thinking of breakfast made my face turn warm because I knew asking Jeffrey to pick up eggs wouldn't ever be a simple request, with nothing read into it.

"Emily?" The voice went high. If accusation and greeting and misery and hope could ever be gotten into the same voice, Cecil'd achieved it. "I'd hoped you would call. At least to see how I was getting through this terrible time."

Mea culpa. "I didn't want to bother you," I told him.

"You'd never be a bother, dear. I'm so alone here at the moment. I was wondering if you could come over. You've finished the chapters I gave you, haven't you? I have more. I've been working so terribly hard. It's the only thing ... my grief, and all ... to keep my mind off of ... poor, dear Lila."

"I can't right now." Nobody was going to get me out of my house and into the dark. Maybe in the morning. And maybe after I finished reading the work I'd lied to him about, saying I'd read it all. And maybe after I got to Leetsville and saw Dolly. Find out where everything stood. But first there was Jeffrey. In a way, I thought, Jeffrey and I were actually taking care of each other. A good thing. And he would be here soon.

"Someone threw a dead dog on my drive today. I'm really not up to …"

"Terrible! Just terrible. Poor, dear Emily."

"Somebody's warning me to stay away from everything that's been going on."

"But what could that be?" he asked. "Oh, you mean that dead Mexican woman. But surely no one would be after you."

I almost brought up Courtney James, but decided against it.

"What about tomorrow morning? I could get there about eleven? Would that be all right?"

He gave a disappointed mewl. "If that's all I can have of you, then yes, of course. I'll see you at eleven. And maybe you'd like to have a look around the ranch? Tomorrow's a big day here. An annual rite you'll find interesting. But I won't spoil it for you. Come. Bring back the chapters you have, will you? I really wouldn't want them to get into the hands of anyone else. I mean, especially now. Your local … constabulary … might misconstrue my work. You understand. I know you do. And will honor our agreement …" He paused, waiting for me to answer. I made a noise in my throat and agreed to nothing.

"Good. I'll have more work for you. And another check. We will sit, have lunch, talk. Make a glorious day of it. Doesn't that sound wonderful?"

He didn't wait for my next throat-clearing answer.

Making 'a day of it' with Cecil Hawke sounded as appetizing as the day I'd just been through. But maybe a day with Cecil Hawke was exactly what was needed.

THIRTY-FOUR

JEFFREY DIDN'T CALL BY dinnertime so I microwaved a frost-covered frozen dinner and sat down with Cecil's manuscript. It took almost more than I had in me to open the folder and pull up the first page.

The first few of the next ten chapters followed the boys, Nelson and Tommy, as they made their way around the British countryside, stealing and running, thinking of themselves as Gypsies. There was almost an air of Tom Jones to it—fun, escapes, country girls gulled by city boys. Plenty of sex now. At least more sex than murder, which I welcomed. In the next chapters things changed again for our Tommy, the boy with the mutilated hand. He was in his twenties and living in Liverpool. Nelson was there, with him, but almost pushed to the background as Tommy claimed he was in love. In love with a wealthy, shy woman.

I read slowly, feeling I was heading into something so terrible I didn't want to know. Liverpool, not Bristol. But still, a wealthy woman.

What was Cecil doing to me? A deliberate game—paying well to keep me silent as he relived what amounted to a confession? He knew I'd met Courtney, knew she suspected him of murdering her mother, a wealthy woman. I sat back and let the manuscript pages settle in my lap. I prayed the story didn't go where I feared it was headed. If it did—I had a responsibility, not to myself and a paper I'd signed, but to Courtney James; maybe even to my own sense of decency.

I looked back at the kitchen clock. Not a word from Jeffrey. He'd promised he would be there. I went to my corner desk and dialed his cell number. The phone rang on and on until Jeffrey's recorded voice answered, telling me to leave a message at the beep.

I let k.d. lang lull me softly, but unsuccessfully, into a safer world. I had Sorrow at my feet, snoring and blowing out his jowls. But the house around me felt foreign and closed in. It wasn't possible to take a deep, freeing breath. I sat as if frozen, listening to a creak from one of my two bedrooms; the refrigerator start with a sudden whirr; Sorrow's nails scratch as his legs pumped in what must have been a dream of running. Small sounds grew huge. They rippled through the house. There was the feel of a breathing malevolence as everyday things joined in against me, seeming to hover just beyond the circle of my reading lamp.

I got up and went to the door. I pulled the gauzy white curtain aside and flipped on the outside light, expecting someone there looking back at me. The porch was empty. My car was in the driveway, shining an odd yellow in the bright light. A skunk skittered back up the brick walkway and off into the dark. Not a single other movement.

I went back to the couch, checked my watch again—ten-twenty—and vowed I would finish the last of this manuscript tonight. Jeffrey would be there soon. Morning would be...

I had no idea what morning would be if Jeffrey finally showed up.

I let my mind sink back to England, and a young man who didn't marry the wealthy woman after all. He didn't kill her either, which I found reassuring. I told myself maybe I could even like this guy—he was charming now, seeming to go out of his way to be polite and kind to women. As if I was in the hands of a magician, I forgot he was a cold-blooded killer and let my mind tag along with him, enjoying time at the races as he bet and won on horses, as he schemed his way into circles of wealth, and seemed soon to be welcomed into manor homes and posh parties. He wooed the rich and lonely older women he called his "Swans, my beautiful swans," while he laughed behind their backs with Nelson; while he and Nelson schemed to steal their jewelry and take off for the Continent.

"Maybe this time—hey, what'cha think—maybe France?" Nelson said as the two young men sat together in the filthy back booth of a seedy pub.

"I've always wanted to go to France," Tommy said. "The women there look so ... so needy."

As I read on, it turned out their next stop wasn't going to be France after all. I would probably never get to know what that next stop was. Cecil had made a mistake. The last of his chapters weren't in sync with the others. At first I thought I'd missed something, or I wasn't getting the structure of the book. Finally I figured out he'd given me work that belonged much farther along in the narrative. Tommy was now Tom. He was in Bristol. Nelson was nowhere in sight. Tom, now much older, maybe in his early forties, was the picture of loneliness, sitting at a sidewalk cafe having afternoon tea. He noticed a lovely woman at another table, sitting by herself. Tom, being Tom, he took in the clothes she wore. She could have bought them in France, or even Milan. At a very expensive boutique. She had long slim legs, blond hair, and a big diamond on her right hand. The left hand was empty—so not married or, at least, not married at the moment.

I read through Tom's detailed assessment of the woman. He might have gotten older but he hadn't changed. He was a jockey figuring the value of a winning horse. I began to get the queasiest of feelings in my gut.

Soon Tom was sitting with the woman. They laughed and her eyes shone. They moved on to dinner, where he listened as she talked about her recent loss. Her husband, Phillip, had been killed in a plane crash. He'd worked in international trade. Tom thought hard and put the woman's value in the thousands of pounds, maybe even up to a million. The smell of a rich woman triggered something in his head. *His senses reacted—nose, eyes, ears—to her upper-class accent. Then other parts of him. He leaned forward to enjoy his hard-on. So much better than sex—this homing in on a woman standing between him and what he needed ...*

I set the manuscript aside for just a minute. Something in his writing, in the character himself, made me feel dirty, as if just by reading this stuff I betrayed me and all the other women in the world. But I didn't have a choice: stop, or go on. Something I needed to know was buried here. Maybe even a message Cecil was sending. As I sat in my own safe living room I could almost hear him whispering.

I read on: Tommy put his head closer to the woman's and listened hard, smiling when a smile was called for, expressing sympathy when that was needed. He made all the right moves. He made her laugh. Lines that creased her forehead disappeared. He watched her face relax and congratulated himself on a truly remarkable talent with women.

———

The next day he was on the way to her house, to meet the woman's daughter, though she assured him she'd never done anything like this before—bringing a stranger home.

"But you know me so well. From that first moment, didn't you feel we'd known each other always?" That line worked before. Tom wasn't above pulling out the tried and true. Women were all emotions, he knew. The right word, at the right time, and he'd be in her bed before he'd barely kissed her, maybe settled into her home, taking care of her, making her laugh, bringing her back to the world of the living. He would tell her how beautiful she was and take her chin in his hand and kiss her slowly.

At lunchtime he arrived with a huge bouquet of flowers. He was there, she'd said, to meet her daughter, a girl who needed cheering as much as she did. Poor thing—left with no father when a girl most needs a man in her life—her teen years.

"She can hardly wait to meet you." Amanda beamed at Tom *when she opened the huge front door of the mansion on Church Road, in Sneyd Park. She was dressed in a pale blue silk dress with marquis-cut diamonds at her ears. Her soft, pale hair was piled on her head and caught there, loosely, with mother of pearl combs.*

The mansion awed him. Riding up in the taxi he'd smiled broadly as he paid the driver, making the tip as small as possible. Best neighborhood in all of Bristol. The house must have cost ... he stood looking up at the white stuccoed walls and deep-set windows. He tried estimating its worth in his head, vowing to check out prices later. Green and leafy Sneyd Park. He'd only driven through once before, thinking then how this was where he truly belonged.

"Courtney will love you. You're such a joy, Tommy." Amanda put *out her hand to draw him into the grand hall. "You're so much like Philip. I haven't laughed and been so relaxed in months, the way I was with you yesterday. I feel so fortunate ... "*

The daughter's name wasn't lost on me. Another bit of poetic license? Use what you know? Maybe, maybe, maybe, I told myself. Or more. How could I be sure of anything? I was through the looking glass, into that place I went myself, into fiction, where nothing was ever as it seemed, where all was made up to fit a storyline.

But this ... ?

What I held was just a story ... just a story. But filled with facts from outside the fictive world. There was a friend ... There was a daughter named Courtney.

I almost didn't dare to read on, but nothing would have stopped me either.

In the next chapter Tommy was in Cannes, enjoying an afternoon aperitif on the balcony of his room overlooking the Mediterranean. There was a phone call...

"Amanda! No! Oh, good Lord. But how ... I'll get the first plane back ..."

Tommy put the phone down, bowed his head over it, and began to laugh until he choked. He did a little dance around the ornately decorated room and chortled, "Has there ever been a friend such as mine? Ever, in the world?" He thought, if only he could have been there ... The basement of that great house would have been perfect—but not with that ugly daughter around.

That was enough for me. I was being challenged. Maybe it was to see if I'd tell others, or keep it to myself. Maybe this was a new game, even more dangerous. Maybe I was Cecil's new Lila.

Or maybe Dolly was right. Too much imagination.

THIRTY-FIVE

AT MIDNIGHT I TRIED calling Jeffrey again. No answer. I left another message demanding to know where the heck he was and when he was going to get to my house. I hung on to the phone even after the machine clicked off. I needed to talk to him. I'd made a decision. I was going to show him a copy of the manuscript. Dolly too. I didn't know if they'd get it right away. If they'd understand what this man was doing; what he was saying in his book.

And maybe Courtney. She needed to know.

Ideas and memories buzzed in my brain. Hadn't Jeffrey said Cecil was out of town the day Amanda slipped into a coma? And he was in plain sight when Lila was shot.

Toomey. That name was like a wasp in my head. Toomey. Nelson. Maybe the same boy/man/friend. This was turning into a puzzle within a riddle, wrapped in a conundrum. Too much to digest that late in the day, when I was so tired.

I shut off the lamp behind me, huddled down into the sofa, and hid in the dark. It wasn't until at least after one a.m. that I fell asleep. By three I was awake again, listening for a car in the driveway. I checked my answering machine, thinking Jeffrey had called and I'd slept right through the ringing phone. Nothing. I brought a blanket from my bedroom, lay back down on the sofa, welcomed Sorrow when he managed to crawl up beside me, and slept until morning.

At eight I called Jeffrey's cell. Nothing. I called the police station in Leetsville and got a busy signal. When I tried a few minutes later, Dolly answered.

"Jeffrey was supposed to come here last night … he thought I should have someone in the house with me … he never made it," I blurted in one long, strung-together sentence, not bothering to identify myself.

"Yeah, Emily. He told me he was stayin' out there," Dolly said. "I was worried maybe it was something more than just watching you. You know, you're kind of weak when it comes to guys."

"Hey, Dolly, focus, will you? He never showed up. I tried calling him last night and again this morning. Nothing."

"Hmm." Dolly switched gears. "Where do you think he got to?"

"No clue."

"Wasn't he hell-bent on getting over to that sheep ranch? Judge almost ready to sign the search warrant, is what I heard. He told those lawyers Cecil Hawke sent that this wasn't New York City where celebrities got different treatment. Lo must've known."

"Then he's probably out there already. I mean, Jeffrey felt so strongly that he had to get on that ranch, talk to some of the workers, would he be hanging back now? Still, why didn't he call me?"

"Okay. Look." Dolly stopped and thought awhile. "I'll keep trying to get him. What are you doing today? You shouldn't be alone."

"I'm supposed to see Cecil at eleven. There's a ritual going on. I guess with the sheep. He thinks I'll enjoy watching."

"You nuts? After that dead dog at your house?"

"Cecil has no reason to hurt me. I'm not, like, a wife or anything."

"Get that jackass to go with you?"

"Which jackass?"

"Your ex, Jackson."

"Cecil's not going to let Jack back in his house. He knows Jack had an affair with Lila."

"Yeah, well this book you're reading for him, you said it's kind of odd? Isn't that what you said? Well, like how odd?"

"Well, like ..." I mimicked her. "Like his main character's a killer."

"And?"

"I don't know, Dolly. It sounds as if he's writing about himself ..."

"And you never mentioned this before?"

"I signed a confidentiality pledge."

"What's that?"

"That I won't talk about the work to anyone."

"You just did. And anyway, so what? Don't you kill off people in your books?"

"But this is different. The main character might be patterned after him, after Cecil. And there's a friend..."

"Aw geez. Emily." There was a groan in Dolly's voice. "We got enough to deal with here."

"You don't get it. Think I should show some of the work to Courtney? See if she recognizes anything. I mean..."

"Thought you signed something that you couldn't do that."

"I did ... but ..."

"Up to you, Emily. Whatever you think. I'm not much of a reader. Don't know if I'd catch what you're talkin' about."

"Maybe I'll wait, see what he gives me today."

"You making copies?"

I hesitated, not wanting to admit I'd already broken the agreement.

"Yes."

"Good for you. That's the kind of brain you need if you're gonna keep writin' mysteries." She hesitated. "Sure wish I could go with you. I can't. Cate's leavin'. I'm takin' her into Grayling to catch a bus. Actually, to tell you the truth, I'm so mad I feel like lettin' her walk the fifty miles but ... guess not."

"I'll call you when I get to Hawke's house. Just so he knows I've told people where I am. And," I got to the biggest thing on my mind, "if you hear from Jeffrey call me there, at Cecil's. Probably something came up. Maybe he had to get back to Detroit, to his office ..."

"And not let us know? What kinda cop is that?"

289

"Thanks, Dolly. You're such a comfort."

"Emily," she said before hanging up. "If you're worried there … I mean, if anything doesn't seem right to you …"

"I know, Dolly. I'll leave."

"And about looking over that farm …"

"It's the only chance we have. Jeffrey's not around. Gotta be me."

"You know what, Emily? Bet anything we hear from Lo today. I wouldn't worry."

That was Dolly's tardy stab at making me feel better.

It didn't.

THIRTY-SIX

We sat in the morning room. Sun, streaming in the leaded glass windows, was dimmed and diffused because the windows were dirty. The dirt filtered the sunlight and made the view from the window hazy: Pointillist trees and Impressionist sky. I would have loved the light, and the pseudo-art on every wall. I would have loved the fragile tea cup in my hand; the chance to be in this *Washington Square* setting; to bring the cup to my lips and sip and then smile and demur and tuck my long skirt back around my legs—crossed at the ankles, the toes of my dainty shoes sticking out, only hinting that I really had legs under there.

I didn't love any of it. I'd called Dolly when I arrived but she was gone. I told Lucky where I was and left the number. "In case you need me," I said as loud as I could so Cecil would hear.

I went back to the tea table, tripping over Freddy, who struggled to his feet to come over and lick my hand. Cecil didn't approve. He shook his head at me but I patted the dog's knobby head anyway.

"Agent Lo, the man with INS who was here the other day?" I said. "He's missing. We don't know if he's gone back to Detroit. We're kind of worried."

"Really?" Cecil showed little interest. He was going over the pages I'd marked with red pencil, shaking his head, or nodding when he came on a place where he agreed with my edits.

"He didn't come here yesterday, did he?"

He shrugged. "Not that I know of. Unless one of the servants…"

Since I had, again, seen no one but the guard at the gate and been let in by Cedric, who'd brought the tea and sandwiches, I doubted there'd been a message.

"Well, if you do—I understood he wanted to talk to you—will you ask him to call me or Deputy Dolly?"

The look Cecil gave me was odd, as if I'd proposed the unimaginable.

"Of course," he said, absently, then pointed to a place I'd marked on one of the pages. "Do you really think I need take out this comma? I mean, it makes so much sense to me…"

Before we got too deeply into commas, I had questions. "I couldn't help noticing, Cecil, that the woman in the last of these chapters is named Amanda."

He looked up brightly, smiling at me. "Yes, I thought that a good touch, don't you? Verisimilitude. Write what you know—that sort of thing."

"Because that was your wife's name?"

He shrugged. "Yes. Using Amanda's name brought back my sadness at the news of her last illness. I wasn't home, you know. Not in Cannes, as our Tommy is, but in London for the day."

"And the daughter—Courtney . . .?"

"I might change that, since Courtney has resurfaced to confuse my life. I wouldn't want to hurt the girl. When this novel comes out it will no doubt shoot to the top of the bestseller list immediately and she would see what I've done. Nothing, not even my art, is worth hurting her feelings. I'm sure you agree. Or would you suggest I remain true to my vision and leave things as they are?"

There wasn't an answer to that question and he knew it. More of the game, I imagined. Make me an accomplice.

"At the end, here." I avoided his eyes, reached across the table, shuffled through the manuscript pages to the last of the chapters, and pointed. "Is this Amanda, Tommy's wife, dead?"

Cecil's eyes opened wide, he threw back his head and laughed so I could see every blunt, yellow tooth in his red mouth.

"Emily, Emily, Emily. What an evil brain you have. That's why you're a writer too, isn't it, dear? To get that evil out on paper." He clucked a few times as if drawing me into a shameful secret with him. "Ill. The woman's ill. Our Tommy is a reformed man. His past is gone, blotted out by the love of a good woman . . ."

"I don't think it's that easy. In the beginning you have Tommy murder his mother . . ."

"You only suspect that. Nothing's stated."

"Then a girl who was his friend . . ."

"Again, no proof. That's the loveliest part of the story, that there is no proof. Tommy's murders take place in the mind of the reader, showing readers what evil lies within themselves. The point of the story, my dear—in case you've missed it—is that evil doesn't exist at all, except in the mind."

"Then I don't think the book works," I dared to say, despite his mounting irritation with me.

His eyes flew wide. "Doesn't work? Doesn't work?"

I watched as he fought for control. I'd found a vulnerable place: the book. He saw it as his message to the world. I was finally getting at what was going on; what my part in all of this was. I let my last comments fall away as I praised his characterizations and descriptions, then went over my additions and corrections. He sat without speaking.

Finally, he slapped his hands on the manuscript and called an end to our meeting. "But, I want you to see the ranch," he said, scooping up the pages and setting them on a table behind him.

"You've come on a most auspicious day. Today my men work directly with the sheep. Very interesting. Raw life, Emily. Ah, yes, raw life. A treat for a writer. You'll see something most women never get to see. Should deepen your work. Won't that be amazing? Your work deepened, maybe approaching the quality of mine?"

We stood. He put a hand on my shoulder, pushing when I tried to pull away from him. I sensed that whatever he had in store for me wasn't about my writing.

We were out the back door before I could protest, and then off across the fields.

"Most of my men are from Australia, where sheep farming is very big. Much easier to own a sheep station there than here, I've unhappily discovered." He talked, excited and out of breath, as we walked. "Your long winters—well, the sheep can't graze the range the way they would there. They have to be put up in the barns. Terrible expense. But, come on. Come on now. The men will be about the business at hand. And I truly, truly, want you to see." He clucked at me again, as if herding hens.

The green lawn was long and sloping. We entered a white gate behind a stand of tall fir trees, then crossed a dirt road toward the biggest of the barns. The barn was U-shaped, with an uplifted, central raised roof running around the U. Cecil took pride in pointing out the unusual form. "For fresh air," he said. "Don't want the smell, or gasses, to build up. The very latest of everything. My wool will be famous worldwide, eventually."

I took note of what I saw. I thought I might need to know the layout. There were other barns and small outbuildings. Then, down another slope, a building with no windows and a steep roof, surrounded by a high, wire fence.

I pointed and asked about the building, thinking I could distract him.

"More room for animals." He muttered, looking where I pointed then waving a dismissive hand.

"And that one?" Another building, windowless, with a flattened roof.

He shrugged, taking no interest now, intent on pushing the high, sliding, wooden door of the big barn open. He put a firm hand on my back again, nudging me to enter ahead of him.

I was under Cecil's control.

The huge interior of the barn was dark except for bright lights near the back. It was difficult to see, though I heard men's voices yelling—one to the other. There were animal noises. The iron stink of blood saturated the air as we walked across the dirt floor. I looked hard at the light but couldn't see much through a thick cloud of dust and straw. I was close enough to see men moving

295

quickly, back and forth, bending, standing, with voices yelling things I didn't understand.

And then a terrible animal shriek.

I pushed back hard at that hand on me.

"What's going on?" I demanded, unwilling to watch a slaughter, if that's what he had in mind.

"I told you." His breath brushed my cheek. "A rare sight. An ancient ritual you'll never see again in your lifetime, Emily. I'm offering you an opportunity. You, the writer, to take part in this ancient rite. Probably illegal here, but then what do Americans really know about such things?"

Something medieval, and ugly, going on—the odd light, the sounds, the smell of fear in the building . . .

"Surely you're not squeamish." His fingers sank into the flesh of my arm. He pulled forward and I pulled back. Maybe this had something to do with Jeffrey Lo. My mind raced everywhere.

Lo's disappearance. Maybe I would have to watch . . .

The murders in his book flew into my mind—each worse than the one before.

All a joke to this man.

It was almost a relief, as we neared the light, to see a sheep being pulled and pushed between the men, then out again, some age-old task accomplished.

"It's called mulesing, Emily." Cecil, his face red and shining with sweat, tongue licking out and in, tipped his head close to mine. His maimed fist stayed firmly at the center of my back. I had to gulp around the stink of him, on top of the smell of blood and manure.

He laughed and pulled me closer to where a man held a young sheep on the ground, his knee deep into the animal's side. A knife flashed.

"They're not killing . . ." I was appalled by what I saw in this place of dark shadows and bright, color-draining light; raised knife hanging in silhouette. The animal, held struggling on the ground, was so white, and then bloody as the knife cut away skin, and wool.

"No, no, no," Cecil laughed beside me when I turned my head and shivered. "The sheep like it. They won't get fly diseases later in the year. Makes them better sheep, with better wool. You understand about being a better sheep, don't you Emily?"

I lowered my eyes so I didn't have to watch. Still, I had to listen as another animal bleated, struggled, and then screamed.

When I looked up, the creature was being pulled from the light, blood running from its hindquarters. The animal's legs kicked feebly.

"My God! Give them something for the pain."

He laughed and held on to me. "But, you see, Emily, this is our power, isn't it? Sheep have to learn that they're only sheep. Do you understand what I'm saying? I hope so. For your sake, I hope you're not a slow learner."

I pulled as far from Cecil as he would allow. Like one of the sheep, I had no choice but to stand there. This wasn't a simple ritual. This was a deliberately cruel and barbaric act, maybe for my benefit. I got the message loud and clear.

I pulled at the hand on my arm again but, with surprising strength, he kept me pinned beside him.

"Stronger than I look, eh?" He gripped so tightly now I couldn't breathe.

"We're all animals, Emily," he whispered at my ear. "They would kill you, if they could. Even sheep. They'd go for your throat, if you didn't show them who the master was."

"You're crazy," I gasped out.

"Remember Tommy, in the basement? Every time I get the chance I think of Tommy, and that dog—what was his name? Ah yes, Freddy. Dear Freddy. That's what an animal will do to you. We have to do it to them first. Can't you see that now? Ah, isn't this a sublime day . . .?"

I hit him hard with my head. He let out a scream and stumbled back, hands going to his nose, where I'd butted him. With as much speed as I had left, and with almost no breath left in my lungs, I ran out of that terrible place with Cecil stumbling, bent double, along behind.

I was at my car, holding on to the door handle and trying to breathe before he caught up to me. He waited near the steps to the house, gasping, a handkerchief pressed to his nose.

"Your purse is in the house, isn't it, dear?" He caught his breath, frowned as he dabbed at his face, then stepped back as if I might hit him again. Which I fully intended to do if he came closer.

"You'll need your keys . . ." He breathed hard, swiped at his nose a last time, then folded the handkerchief and stuck it into a pocket. He smiled a sad, paternal smile as he shook his head.

I ran up the front steps and through the door, not afraid any more of this pudgy man with a high voice who had nothing more than a gigantic ego going for him.

My purse was in the morning room, along with the new chapters. I looked at the manila envelope on a side table. There was another check clipped to it. I wanted to tell him what he could do with his filthy book and his filthy money but I said nothing. I stood without moving, trying to think.

"This doesn't mean you won't finish editing my book, does it?" He clasped his hands at his chest and gave me a sorrowful look. "I know you didn't mean what you said before—about my book. Only a lapse. Stress, no doubt.

"You're kidding? After that . . .?" I yanked my head in the direction of the barns. "You think I don't recognize a threat when . . ."

"No, no, no. I'm sorry it upset you." He spread his hands and gave me a deeply hurt and innocent look. "I had no idea you were so . . . squeamish. Just one of the rawer sides of life, Emily. You say you love living up here so much, so close to nature. I thought you'd want to see what farm life really is, what this nature you worship is truly about."

"Cruelty," I said. "Stupid."

He tipped his head and tsk-tsked prettily at me. With his hands clasped in front of him, he clucked one more time. "Ugly, yes. But surely not stupid. You know better . . ."

I shook my head, then shook it again. A weak gesture but I'd never dealt with a man like Cecil Hawke before. Nothing was right—not his reactions, his emotions, his sympathy, his humor.

Everything in this world I'd entered was skewed, turned on its head. If I stayed here, in Cecil's idea of life, I'd be a mess. He was so much about death, and dying, and cruelty. It wasn't a place where a normal human being would choose to exist.

THIRTY-SEVEN

I PULLED OUT THROUGH Hawke's front gates, ignoring the guard who tipped his uniform hat at me. Not far down the road, I pulled over, my hands on the wheel. I gulped in fresh air and leaned back against the seat. There was no way to stop the overwhelming sense of helplessness rushing through every inch of my body. That scene in the barn. Maybe not slaughter, but something so close.

I picked up the new manila envelope, hoping for something explicit, for the details of Amanda's murder, a kind of ending for Cecil and for me.

What I read, sitting there, was nothing. Cecil was back to where he'd left off when Tommy and Nelson were in their twenties. More sex. More celebration of bigger and bigger thefts. The book had stagnated. Cecil had become boring. How I would love to tell him that fact. I imagined boring to be the most painful barb I could throw at him. I tucked that fact back in my brain. I was going to need a bigger arsenal to go after him, but 'boring' was a beginning.

I put the pages back in the envelope. What I had to do, I told myself as I gripped the wheel and stared out at the thick woods on both sides of the car, was think. First: why was I feeling sick to my stomach and scared in a way I'd never been scared before? Down in my brain, at a center, something was misfiring. What had happened back there? That wasn't a routine farm procedure. Not some glorious rite of summer. Maybe in Australia it was legal, the way Hawke said, but here, in the United States? Were we still at that level of cruelty?

Something bothered me but I couldn't pin it down. It was like chasing a worm crawling in my head—always just out of reach. An evil so deep I couldn't face it.

I tried to relax. This wasn't who I thought I was. This shaking, scared woman.

I held my hands out and made them be still. I took three deep breaths, had a good talk with myself, and went for logic. What I'd just been through wasn't pretty. It wasn't only those mutilated animals—that was bad enough—but something else. If I hadn't gotten so scared I would have seen it. And if I hadn't let myself dissolve into jelly I would have hit him with a knee to the groin.

Well, maybe not...

But the message had been so clear. It lumped me with Lila, and even Freddy—alive only through Cecil's mercy.

Those sheep had been me to Cecil Hawke. I was the thing bought and sold. He could harm me at will, he was telling me. Hurt me whenever he wanted. Teach me some terrible lesson he thought I needed to learn.

I tightened my hands into fists. How did I begin to fight a monster like Cecil? Futility took on new meaning.

And I was fighting darkness, a kind of shutting down. Or giving up.

Everything in me shouted: Run. Be an unapologetic coward—for just a little while. This was my life. And possibly my death.

I looked at the woods around me, dark between the tree trunks, movement in lower branches. Something could materialize at any minute.

I rolled up the car windows, not caring about the heat. I locked the doors.

I could be murdered by a ghost, I told myself. Toomey was out there, waiting for word from Cecil. Yesterday—that dead dog was the opening shot.

I put the car into gear and pulled out into the road. Behind me I saw only a thick cloud of dust from the gravel road, but there could be something there, at the center of the dust, something dark and formed.

I drove home and called Bill first thing, to warn him Cecil knew where Courtney was.

"I'll take care of it, Emily," he promised.

"How is she?" I asked.

"Fine. She's told me a lot of things I think you and Dolly need to hear. Whatever the Bristol police said about her, they're wrong. Courtney has letters her mother wrote to her when she was away, visiting an aunt in Cornwall. Her mother called Hawke an evil man. The will, leaving everything to him, has got to be a fraud. What the kid needs is a good lawyer. What you need to do is protect yourself. This Hawke is smart. But no conscience. Let the cops handle it."

"I'm in it, Bill. Lo's missing. I've got to stay at the center."

He sighed. "Be careful. And don't worry about Courtney. We're getting out of here right now. Call my cell from here on in."

I threw a few things into a garbage bag—in lieu of a suitcase—and packed dog food and dog bones, got Sorrow, happy as usual, into the car and drove away from my house.

———

I picked Jackson's cottage out on Spider Lake because I didn't have a lot of choices. Maybe I could have gone back to Ann Arbor, but that was too far. Cecil Hawke, along with his friend, Toomey, wasn't a problem that would go away. I could run forever and still know they were around the next corner, able to find me whenever they wanted.

Jackson wasn't exactly happy to see me. I explained about the dead dog left in my drive, about what happened at Cecil's that afternoon. I left out the fact that Jeffrey Lo was missing, in case we were wrong and he'd left for reasons of his own. I did use Jack's phone to call Lo's cell again and got the same voice mail. I called the Leetsville police station, but Lucky's wife told me Dolly was off duty and hadn't called in. I left a message for her to call me at Jackson's number.

"Of course you can stay with me," he said when I got off the phone. He warmed when I explained how Sorrow and I needed a safe place.

He caught on fast, that I was a damsel in distress.

"And Toto too…" he added, nodding at Sorrow, then laughing, liking his *Wizard of Oz* joke.

Jackson became solicitous, urging me to sit on the deck and put my feet up. He brought me a glass of pinot grigio and a bowl of grapes. Jack's form of solace. When I'd settled down a little I watched fishermen out on the lake, and kids floating by in kayaks. Amazing, how ordinary the world looked here, away from my life.

I told Jack the whole story and about how I felt Cecil and Toomey were connected and that Toomey probably did Cecil's killing for him.

"When you first met him, you told him things about our divorce." I looked around at Jack who had settled in an Adirondack chair beside me. "If he thought I was some grasping woman…"

He shrugged. "I might have painted you as a little bit grasping. Maybe I mentioned how much you drained my resources…"

"Your resources! We split everything down the middle. I got exactly what you got. It wasn't like I hadn't worked…"

He waved a hand, stopping me. "Just talk, Emily. Just talk."

"Well, you got me into this. Back when he was your friend he probably thought killing me would be a favor to you."

"That's insane."

"Yeah. My point exactly."

After a long quiet time, Jackson, looking contrite, reached from his chair to mine and took my hand. "I'm truly sorry, Emily." This was an unusual Jackson, more the man I'd once thought was inside there. "If I can do anything, make it up to you in any way…"

"I thought you were leaving," I said. "You know you've been cleared of…"

He shook his head. "I won't leave. I'm staying…for you. And for me, of course. I should have seen what a phony he was. This Noel Coward business…really. Says a lot about me, doesn't it? Maybe I'm learning…"

"Not Noel Coward," I told him. "Not his book."

I explained about Hawke's book—a long, sick confession by a sick man—then watched as Jack's face turned a muddy shade of gray beneath his tan.

When the phone rang I leaped out of my chair. It wasn't my house but I was expecting someone to call me: Lo, Dolly—anyone. I ran into the living room and grabbed up the phone.

"Emily?" Dolly. I was almost disappointed.

"Yes."

"What in hell are you doing there?"

"I had to find a safe place. We've got to talk. It's Cecil Hawke…"

"Okay. Listen," she interrupted. "I've got something to tell you. I don't know yet if it's what I think it is, but it's bad any way you look at it. Timothy Chesney, out on Valley Road, just found a body, dumped in the ditch in front of his house."

"Oh, my God, no!" I dreaded asking what I needed to know. "Man or woman?"

"It's a man's body, Emily. I only hope…"

"Where?"

She gave me directions. I promised to be right out, that I'd meet her at the site. I hung up and told Jackson, who wanted to go with me. I'm not sure what I said, but I brushed him aside. I could only keep one thought in my head: that the dead man in the ditch not turn out to be Jeffrey Lo.

THIRTY-EIGHT

DOLLY WAS OUT AT Valley Road ahead of me. I parked in front of an old stone house, jumped out, and headed for her broad blue back. She stood, along with other officers, at the edge of the ditch, among tall weeds and black-eyed daisies. Lieutenant Brent was there, little Omar Winston, and a lot of other cops I knew. As I walked toward them my feet grew cement shoes. I picked them up and put them down, not much wanting to get to that place where I might see a dead guy in a nice blue suit and Nikes.

I tried to read Dolly's face. She looked back at me, giving me a blank stare, deep in thought.

"Dolly?" I asked, drawing closer, and trying not to look at the body laid out at the bottom of the ditch, face down in a slow, moving stream of water.

She nodded at me. "Take a look," she said.

The body was laid out lengthways, partially covered with dirty water and grass. The face lay in the murky water. No blue suit. No sneakers.

From what I could see of the side of his face and his hands, turned up and tied behind him, this man was tall, dark haired, and olive skinned.

Brent followed the medical examiner into the ditch and turned the body.

In death the face was benign—no sneer, no menace. I recognized who he was. Certainly not Jeffrey Lo, which almost knocked the wind out of me. I'd been so sure. This man wore dark work pants and a blue, short-sleeved shirt with a huge, wet stain covering most of the front. I recognized the boots on his feet—scuffed, heels worn away. I recognized him. Toomey, the man Lila hated; the man I'd seen at the Hawkes's party.

Murderer and ghost.

THIRTY-NINE

MY HOUSE WAS STILL. And lifeless. Jack was bringing Sorrow home later. I walked through my few, small rooms and remembered how it felt when Jack and I were officially divorced and I'd stood in the middle of my Ann Arbor dining room, listening to a clock tick somewhere, and thinking, then, the worst thing that could happen to me was to be alone. I knew better now. There are worse things.

Like being so confused I couldn't finish a thought before an opposite thought took over.

The guy I feared most was dead. Who did I fear now? Cecil? But he was the puppet master—he'd pulled Toomey's strings, sent him out to kill.

Toomey was dead. Was there someone else I didn't know coming at me? How did you fear an empty face? A void? How did you fear a thing without substance?

I looked over at the kitchen counter and saw Cecil's manila envelope, with his check on top, and I knew with every inch of skin on my body, with every pore, every strand of hair, every organ—that I was in a fight for my life.

Maybe he would come. I didn't put it past him. Or maybe I'd go to him—to return the envelope, the last of his filthy manuscript, and the money he'd given me. Face him down and take my soul back.

It was all such a bad joke. I'd been so thrilled to read his destructive prose. For what? To pay a gas bill? To buy sheets? Maybe get an oil change? Can a person really sell bits of herself for next to nothing?

It wasn't just my life anymore. There was still Jeffrey. Cecil had him. I knew it the way I knew the sun was coming up in the morning. There was nowhere but Cecil's, unless Jeffrey was dead and rolled, like Toomey, into a ditch, down a ravine, into a shallow grave in the middle of a thick wood.

If I could have cried, I would have welcomed it. But there's a point beyond tears; a place so hollowed out and empty that to go there meant the end of self pity, maybe the end of all pity. A place where I stood at that moment, thinking of murder.

The French doors were wide open. I didn't bother to close and lock them. Overhead the fan turned with a solid creak, not stirring much of the hot air in the room. A whippoorwill sang his forlorn and cruel song in one of the maples down by the lake; one of the trees that refused to die, coming back to life, new leaves fuzzing the branches. The trees looked lacey now, in silhouette against the red, sunset sky. A kind of resurrection.

They were all coming to my house, after Courtney identified Toomey. She was the only one who knew him. I'd had only glimpses of the man. One in his farmer's clothes at Cecil's front door. One as Abe Lincoln at the *Blithe Spirit* party. But I knew who he was. I'd thought, for those first few minutes after seeing his dead body, that it was all over—for us, for the migrant workers, for Courtney.

From the corner of my eye I saw the light on my answering machine flash. I checked, hoping, stupidly, it could be Jeffrey. That Madeleine Clark had called was more than I could take right then. There wasn't even a question in my mind what she wanted. Life's jokes are always huge, and often cruel. This one would be no different.

Dolly, Lucky, Courtney, and Bill were the first to arrive. Straight from Gaylord and Toomey's stiff body laid out on a metal table. Courtney'd probably never seen him with his eyes closed. Probably never saw him when he couldn't stare her down and seem to promise more of what he'd given to her mother. I felt bad for the girl, but no more than I felt for all of us.

They shuffled in single file, Dolly—who swore she hated dogs—hunting around for Sorrow. "Where'd he go?" she asked. "Thought you at least had a dog here with you."

I told her Jack was coming with him and offered cold drinks, chairs—all the caretaking things a woman does.

Bill was more subdued than I'd ever seen him, that mop of thick hair wild from his hands running through it again and again. He looked over at me and tried to smile. I shook my head at him. These weren't normal times. And we weren't normal people.

"How you holding up, Emily?" Bill asked finally, settling his big body down in a corner of the sofa.

I shrugged. There are times in life that have no words. This was one of them.

"I'd like Courtney, here, to take a look at that manuscript you told me about," Dolly said, breaking a kind of silence we'd imposed on ourselves.

I nodded and went to get everything I'd copied. I gave her the chapters about her, and about her mother.

Only the squeak of the overhead fan broke the silence as she read, her neat head bent to the papers in her lap. From time to time she turned sad blue eyes up at us and took her bottom lip between her teeth, chewing at it, then turning back to the manuscript. She skimmed some of the pages, and reread others. When she'd finished she lay her hands on top of the manuscript and looked around at each of us, as if afraid to talk.

"That's my home," she finally said, slow words consciously formed. "The house on Church Road, Sneyd Park, back in Bristol. He describes it here," she said to everyone; each of us in turn. "He sold it after she died, along with all her things—the lovely things she'd touched and cherished. There was a clock from my great-grandmother, and my father's chess set. Her will left him everything. No one would believe that it was forged. That my mother would never have done that to me."

She bent back to the pages, read, and looked up again.

"And that's my mum, the woman he's talking about. I know that dress, and her favorite brooch. How he tricked her, because she was lonely and she thought Cecil was funny. Not a serious man, she said to me one day, telling me not to worry, he'd never be my stepfather. She swore to me Cecil wasn't someone she might marry—until she did, and it was too late. Before she went into that coma, she'd told me, even wrote to me while I was away with my aunt in Cornwall, that she was going to divorce him. He wasn't the man she'd thought he was, she said. I wish I'd kept her letters but how was I to know it would be the last time I'd ever hear from her?"

Courtney's eyes glazed with tears. She'd had her mother taken from her, her family home, all the money that should have been hers. There was a lot to cry about. I didn't blame her.

"The murders, did you ever know anything about what he'd done before your mother met him?"

She shook her head. "But that bit, about losing his finger, I know I asked him once and he told me a dog bit it off. Of course, he'd laughed so I thought it was just one of his jokes. But now ..."

"What about the friend in the book?" I asked. "Could he be Toomey?"

"The description of the man matches Nelson Toomey. And the cruel eyes, and that laugh he'd give—not very often, but then you didn't want to hear it often." She shuddered. "If this is real and not fiction—I wouldn't put it past either one of them. And this—here at the end." She leafed back through the pages, pulled out two and held them out to me. "About him being in Cannes when this fictional woman dies? That's where he was when my mum first went into her coma. Out of the way, he was. Nothing to do with it, of course. But here ..." She pointed. "And here ... he calls her Amanda. That was my mum's name. And the daughter ..."

She looked at me, eyes wide, something of what I'd been feeling settling there. "He's called her Courtney."

Nobody spoke. Finally Dolly shuffled her feet and slapped her hands together. "Gotta do something."

Lucky agreed, then turned to greet Lieutenant Brent, Omar Winston, and two other state police cops as they filed in and stood behind the sofa.

"How are we going to handle this?" Brent looked around at the others.

"We've got a missing agent here, Lieutenant," Dolly snapped.

"You have reason to believe he's out there at Hawke's?"

"Hell, yes."

"Somebody saw him? He said that's where he'd be? He left a message, a note, something back in his motel room? Lord, Dolly, give me anything."

"Let's at least go talk to Hawke," she demanded.

"That'll just warn him. Could force his hand. Maybe even make him kill Agent Lo."

After a long silence, I spoke up. "I'm going back."

"Don't be nuts," Dolly said without even looking at me. "You're not goin' anywhere."

"I can get in." I came around to sit beside her, looking from Lucky, to Brent, then back to Dolly. "He'll be happy I'm back. I know him now. He'll think it's some kind of victory…"

"That man's the worst kind of crazy," she said. "He's smart, and insane. That's as bad as it gets. No civilian is stickin' her nose in…"

"I can get in the house, Dolly. You can't—not without setting him off. With me in there you've got an excuse to break the doors down if you have to. I'll back all of you, say I asked you to come

315

get me if I wasn't out in fifteen minutes, that I felt threatened, knew the man was a killer ..."

"Dolly's right, Emily," Brent finally said. "I can't, with good conscience, let you get anywhere near him. That's not a civilian's job." He shook his head again and again.

"So? What about Jeffrey?" I kept my voice low and tense, the way I was feeling. "You want to find him dumped in a ditch?"

Nobody answered.

Soon, with nothing settled, they all got up to go. Bill put his arm around me and squeezed. I hugged Courtney and told her not to worry. They got out to their cars just as Jack's white Jaguar pulled down the drive with Sorrow in the front seat.

FORTY

THERE WAS PLENTY OF day left. I drove to the one gas station on 131 that had a pay phone where I called Dolly and told her what I was going to do.

"I'm jumping in my car. I'll beat you out there..." she exploded, yelling, her little voice reaching registers only a dog should hear.

"Fine," I said. "Just give me ten or fifteen minutes. I've got to get inside. I know a little about the place. And Cecil will talk to me, Dolly. If he thinks I'm alone..."

She made a disgusted noise, then thought a minute. "Okay, but I'm bringin' everybody. You wait until you see our cars before you go in. You hear?"

This was Dolly angry and ready to turn all guns loose on me.

"I'll park out by the road until I see you pulling into the trees. Give me ten, at most fifteen, minutes. You'll have your excuse to come in—that I said he was going to kill me. Got it? Jeffrey's somewhere in that house or in the barns. And that Diaz family—

317

they're still missing. Don't forget them. I just wouldn't put anything past this guy, Dolly. We can't take the chance he might get away."

"Honest to God, I wish you wouldn't do this, Emily. We'll figure it out. Probably get a warrant for his arrest no later than morning…"

"Too late. He's had Jeffrey three days. Who knows…?"

There was quiet from the other end of the line. When she spoke her voice was different, more concerned than businesslike. "I'm scared crapless for you right now. You're takin' on something… well… I could tell you were really bothered and I don't mean about all Hawke's stuff. Not even Agent Lo. It's personal. Isn't it? Something you got yourself into…"

"Yeah," was all I was going to give her. "It's personal. So, just get out there. Call every big cop you know and get them to Cecil's. Swear to God, I'll wait 'til I see you guys coming down the road. Then I'm going in."

I hung up. It was settled. There was nothing else to do. No gun—but that was probably a good thing since I had no idea how to use one. Only me. And Cecil. If he got out of hand I'd tell him the cops were on their way. That was all I had. It had to be enough.

I made one more phone call.

"I have to see you," I said when Cecil answered, no phony maid as go-between.

"Of course you do, Emily." He laughed a knowing and condescending laugh that came from deep inside his body. "I'll be here. But, Emily, I really think our relationship is at an end. Don't you? There'll be no more money. Please return my manuscript. All of it. I'll be leaving soon."

I hung up. The sound of his voice had turned my skin cold. I was afraid. Dolly'd gotten all the bravery I had left in me. Alone, I was stuck with the other me—the shaking woman who had no choice.

Getting back in my car took a huge effort. Turning the key—deliberately going slow, taking a deep breath, listening as the engine came on—took all I had inside me. I put my right hand at the top of the wheel and drove—out of the gas station, across the highway, up Plum Valley Road, then other roads, turning and signaling and turning—all against my will. I felt like a little kid facing everything her mother and father and church and school told her to run from. And then something even colder ran through me. I was someone very old, facing something even older.

I turned down Cecil Hawke's gravel road and stopped before I got to his fence and gate house. I was scared, sitting there in my car waiting for something to happen. There was no sign of Dolly or any blue state police cars. But they were coming. I'd never been more certain of anything in my life. Dolly would never let me down.

I couldn't wait any longer or my nerve would be gone. I drove on through the gate, waving at the guard, then up the drive to the long, low house built into the hill. I parked under the portico, grabbed the manuscript I'd brought, and walked up those wide front steps. The door opened before I had the chance to knock.

Cecil Hawke waited in one of his gaudier smoking jackets, a fringed belt around his ample waist, his blond toupee neatly centered and brushed back around his ears. He held a tea cup in his hand.

"Ah, Emily. So good to see you, and so very, very soon. Come in. Come in." He stood back. I brushed against him as I entered the long hall, getting a whiff of that awful cologne he wore. Or more than a whiff. It was thick enough to stick in my throat. I forced myself to breathe around it, then stood as far from him as I could get.

I tried to think of something to say. I was afraid my voice would give away my nerves. I looked around for Freddy, who I now thought of as my only ally here, but he was no where in sight.

"So," Cecil closed the door, then leaned back on the heels of his shiny black shoes. "What can I do for you? I see you've brought my manuscript. Finished, I hope." He nodded at the manila envelope.

"And that last check." I handed both to him.

"But you've earned it. The money's yours."

"I ... I would have brought all the money, but I've spent it."

He frowned. "You sound so angry." He worked deep hurt into the words.

I shuffled through ideas for something that would derail him long enough for the others to arrive. What I wanted was to ask him about Toomey, and Jeffrey Lo.

"I should have been honest with you from the beginning," I said. "The book is just ... well ... not good enough to find a publisher."

He rocked back on his heels, set his tea cup down on a small table, and fixed me with an open-mouthed glare. "And that from a failed writer. Is there jealousy at play here?"

He threw back his head and sighed again. "Ah, Noel Coward knew this well. '*Criticism and Bolshevism have one thing in common,*' the great man said. '*They both seek to pull down that which they could never build.*'"

"You're an evil man, Cecil." I said before thinking, then was pleased with myself. It was what I'd come to say. I'd come to let him know I wasn't a fool, that he hadn't put anything over on me. "I've shown the manuscript to Courtney James. She recognizes her own house, and that you were in Cannes when her mother was put into that coma—probably by your friend, Nelson Toomey?"

His eyes went wide, chin dropped. His whole body shook with indignation. "You showed my work to that terrible girl?"

He sniffed and walked away from me, turning further down the hall, his face red, his hands knotted into fists at his side. "I'll sue you. That's the first thing I'll do." He paced back and forth then turned to hurry over to where I stood. "Or, maybe, there are other ways…"

"Your friend is dead. Toomey. His body was found in a ditch. But you knew that."

Cecil waved a hand, swatting the image from his mind. "Nothing to do with me. The man really was a pest. Troublemaker, you could say. Everything was going so well here and he had to hire those migrants. Too much work for the men he'd brought from Australia, he said. But for heaven's sakes—that was their job: the sheep, the barns." He shrugged and sighed. He put his hands deep into his jacket pockets, brought his shoulders up, and grinned a childish grin at me. "That's what started it all. The trouble. Those heavy-handed threats of his—dead dogs, for God's sakes. All I did was point out that the migrants would tell others about our ... well, about my little business venture. Profitable, let me assure you. Friends from everywhere fly in. Just a sport. A man's sport. Unfortunately he carried his threats too far. Then that woman came—the agent. I just wouldn't have it. When I leave here—and I'm forced to now—I didn't want him trailing after me this time. There's been too much mishandling of my ... well, but it's none of your business, is it? Never has been."

"And Jeffrey Lo? What did you do to him?"

He gave a disgusted grunt. "Do you really think I'm to blame for everything that goes wrong in this Godforsaken place? Well, hardly ..."

I edged back toward the front door. I'd only been there five minutes. Maybe less. The cavalry was coming.

"Are you expecting someone?" He shook his head and frowned as I put my hand on the doorknob. "Not your friend, Dolly, I hope. I called her. I told her I had an appointment with you but had to cancel and that I would be in at noon to tell her anything she wants to know. I don't think ..."

He smiled sadly and shook his head. "People only hear what they want to hear, Emily. I'm sure she's trying to contact you even as we speak. She won't be coming."

"I wasn't expecting ..." I began but choked on the words.

"Fine. Then let's part as friends, shall we?" He clapped his hands together. "Let me show you what I've been doing recently. It's very interesting. You'll be fascinated."

"I think I'll leave now. You've got your manuscript. And your check. Everything else—well, maybe I jumped to conclusions. But that's all I wanted to say to you—about the book."

"Bad judgment there, girl. You'll be sorry. You won't be thanked in the acknowledgments, as you might have been. Still," he reached forward and grabbed my arm, his fingers closing down hard just above my wrist. "There are things you really should see, so you don't think so badly of me..."

He pulled me across the hall. I pulled back, until he turned and reprimanded me. "Emily, don't be a child. I really would like to share the game with someone—before I leave this place."

Nothing was sinking into my head.

"The game, Emily." His voice shook. "It's about the game. You knew, didn't you? You were playing 777 too."

"Look, Cecil. I don't know what your problems are, or how your mind works. But I'm getting out of here. And yes, Dolly is coming. I doubt your phone call would stop her. You've underestimated all of us, all along. And overestimated yourself. You're not an intelligent man. You're just a sad, evil human being." The words were true and it felt good to say them to his face. All of it was so simple—just a human being who wasn't smart enough to put his past behind him. And I'd been so afraid...

"In that case, we'll have to hurry, won't we?" Cecil smiled, put his hand back into the pocket of his jacket, and brought out a small but lethal-looking gun he pointed straight at me as he went on smiling.

I caught my breath. I hadn't expected this. Somehow a gun didn't seem to be his style. It didn't make me any more afraid.

"Here is where our tour begins." He pushed the gun into the small of my back. I felt it at kidney height, pressure and pain at once.

"You will so love this place I've created. Perfect."

He pushed harder against me, forcing me to move, one foot after the other. We crossed the length of the hall, into the empty kitchen. Then we were out the back door, and down the lawn toward the barns. Walking wasn't hard, though I stumbled often. There hadn't been any rain lately so I wasn't mired in mud; but with someone pushing, and my own fear, it wasn't an easy trek.

Sheep grazed in the barnyard, behind the fence, and out in the pastures. No one was around. There didn't seem to be a single farmhand anywhere.

"Don't be afraid, Emily. Nothing's going to happen to you ... here. I'm doing you a favor. Giving you an experience. As a writer, you know how important experience is, don't you?" He was too close. I could smell that awful cologne.

I wondered if I could elbow him in the gut, then kick him, all in one turn. I pictured a high, karate kick to his chin. But I'd never studied karate. And if I missed, he'd just shoot me. It was funny how the gun was what kept me in place but wasn't what really scared me. It was the man behind me, able to touch my skin, having power over me. That was the worst of it. My brain kept clicking. I figured he'd lock me up somewhere. But that was okay since Dolly and every cop in the area would be there soon. I'd be all right. Just had to keep my head and lead him on.

Around me the rolling, green hills had become a backdrop to evil. The white dots of rounded sheep's bodies, way off in other pastures, weren't real. More like dots on a canvas.

We walked by the big barns and the fenced-in sheep. They gave low baas as we passed. I searched for a worker, someone among the sheep. We were out in the open. There had to be a shepherd somewhere.

Behind me, Cecil said, "There's no one, Emily. I've fired the help. A farmer down near Grand Rapids is coming this afternoon to make arrangements for the sheep. The rest ... well ... I'll leave it all behind. Maybe a fire. Hmm. What a fine idea. I'll leave Courtney a pile of ashes. I'm bored here anyway. As Coward said, '*I will accept anything, provided it amuses or moves me. But if it does neither, I want to go home.*' So, time to move on. The world is truly my oyster, Emily. A slimy thing that sticks in my throat."

He laughed heartily as he forced me toward a building I'd only glimpsed before. Bunker-like, the structure sat low to the ground. There were no windows in the gray walls. It had only a single, low wooden door built into the front wall.

"Here's where the game begins in earnest." Cecil leaned close. I felt his excitement as his breath brushed across my ear. He gave a short, happy laugh.

"Knock," he ordered. "Go ahead. Knock."

I reached out, keeping one hand clamped over my nose against the odor of him, and tapped at the wooden door with one knuckle.

"I said knock. Give it a good one," he ordered, poking the gun barrel against my spine.

I balled my hand and hit the door hard.

"Listen." He put a finger to his lips, shushing me. "Move in closer. Put your ear to the crack. You'll hear ..."

"Please ..." The word came from the room beyond the heavy door.

I listened harder. "Jeffrey?" I yelled and pounded hard at the door.

There was nothing. After a while the voice, very weak, almost unrecognizable, called again, "Emily? It's dark. There are ... dead bodies in here."

"Oh my God, Jeffrey. People are coming ..."

The gun dug into my back. "Would you like to join him?" Cecil was close, whispering at my ear.

I turned to face him. The worst he could do was kill me.

"Let him out of there, you bastard."

He pushed the gun against my stomach, slowly, looking as if he enjoyed the closeness. "Think of it as punishment for trespass. I found him where he didn't belong. Like that other agent, the woman. But don't worry. He won't last much longer."

Cecil cocked his head back and gave me a speculative look. "But you, Emily. You've hurt me badly, all that twaddle about my book being no good. Why, I think you're the evil one. What a cruel thing to say to another person. Especially when you haven't the talent to recognize good writing when you see it."

He backed off and motioned again with the gun, forcing me down the hill toward an octagonal building I could only partially see. "I've something better for you. Wait until you see. Remember the sheep? Oh, this is so much fun."

I walked ahead of him feeling as if I'd left my real body behind. There was a disconnection, a truly out-of-body moment, when my brain took me from where I was, who I was with, and what was happening to me. As if I stood aside and watched with interest, as I was prodded on down the path, my mind noticed dandelions still in bloom, it noticed that the sky, to the north, was getting dark, and that my shoe was loose, as if my feet might be shrinking.

I forced myself back to Cecil and the gun, watching for an opening to elbow Cecil in his stomach, or trip him and fall on top of him while grabbing the gun, or I would point at something and distract him long enough to run.

All I had to do was stall. If I kept my head, it would be over soon. Dolly and the other cops would get there. Jeffrey would be released.

"You killed Lila." I pretended the idea had never occurred to me before.

"You know I didn't. I was in the hall with you."

"Then Toomey did it for you. He killed for you, like a trained dog."

"Oh, you've guessed our little secret." He sighed. "She was useless. And she really was leaving me. Can you imagine? Not with Jackson Rinaldi. No, Lila's death was just for fun. Ending the party with a death. What a lark! Like one of our English mysteries—death in the library and all of that. Noel would have loved my twist on *Blithe Spirit*."

As we made our way down the grassy slope, I turned to look hard behind us, expecting cops with guns coming up over the slope of the fields to our left. For a second I thought I saw Dolly, ducking behind the corner of a tall corn crib. I was sure that was her head. But the sun was high and hot, blinding me so I saw nothing but grassy slopes and more buildings.

"Where are we going?" I dug my heels into the grass.

"You'll be amazed," he chortled as he put his fat hand on my neck and squeezed. I thought I was going to fall to my knees. My disgust at his touch was nearly more than I could take. I tried shaking him off but he only laughed again and hung on. There was no stopping what he planned for me.

"Too bad it has to be the way it is—if only you'd been smart enough … well, here we are."

We stopped in front of the almost-circular barn. The building was gray with a dark-green metal roof, no windows. It had the look of a fortress. The double door was shut, and locked. I heard the jingle of keys behind me. Cecil reached around and put a key in the lock, turned it, and easily pushed the door aside. I kept my eye on the gun as much as I could. I looked over my shoulder for what I figured was a last time and prayed I'd see Dolly creeping toward us, ready to take Cecil Hawke down at any minute.

As the door opened, sound came at me. Growling, barking. Dogs waiting to attack, or attacking. There was a cacophony of snarling and yipping—a dog in pain. I looked down hard into where he was forcing me and was instantly blinded by high over-head lights. Then blinded again as Cecil, chuckling behind me, turned on more lights.

That awful cologne of his got into my nose. It was thicker than before. It mixed with his sweat and his apparent sexual arousal. The smell of him was feral.

The room, what I could see with part of it in glaring, white light and the other in deep shadow, was some kind of amphitheater. There were benches—rows of them going down from shadowed places toward a central, brightly lighted circle. The lights focused on that central pit. There were no ropes. Only a waist-high wall surrounded the ring that wasn't a ring.

The barking started again. Snarling—louder than I'd ever heard.

Cecil prodded me forward. Pushing me toward a row of rough steps between the benches. I had to watch my footing. Though the center of the building was well lighted, the aisle was shadowy, the steps crude and steep.

I stumbled, and grabbed at a bench. My mind ran back and forth. There had to be something I could do. A moment when he would be off guard. I looked ahead of us, down into the dirt ring below.

Dogs. There were two bloody dogs down there. The growls and screams were terrible as the dogs locked in mortal combat.

I looked at my feet. That was all I could think to do: watch where I walked; hold on tightly to every row of benches; move ever so slowly. Dolly would be there.

One slow step…

I wasn't going to let him get me all the way down to the pit. I would run. Let him shoot.

I knew one thing—I wouldn't go into that pit where two dogs were tearing at each other's throats.

FORTY-ONE

ONE BENCH AT A time.

He didn't hurry me now. He stepped down as I stepped down, talking to himself from time to time, laughing, then waiting behind me.

I bent forward, feeling my way along the crude wooden benches until there was only a single row of benches between me and the edge of the pit where I hesitated, thinking hard and fast, listening for something behind us.

I felt Cecil's foot at my back. I gasped as he kicked me hard, sending a burst of pain around my kidneys. I fell forward, into dirt and sawdust, where I lay sprawled. As good a place as any to hang on, I told myself. He poked me with the toe of his shoe, then bent and put the gun down beside my ear. I got up slowly, grabbing at the edge of the wall in front of me. Once on my feet, I glanced over the wall into the pit.

I stared straight into hell.

The dogs were huge, and yellow. Both had torn strips of flesh hanging from their bodies. On one I saw the white flash of an exposed bone. Bloody spittle flew around their heads as they shook, quivers running along their sides and flanks.

The place stunk of shit and heat. Overheated—all of it. If death had a single stink, I was smelling it.

Off somewhere up around the edges of the arena, other dogs barked and howled, and rattled cages.

"*Mad Dogs and Englishmen ...*" Cecil sang in a falsetto voice, maybe mimicking me, a woman, or Noel Coward, or just enjoying himself. I didn't care. I pretended to trip again, falling sideways. As I fell I twisted my body, kicking out hard at Cecil, catching him midway, in the stomach.

He grunted and fell to his side, down into the dirt. He righted himself immediately, before I could roll out of the way, or move. He leaned toward me and pushed the gun against my right cheek. The cold barrel hurt my teeth. It would go off now and I was too tired to care.

"That was good, Emily." He was in my face, his eyes cold, even amused. "I was afraid you were going to go without a fight. Wouldn't that have been a shame? We've had such a good jousting relationship. You've really made for a great game. I'd hate to have you disappoint me now."

He pulled me to my feet, the gun going to the back of my head, forcing me against the wall that came to just above my waist. I put out a hand, grabbing the edge and steadying myself. As my fingers closed on the concrete, one of the dogs flew toward me across the pit, teeth snapping at the hand I pulled back just in time.

I tried to fall off to the side, maybe push my body so close to the wall he couldn't move me, but Cecil pressed his body against mine, closed his arms around me, and whispered something I was too panicked to hear.

I thrust hard, with all I had left in me, against him, keeping my face from the edge of the wall where, I knew now, one of the dogs could spring up and tear my face off. I used all my force, but Cecil was too strong and had too good a position behind me, bearing down, his body close and hard so the wall of the pit pressed into my stomach. There wasn't an inch of room anywhere. He forced my face higher above the wall.

I looked into the pit through blood streaming into my eyes, trying see where the dogs were. One had moved to the other side of the ring. It stood there, bleeding from bites all over his body, watching me as if in speculation: how much of a leap it would take to pull my head off.

The other dog stood at the exact center of the dirt pit. I breathed hard and looked at him. He could be at me in a second.

This dog bled too. Ragged tears of skin hung from his body. His sides heaved in and out with what he'd already been through. His breathing was loud. It rattled over the barking of the caged dogs behind us.

Cecil lay against me, whispering things I wouldn't hear.

The dog I stared at had only one eye. The other eye was sewn shut, running with fluids and with blood.

Freddy.

I would have laughed, if I could. Cecil was going to throw me to Freddy, a dog I'd tried to befriend.

I looked at the one-eyed dog and held my breath. Freddy looked back at me, that one eye wild and murderous. He was crazed with the smell of blood and by his own pain.

Cecil stopped pushing me. I felt a hand at the waistband of my jeans, and one at my hair, pulling.

"All for you, Emily," he said and lifted me into the air. I was going over the edge. I tried to get a hold on him, reaching out for his jacket, his eyes—anything I could hang on to or gouge out, but I felt the cement of the wall scrape against my bare stomach.

There was a sudden, hard crash from behind, straight at me. Cecil was off my back, flailing at the wall as I had been, his gun arcing into the air. He was over the edge into the pit, with someone hanging on to him. A blue uniform. A flat hat flying.

Dolly fell into the pit with Cecil, hitting him with everything she had as Cecil fell to his knees and hands. Dolly was on him when he tried to crawl away from her. She straddled his back and choked him.

I screamed, watching the dogs stand at attention, interested, then taking a step closer to the two rolling bodies.

"Dolly." I threw myself as far over the wall as I could reach. "Take my hand!"

She turned wild eyes at me and then back down at Cecil. She pushed his face into the muck of the pit. The toupee was gone. There was no hair to hang on to so she grabbed the ears and pushed his face back into the muck. For a moment he lay there stunned as she scrambled off his back and reached up for my hand.

I grabbed on to her and pulled. She used her other hand to grasp the wall, then moved her feet up the cement. With a deep grunt, she launched her body hard over the top and down beside where I stood, still hanging on to her. She lay there for just a moment. Then the moaning began. She grabbed at her stomach.

Behind us I heard the running feet of the big cops I'd prayed for. Brent was there. Omar was there, kneeling beside Dolly.

"Get an ambulance," I yelled at them. "Don't let her lose her baby."

When I got to my feet and looked back over the wall, Cecil stood clumsily, bent double, his face smeared with excrement and dirt.

Freddy watched, standing very tall and straight, his head high, ears up like a show dog's. He looked at Cecil with an almost quizzical twitch of one of his eyebrows.

Cecil hissed something, then hissed again. Maybe a signal for Freddy to kill the other dog.

For a brief moment, Freddy turned that one seeing eye up toward me. It burned with something buried there. Freddy began to move, not away from Cecil but toward him. There wasn't time for me to look away. I stood frozen, the way Cecil Hawke was frozen, staring at his dog.

Around me, no one moved, or made a sound.

Freddy took a few more hesitant steps, then broke into a run. He leaped high, hitting Cecil with tremendous force so his body rose up and backward. Freddy grabbed his master by the throat, sinking his huge teeth into flesh and then, with snapping sounds, into bone. He began to shake the man.

Cecil's screams went on until one of the cops near me took out his gun.

The sound of that single shot overpowered everything else in the echoing building.

FORTY-TWO

THEY BROUGHT ZINNIAS, ANTIQUE roses, daisies, black-eyed Susans, and pansies. Tall delphiniums and foxglove were brought in by pickle jar and mayo jar and canning jar. Lavender came in antique vases or clutched in sweaty fists. Leetsvillians stripped their gardens and the surrounding summer hillsides, bringing their offerings. A constant stream of neighbors and friends tip-toed into Dolly's hospital room: formally presenting their gifts to our newest town hero.

One by one and two by two they came to stand in awe at the foot of Dolly's bed, staring in admiration at the woman the *Northern Statesman* credited for the capture of what Bill called "The Monster of Torch Lake."

More brownies than any woman should eat were dropped off on paper plates and old china. Orange and applesauce cakes appeared. The hospital brought in a long table for the food: casseroles and plates of ham, homemade breads and 'put-up' pickles, lots of macaroni and cheese, and even a bowl of Harry's canned fish, though it wasn't going as fast as the ham.

Women from the library came with books; Eugenia and Gloria from EATS came with meatloaf. Farmers and their wives brought eggs and one whole chicken. A steady stream of migrant workers came with holy cards and plates of tostadas and enchiladas. Men from the gas station and the small engine repair brought bags of chips. People from the Skunk Saloon, among the first to arrive, brought beer but got kicked out at the first pop of a cap. Jake Anderson, the owner of the saloon, brought goldenrod in an old catsup bottle. The flustered nurse made him take it away at the same time she cleared the room of beer drinkers.

Dolly's plain hospital room—a private room since the floor nurses couldn't contain the crowd, nor the eating, nor much of anything else—was filled with celebration, with Dolly holding court from between the sheets, dressed in an open-down-the-back green hospital gown which required the room being cleared when she had to get up and go to the bathroom.

I sat off in one corner most of that day, watching the procession of well-wishers and Dolly, laid out on her glowing white bed, caught in long rays of sunshine coming through the large windows that overlooked the hospital laundry.

Dolly's obstetrician, Doctor Cornell, came in three times that afternoon, garnering admiration from the collected crowd.

"Baby's doing fine," the elderly gentleman told everyone again and again, bowing his great head of white hair as if serving the queen. "Dolly's pain comes from three broken ribs. I'm keeping her a few days to make certain everything stays okay with the baby."

At this point Dolly frowned hard at me. "You pulled me too damned hard," she groused.

I smiled and reminded her I'd saved her life.

Then I thanked her for saving mine. We'd decided early on we were even on that score.

Cate, Dolly's grandmother, was there, back from the world excursion that never happened. She'd gotten as far as Grayling, turned around, and found a young couple to bring her back to Leetsville. "I knew it in my bones," she told everyone. "Knew my Delores needed me."

Cate arranged the flowers on the windowsills or set them on the floor. She bustled around the hospital room in her funny shoes and feathered hat like an elderly, come-down-in-the-world queen.

Jeffrey was gone before evening. Dehydrated from no water or food for three days, he'd been treated and released. When he came into Dolly's room to say goodbye I could see, in his eyes, that physical pain wasn't the worst thing he faced. The Diaz family— father, mother, and two young boys—had been in that dark room with him. Dead. For three days he'd felt around the walls only to stumble over another cold body, until he'd confined himself to a single corner, waiting for someone to come. "Or to die," he'd said.

When he was leaving I hugged him. "Come back whenever you can," I said, very close to his face. Meaning it. Sorry to see him leave.

He looked directly into my eyes. There was a wistfulness there, a kind of cautious hope. His smile was rueful. "Sure will..." he began, then stopped.

I figured I'd never see Jeffrey Lo again. The north country didn't hold good memories for him.

I watched him walk out the door, that neat blue suit rumpled, his shoulders slumped, the Nikes dirty. Confrontation with true evil can do that, I thought, knowing I'd never be the same again either.

"Where am I supposed to put all these things?" Dolly groused as Flora Coy struggled through the door with a bucket of lavender stalks.

"It's for your bathroom," Flora whispered in her carrying voice as she pushed her big pink glasses back up her nose. "You know what they're like in the hospital."

She carted her bucket into Dolly's private bath.

Bill Corcoran dropped by after taking Courtney to the airport, on her way back to England. She would get everything left of her mother's estate, including the Michigan ranch—since Cecil Hawke used stolen money to buy it, and left no other heir.

At a little after six, Lieutenant Brent and Officer Omar Winston walked in. They had been involved in the investigation all day. Brent, as usual, sucked the air out of the room with his big, uniformed body. He went to stand by Dolly's bed, at full attention, delivering his thanks, on behalf of the Michigan State Police, for Dolly's heroic actions in stopping a murder.

Mine.

Omar Winston was too small to be much of a presence, but his face showed real concern for Dolly. He went straight to her bedside, a large wrapped box under one arm and a big bouquet of pink roses stuck out in front of him like a shield.

Dolly looked at the huge bouquet and groaned. "Now where in hell am I gonna put more flowers?" she demanded. "Makin' me sneeze already."

Cate shushed her and took the roses from Omar's fist. She pulled a chair close to the bed for him to sit while Brent remained behind him, hands crossed, shoulders back in his usual military stance.

Omar set the wrapped package on the bed beside her.

"What's this?" Dolly scowled at the prettily wrapped box with a baby rattle attached to the bow.

"It's not for you." Omar cleared his throat. He reddened from his forehead to his chin and out to the edges of his ears.

"Then who?"

"Who do you think?"

She made a face, pulled herself up in the bed so Cate could plump her pillows, and pulled the box toward her. "Hope you didn't spend a lot of money."

He shook his head. "You might call it a present from all of us at the post in Gaylord. Just to thank you…"

Dolly carefully removed the ribbon and handed it to Cate. She pulled off the paper and handed that to Cate too. The box was securely taped so Dolly swore, then ran a fingernail along the edge, cutting the top free. She opened the box and pulled back the tissue paper, seeing what the rest of us couldn't. Her mouth dropped open. Her eyes took on an unDolly-like softness.

"You gonna take it out?" I asked, as curious as the others gathered around, gawking over each others shoulders.

She reached in and pulled a little blue suit from the box, holding it up in front of her.

"Is this what I think it is?" Dolly frowned hard at Omar.

"Lieutenant Brent's wife found it for me ... er ... us."

She sniffed a few times, then held up a tiny cop suit with epaulets, a painted-on gold star, and snaps along the inner legs.

Eugenia and some of the others snickered, drawing an angry face from Dolly.

She ran her hand over the little uniform. "Can't wait to see her in it." She beamed up at all of us.

"You know it's a 'her'?" I asked.

She shook her head, then stole a quick glance at Omar Winston. "Just guessin'."

"I didn't mean what I said about you not being the godmother," Dolly looked back at me slyly, from the corners of her eyes.

I nodded. Fair enough. I wouldn't have let her get away with it anyway. We were friends. Friends stand by each other.

"You can be the godfather, Omar," she said toward the anxious little man. "If you wanna be."

He began gulping and looking from side to side. She'd silenced him.

Soon she was grumping about the mess on her bed, brushing off the box and wrappings, but holding tightly to the tiny cop suit with gold buttons.

It was late. People began to leave. Lieutenant Brent soon excused himself.

I looked over at Omar, expecting him to go with Brent. He sat with his hands folded in his lap, back straight against the upright chair. He never cracked a smile, just sat there with his eyes on Dolly, who intentionally ignored him.

"Hope you get back to work soon," he said once, leaning toward her, his voice tiny. He tried to take her hand in his.

Dolly whipped that hand away and stuck it under the blanket where there was no chance of him grabbing her.

Omar sniffed and sat back. The place under his left eye started ticcing away. He blinked again and again and licked out at his lip.

I got up and stretched, hoping he'd get the hint. He didn't. Didn't even turn to look at me. He just sat on, that little nerve under his left eye ticcing.

I pulled my shoulder bag from the back of the chair. I was figuring I'd have to nudge the guy out of the room so Dolly could rest. He was a guy bent on doing his duty, and the police post in Gaylord had sent him to deliver their thanks.

I stood in the doorway, after waving goodbye to Dolly.

Dolly's left eye stayed right on the little blue cop suit she still held in her hands while her right eye wandered off, exploring the room.

Omar's nervous cheek kept ticcing as he licked at his bottom lip and cleared his throat again and again.

I looked from Omar to Dolly, truth finally dawning.

Tic. Tic. Tic.

That wandering eye ...

Ticcing.

The eye off looking at nothing.

Oh lord, I groaned, as a picture of a tiny baby girl flashed through my head.

Tic. Tic. Tic.

That eye wandering off on its own.

All I could think, as I went out into the hall and pulled the door shut behind me, was ...

Oh no.

Poor baby.

EPILOGUE

IT WAS THE MIDDLE of August when fall first hit the edges of the woods, slowly turning the leaves a deep, blood red.

The tent worms were gone—at least for that year. From time to time, as Sorrow and I walked the woods, I stopped and put my hand against the rough bark of a tree, letting my skin become accustomed to the feel of deep grooves and scaly surfaces. I wanted, for just a moment, to transfer my pity to the mute, tall giants; give them my fervent hope that the evil worm wouldn't come back again in spring.

I'd read that trees produce an enzyme that would protect from future worm attack. It seemed so smart to me, to outwit evil.

Like the worms, Cecil Hawke's evil was gone from our woods too. I was proud that Dolly and I had faced it, saved each other, and done away with him. But we had no enzyme to protect us from the future.

I'd kept the copy of Cecil's book. The original was taken by the police to molder in a dark evidence room until someday it would disintegrate into nothing.

At first I thought of inviting Dolly and Bill and Harry for a ritual burning of the book, but I couldn't. Burning evil, I realized, was best carried out alone. Best done as the sun went down, the pages thrown into a blazing log fire set at the bottom of a deep pit.

I chose a night and did the burning furtively, with only the natural world as witness. It doesn't take more than one who has seen true evil, to keep watch and know as flames lick the papers; as words ignite—letter by letter and page by page.

I watched alone down at the shore of Willow Lake while the sun set and the water behind me turned black. As self-appointed gatekeeper, I poked my stick at papers trying to escape the flames, separating pages, letting the fire lick up between them. The burning embers rose and soared toward whatever was out there in a sky slowly filling with a million stars, but no moon.

I made sure not a single word escaped whole. I poked and burned until the last of the flames disappeared and the world was cleansed of Cecil Hawke.

It was deep night by the time the fire burned to a single flickering spark. I stepped down on that last spark, grinding it beneath my shoe.

I could leave then, parting the ferns and making my way toward my brightly lighted house where the dog I loved waited, where a phone call could change my life, where there was possibility and hope and absence of evil.

No breeze ruffled the ferns.

No late, nesting bird sang off among the willows.

There was no one nearby.

Still, as I walked silently along my path, I thought I heard a thin, high voice coming from out over the dark water behind me.

I stopped to listen.

Lilting words at the edge of hearing.

A Noel Coward song.

Karen Youker

ABOUT THE AUTHOR

Elizabeth Kane Buzzelli is a creative writing instructor at Northwestern Michigan College. She is the author of novels, short stories, articles, and essays. Her work has appeared in numerous publications and anthologies.

www.MidnightInkBooks.com

From the gritty streets of New York City to sacred tombs in the Middle East, it's always midnight somewhere. Join us online at any hour for fresh new voices in mystery fiction.

At midnightinkbooks.com you'll also find our author blog, new and upcoming books, events, book club questions, excerpts, mystery resources, and more.

Midnight Ink Ordering Information

Order Online:
- Visit our website www.midnightinkbooks.com, select your books, and order them on our secure server.

Order by Phone:
- Call toll-free within the U.S. and Canada at 1-888-NITE-INK (1-888-648-3465)
- We accept VISA, MasterCard, and American Express

Order by Mail:
Send the full price of your order (MN residents add 6.875% sales tax) in U.S. funds, plus postage & handling to:

> Midnight Ink
> 2143 Wooddale Drive
> Woodbury, MN 55125-2989

Postage & Handling:

Standard (U.S. & Canada). If your order is:
> $25.00 and under, add $4.00
> $25.01 and over, FREE STANDARD SHIPPING

AK, HI, PR: $16.00 for one book plus $2.00 for each additional book.

International Orders (airmail only):
> $16.00 for one book plus $3.00 for each additional book

Orders are processed within 12 business days. Please allow for normal shipping time. Postage and handling rates subject to change.